Copyright © 2020 by Roberta Kagan

ISBN (paperback): 979-8647185273

ISBN (hardcover): 978-1-957207-30-8

DISCLAIMER

This is a work of fiction. Names, characters, businesses, places, events, and incidents are either the products of the author's imagination or used in a fictitious manner. Any resemblance to actual persons, living or dead, or actual events is purely coincidental.

SARAH AND SOLOMON

ROBERTA KAGAN

CHAPTER 1

SOLOMON COULD HARDLY CATCH HIS BREATH AS HE LOOKED INTO HIS mother's eyes. "Take care of your sister," she said somberly. Solomon rubbed the sleep out of his eyes. And even though he was in the familiar small room that he shared with his sister, Sarah; his mother; and his mother's friend, Benjamin Rabinowitz, it was the middle of the night, and the stars that came through the window gave the small space an eerie glow. For a moment he felt that the entire situation was not real. His heart was pounding. Perhaps, he thought, he might be trapped in a terrible nightmare.

"Mother?" he said, sitting up in bed.

"Yes, Solomon."

"Am I dreaming?"

"No, son. I wish to God that you were. But this is not a dream. So you must wake up quickly, and get your wits about you. Now, I know I am asking a lot of you, and what I am asking is a big responsibility for a boy your age, but you have always been my little man. From the first day I held you in my arms, I knew you were special. You have an old soul, Solomon, and I love you more than you'll ever know. But, my son, my dear beloved child, I have no choice but to send you and your sister away."

So it was true. He'd heard her correctly. It was not a dream at all. His mother was sending him and Sarah away from the ghetto, and she wanted them to leave immediately.

Zelda, Solomon's mother, continued as she stroked his hair. "My son, my dear sweet boy. My Solomon. As much as I would like to keep the two of you here for as long as I can, and every moment I can share with you and your sister is precious to me, I know that we must act quickly. There is no time for sentiment. As much as it hurts me, I know in my heart that this is the only chance the two of you will have to survive the Nazis."

She wiped a tear from her cheek with the back of her hand.

Then she touched his shoulder. "My babies, my two precious babies."

"We're not babies anymore, Mama. I'm nine, and Sarah is five," Solomon said, trying to sound strong.

"Of course you're not. But to me, you will always be my babies." Then she forced herself to smile. "Now, I know how smart you are, Solomon, and I am depending on your quick wit. You'll need to be smart and alert at all times." She went on. He could see, by looking at the pain in her eyes, just how distressed she was, and it frightened him.

"I know what a strong boy you are, and I'm counting on you to use every bit of street savvy you have to protect Sarah," she said, touching his cheek softly. "Your sister is only five, and she has been protected and is not nearly as wise as you. She is going to need you, Solomon."

Solomon felt the bile rise in his throat. He wished he were still asleep, still an innocent child trying to keep his mother from finding out that he'd been sneaking out of the ghetto or palling around with a wild bunch of older boys.

"Tomorrow, Mordechai Rumkowski . . ." she said, and he turned away from her, not wanting to face the truth that she was about to share with him.

He knew who Rumkowski was. He was the head Judenrat of the Lodz ghetto.

Zelda gently took her hand and put it on his chin. Then she

turned his head back to face her, and her eyes fixed on his. "Rumkowski made a speech today. He said that tomorrow all of the children, who are under ten and living here in the Lodz ghetto, would be sent away on a transport to fulfill a quota for the Nazis. He didn't tell us where they would be sent. But everyone who has been living within these prison walls of the ghetto, knows that those who are sent away on transports, never come back."

Solomon had heard that anyone who went on a transport was murdered. "I've heard the rumors. I've heard that the people who are sent away on transports are murdered."

Zelda could not speak. She let out a gasp as she pulled Solomon close to her and buried her face in his hair.

"Mama, you're crying."

She nodded. Zelda found it hard to believe that even the Nazis could be so cruel as to murder her children. However, she dared not trust them or Rumkowski. These two precious lives must be forced to leave her and get as far from the ghetto as they could. Then maybe, if God would only watch over them, they might have a chance to live. Her mind whirled with terror. She searched for any other solution, but could not find any. Her two children would be all alone. Wandering the streets of Poland with no money and no food, they would be at the mercy of strangers. But if she went with them, they would most assuredly be caught.

The children were small, and Solomon knew how to slip in and out of the ghetto wall, but she was too big to get through. *Dear God, what am I to do? Am I making the right choice? How will they live? What will become of my babies? These two precious lives, lives that you, God, have entrusted to me.* She closed her eyes and remembered how she'd held them in her arms at night when they were sick. How she'd rocked them to sleep when they were scared and taught them as much as they could comprehend about reading. She'd shared books with them and given them her own food when the family had run short. And now, her only choice was to entrust them back to God. If they stayed here with her, they would be ripped from her arms in the morning. *Watch over them, dear God. Please keep them in the palm of your mighty hand.*

3

Although Solomon was very young, only nine, he was tough. His friends were less-than-savory characters, who were much older than he. They'd taught him how to maneuver his way in out of the ghetto walls. Solomon knew where every opening was and how to get through. He prided himself on how easily he'd learned all of it. He was tall and muscular, looking much older than his nine years. And he'd already had several years of experience slipping in and out of the ghetto at night to make deals with the Polish underground to buy and trade on the black market. His mother had begged him to stop. She was afraid he would be caught, but he was incorrigible, running around as if he were indestructible.

Many nights he would make his quiet escape from the bed he shared with his sister after she fell asleep and return before sunrise with necessities, like extra food for his family and a little more to sell. It was dangerous, of course, but at that time, at least he had been able to return to the apartment where his family lived. After tonight, he knew he could never come home. When his mother awakened him, she warned him that no matter what happened, he and his sister must never return to the ghetto. He'd steeled himself, trying hard to be a man. But the truth was he wanted to run into his mother's arms and cry like a baby.

"When this is all over, I will find you and your sister. But for now, you must stay far away from here," his mother warned.

"How will you find us?"

"I don't know. But I will. Now, you must trust me. And go, hurry, get as far away as you can before the sun comes up." Zelda wiped her tear-stained face on her nightgown.

Benjamin Rabinowitz awakened. He'd crawled quietly out of his bed and was now standing by Zelda's side with his arm around her shoulders.

Solomon glanced at Benjamin, who looked worn out and very sad.

"Mama, I don't want to go," Sarah said. "I want to stay here with you."

"I know. But you must go with your brother. And you must mind him. Do you understand?"

"I don't want to go," Sarah moaned again.

Solomon took both her hands in his. "Listen to me. I'll take care of you. And before you know it, Mama will come and find us."

"I don't believe you, Solomon."

"Have I ever lied to you?"

"No."

"I won't this time. I promise," he said. "Now come. We must go."

Zelda hugged her beloved children for several moments. Her mind went wild with worry, sadness, and terror. How could she be sending these two little children out into the world alone. But . . . she had no other choice, and she knew it. If she didn't send them away, Rumkowski would take them.

"Go. Please go, and hurry." Zelda had wrapped all the food she had left from her rations in a clean towel, which she gave to Solomon. Then she placed his father's gold ring into his hand. "This was your father's. It's real gold. Sell it to buy food or whatever else you need. I know you'll be careful," she said as her body was trembling.

Sarah saw her mother give Solomon the ring. "That's Papa's ring," she said angrily. "He'll want it when he comes back."

"It's all right. Papa told me to give it to Solomon," Zelda said. Her husband, Asher, who had been a volatile and abusive man, had been sent away on a transport. She didn't know if he would return. But if he did, she would worry about the ring then. Right now, she wanted Solomon to take it and use the money to provide for him and Sarah.

Solomon took the food. He plunged the ring deep into his pants pocket. Then he grabbed Sarah's hand. "Let's go. The guards in the tower are less likely to notice us while it's still dark."

"Mama? Are you sure I have to go?" Sarah said, shaking and holding her doll tightly.

Zelda nodded, then she said, "Sarala, I love you. Solomon, I love you too, my little man."

He nodded, trying hard to hold back his tears, then he forced himself to smile at his mother, hoping he was reassuring her as he gently dragged his sister out into the darkness. He felt his stomach lurch with fear. But he couldn't stop. He knew he must do as his mother asked. So, still holding tight to Sarah's hand, he pulled her, and within seconds they disappeared onto the route that he'd come to know so well. Before long, he knew they would come to the crack in the ghetto wall where he would push Sarah through and then follow behind her.

The streets were dark. Sarah gripped Solomon's hand tightly. He moved fast, but all his senses were on high alert. He'd done this a million times before but never with a five-year-old child hanging on to him. From the intensity of Sarah's grip, he could feel her terror. She needed comforting. He knew that; he could feel it. But it was not safe to stop and coddle her right now. He had to stay as vigilant as possible and get them out as quickly as he could, so even though he could hear her softly sobbing, he just squeezed her hand and pulled her along. Her short little legs made her slower. He was annoyed, but at the same time he felt sorry for her as she struggled to keep up with him clutching her doll in her arm.

"Who goes there?" It was the voice of one of the Germans. Solomon thought he could tell the Judenrat henchmen from the Nazi guards. This was a Nazi. *Damn*, he thought, breathing heavily.

When she heard the guttural German voice of the Nazi, Sarah let out a gasp. Solomon yanked her into an alley that was on the side of a building and put his hand over her mouth. She struggled to break free.

"Shh," he whispered into her ear. "If you promise not to say another word, I'll let you go."

She nodded, but when he let her go, she said, "I couldn't breathe with your hand over my mouth, Solomon! I'm telling Mama you hurt me."

"Shhh . . . I said shut up." He was harsher than he'd meant to be. He felt bad, but there was no time to explain. He had to get them out of there and fast. If they were captured, it would be bad, very bad. Sarah's body was shaking. She was crying silently now. He knew she'd been crying since they left, and he knew she was scared.

Solomon's hearing perked like the hearing of a dog as the

guard's bootheels hit the pavement. The Nazi was getting closer. Solomon knew he must act immediately. There was no time to think, only to act. He grabbed Sarah's hand roughly and pulled her along. He was pulling her so fast that she tripped and fell and skinned her knee. She let out a cry, but Solomon did not stop. He only dragged her harder and faster until they arrived at the wall. Then without stopping for a second, he pushed Sarah through the crack and followed her. Once they were on the other side, he lifted her up and ran with her until they reached an alleyway behind a general store. Then out of breath, he put her down.

"Stay quiet. We aren't safe yet," he whispered.

"I lost my dolly," Sarah said angrily. "She fell out of my hand when you pushed me. You pushed me so hard, Solomon. Mama would be angry if she knew. You hurt me. And you made me fall down and cut my knee too."

"Sarah, be quiet. You have to be very quiet. If they find us, they'll kill us. So don't make another sound." His tone of voice was harsh. She glared at him, but she didn't say a word. Instead, she put her thumb in her mouth and whimpered. Solomon glanced at her as she sat there looking small and frightened with her tear-stained face illuminated by the moonlight. He was sure she'd stopped sucking her thumb a year ago. But she'd reverted to it to comfort herself. Well, he didn't care if she did it now. He didn't care what she did so long as she kept quiet.

Solomon let out a long, low whistle like the call of a night bird.

It was several minutes, and then Solomon let out the whistle again. Just as Solomon expected, a man slipped out of the darkness. "Sol," he said. It was Wiktor, one of the men he dealt with from the Polish underground, who acquired things for him through the black market.

"It's me. I'm here," Solomon responded.

"What are you looking to buy?" Wiktor asked.

"Food. A gun, bullets."

"How much you got?"

"I got a gold ring. It's solid gold."

"Can't be worth much. Besides, how do I know it's real gold?"

"You're just gonna have to believe me. That's all. I've been working with you for over a year. I haven't tricked you yet. Why would I start now, Wiktor? This ring is worth plenty, and you know it."

"Sol, for a kid so young, you sure got a good head on your shoulders. All right. I'll get you a gun and bullets. I'll do what I can as far as the food. It's so damn scarce. But I'll try."

"And listen," Solomon said as he looked back at Sarah, who was huddled in the corner where he'd left her. "Can you get me a doll? Doesn't have to be a new doll or an expensive one. Just a doll."

"A doll? You want to waste your money on doll? Are you crazy?"

"I might be crazy. But I need a doll for my baby sister."

"That should be pretty easy, but it sure is a waste of money, don't you think?"

"Of course it is. Don't you think I know that? But . . ." Solomon looked back at Sarah, who was watching him with wide eyes. "Get it for me anyway."

"You want to pay? What do I care? I'll get you a doll. Meet me here tomorrow night. After dark, say eleven?"

"I'll be here," Solomon said.

CHAPTER 2

Ludwig Beck wiped the sweat from his brow on the sleeve of his green uniform. He was glad the sun was rising and his shift would soon be over. *I should be grateful to have a job, and at least I'm not fighting on the front lines,* he reminded himself as he did each morning before he finished patrolling the Lodz ghetto. When the father of his girlfriend, Hedy, had gotten him this job working for the Ordnungspolizei, or better known as the Grüne Polizei, he had no idea he was going to work all night to make sure that sick and filthy Jews did not escape the ghetto. This place was foul, and his work here was a far cry from what he'd originally hoped for when he joined the party and became involved with Hedy Keller. Ludwig had envisioned himself walking through the streets wearing the starched black uniform and shiny boots of the SS, commanding respect. But that was not the case.

It was a beautiful sunrise. The sky was clear, crystal blue, like sapphire. Making his final walk-through for the night, he tripped on something as he strolled along the edge where the wall and barbed wire kept the prisoners from daring to leave. When Ludwig looked down he saw the strangest thing, a doll. A torn and dirty rag doll. *A child would dare to come this close to the edge of the ghetto?* he thought as he bent down to look more closely. And as he did, he spotted a small hole in the wall, just large enough for a child to push through. *Why haven't I see this before?* he thought, but he knew why. It was because he made a habit of not looking at anything too closely. If he had his way, he would just count the hours until the end of his shift and then collect his pay. He was not interested in heroics. At least not until now.

CHAPTER 3

LUDWIG STUFFED THE DOLL INTO HIS JACKET AND LEFT THE GHETTO. As he boarded the bus, he felt self-conscious wondering if anyone noticed the bulge in his breast pocket. But no one paid any attention. The morning commute was filled with workers who had their own concerns. He took a seat alone in the back and rode quietly until the vehicle arrived at his stop. Once he left the bus, he walked for almost a mile to the small flat where Hedy lived. Technically, they were not living together, but he stayed with her much more than he stayed at home with his parents and sister.

Quietly, he turned the key in the lock and went inside. Expecting Hedy to be asleep, he sat down on the sofa and began to remove his shoes.

"I'm glad you're home," Hedy said, walking out of the bedroom.

"What are you doing up so early?"

"I had a terrible nightmare. I dreamed that you were shot."

"I'm here," he said as she ran into his arms.

"What is this?" She felt the bulge in his jacket and reached inside. "It's a doll? It's filthy. Do dolls and other inanimate objects carry lice?"

"I don't know," he admitted.

"Why, pray tell, do you have a doll?" she said, cocking her head.

"I found it by the wall of the ghetto."

"And you brought it home? Why would you ever do that? It's probably filled with lice. You should have put it right in the trash."

"I have a dilemma. Maybe we can talk about it? The truth is I don't know what to do." Ludwig shook his head. He gazed at Hedy. She wasn't his dream girl by any means. They'd met in the Hitler Youth program at a campout last summer. She liked him right away. He was not as taken with her. It wasn't that she was ugly—she wasn't. But no one would have called her a great beauty either with her long honey-colored curls that she wore in braids on either side of her head and her strong, stocky build. When his family met her, his mother referred to her as a sturdy and stable girl, the kind of girl who makes for a good wife. It didn't hurt that Hedy's father had friends in the Grüne Polizei, the green police, and when they became engaged after a short courtship, he'd helped Ludwig to secure this job. It paid well enough for Ludwig to help his family out a little, and for that reason his parents thought the marriage was a wonderful idea.

"Talk to me. Tell me what is bothering you, liebhaber," she said. She'd taken to calling him *lover* lately.

"You know how I like to keep to myself and not get in the middle of things, right? As I have told you before, sometimes when people get involved in things that don't concern them in the ghetto, they can end up in trouble."

"Yes, I know. You've said this many times."

"Well, this doll was lying right next to an opening in the wall that was large enough for a child to get out. And I think this child may have escaped."

She shrugged her shoulders. "Would anyone be the wiser?"

"I don't know. If today were a normal day, I would say no. But today is the roundup."

"Oh yes, I remember you mentioning this. Isn't this when they are taking all of the children on a transport?"

"Yes, they are going to be exterminated, but the prisoners don't know that. They are sending their children off."

"Nasty business," she said. "Would a single child make that much of a difference?" Hedy asked, lighting a cigarette.

"Perhaps. There is a ten-thousand-person quota that must be met."

"Ten thousand? One probably wouldn't make any difference. Do you want a smoke?" she asked.

He nodded and took a cigarette and lit it. "I don't know how many got out. Maybe just this one."

"Yes, maybe. But . . ."

"Yes?" he asked.

She paused for a moment inhaling a long, deep puff of smoke then she continued. "I was thinking. You know how you have been hoping for a promotion? And we've talked so much about how we would be happier and able to spend more time together if you were able to get off the night shift?" she said.

He nodded.

"Well, what if you could find these missing little rats and turn them in. Wouldn't that make you quite the hero? Then perhaps we would have some leverage to ask for favors."

He bit his lower lip and considered her question. "If there are several of these children, then yes, it might be possible."

"Even if there is only one. You will still have made quite the impression on your superiors having gone out of your way to uphold the law."

"Yes, that's true. But it somehow feels wrong to be hunting children."

"Does it? Think of them as demons, little Jews waiting to grow up to be big Jews. Besides, the one who escaped or the one who plotted the escape, must be a cunning little beast. Just imagine what she could be capable of doing to our beloved fatherland if she were allowed to grow up. Better to rid the world of these vermin while they're small. Don't you agree?"

He nodded.

"Then it's settled. You must find a way to hunt them down and return them to their captors."

CHAPTER 4

The following day, Solomon left Sarah hiding under the stairs in the back of an apartment building. "I'll be back as soon as I can. Don't move. Don't talk to anyone. Stay here and stay out of sight."

"I'm scared. I want to go back to Mama," Sarah moaned.

"We can't," Solomon said. He was tired and annoyed. "I'm hungry too."

"I know. Here, take the food Mama gave us, and eat some of the bread."

"What about you?"

"Don't worry about me. I'll be fine," Solomon said, taking off his jacket with the yellow star on it.

"You can't walk around without the star on your clothes. You'll get in trouble."

"Don't you worry about me. Now do what I told you, Sarah," Solomon said as he slipped out from under the stairwell and began strolling leisurely. *The main thing is to look as if I belong here,* he told himself. *I must act as if I'm just a Polish kid walking down the street. The worst I can be accused of is skipping school, and nobody will bother with that.*

He walked into a used clothing store and scanned the little girls' coats and dresses. Hating to part with the money, but knowing it was very necessary that Sarah must not be wearing anything with a gold star, he picked up the cheapest dress he could find and an inexpensive but warm coat he thought would fit. Then he went up to the woman at the counter and smiled. In his most charming voice, he said, "It's my sister's birthday. I want so badly to buy her a gift, but I don't have much money. Can I perhaps wash the windows here at your store in trade for these two small pieces of clothing? My little sister doesn't have a nice church dress, and I think she would love these." Solomon thought about removing the yellow stars from their clothes, but he was afraid that there would be a discoloration in the fabric where the stars had been, and it could give them away. He decided it was better if he were able to get his hands on new clothes.

The woman at the counter looked at the items and then at the boy. She looked to be in her late thirties. Solomon assumed she was probably a mother because she smiled at him, and when she did, it reminded him of his own mother. "Yes, all right. These aren't worth much. Go on. The windows are very dirty."

"Thank you so very much, ma'am."

Solomon washed the windows, and when he finished, the woman wrapped his package in brown paper. "I hope she enjoys her gifts," she said.

"I know she will, and thank you again for your kindness."

After Solomon left the clothing store, he grabbed an apple from the cart of a street vendor, who was busy selling to another customer. He tucked it into his jacket, then as soon as he turned the corner, he took it out and bit into the sweet, juicy flesh. *I sure am hungry*, he thought as he continued walking. An old woman was selling used pots. He gave her a sweet smile and asked where the Catholic church was located.

"You're not from around here?" she asked.

He was suddenly afraid that he'd made a terrible error. Why had he been so dumb as to ask a stranger for help? She could turn him in easily. Solomon thought about running away, but that would only cause her to be more suspicious. He'd talked to the men from the black market about their religion. Sometimes he'd heard them mention going to confession. "I'm not from Lodz," he said. "You see, I'm from the country. I've come to Lodz to visit my aunt who is sick, but I wanted to go and see a priest to do a confession."

"A confession? How old are you? What could a child your age possibly need to confess?"

"I'm small for my age. I'm actually fourteen. And I need to see a priest. It's about a girl."

"Oh." The woman turned red in the face. "Turn right at the corner and walk two blocks then turn left. You'll see the church."

"Thank you, ma'am."

The truth was Solomon was big for his age. He took after his father in that way. He was only nine but could pass for a young-looking fourteen with his broad shoulders and already developing muscles. And as far as girls were concerned, he might be only nine, but he had an idea of what went on between a boy and a girl. After all, he'd had a few clumsy encounters with older girls. Nothing really to speak of, a kiss here, a squeeze of the breast there. But enough for him to know that there was a world beyond the innocence of child-hood. And when he was talking to that woman who was selling the pots, he sensed that alluding to that world of men and women and sex would embarrass her enough to make her want to get away from him and the conversation as quickly as possible. His instincts had been correct. Solomon smiled a half smile as he walked toward the church.

Being forced onto the streets at a young age had not been easy. At first the older men who he worked with in the black market took advantage of him. They laughed at him and took his money deliv-ering insufficient or low-grade goods which he'd been hard pressed to sell for enough cash to buy more. However, he'd found ways to stay in the business. He'd also learned their slang, never letting them know that he understood what they were doing when they were making a deal. And as time passed, they learned to respect him, and then they even learned to like him.

Solomon entered the church and walked around. He'd never been inside a church before. But he had heard the Polish men from the underground mention that they had been to confession, so he knew that if anyone asked what he was doing there, he could say he needed to see a priest to confess even though he had no idea what that might entail. The main room inside the church was large with beautiful polished wood benches and a stained glass window that reflected an array of colors on the wood floor. It reminded Solomon of the synagogue he had gone to on high holidays before the Nazis had imprisoned him and his family in the ghetto. He didn't miss going to synagogue. He'd never cared much for religion.

No one bothered him as he walked through the rooms. He was hoping to find a store inside the church that sold a necklace with a cross hanging from it that he could purchase. But he found nothing. He sat down on the bench and sighed. *I'll have to talk to Wiktor or Majec and ask them if they can find me a cheap cross pendant.* As he stood up to leave, a man wearing a black robe came out from a back room.

"Hello, my son," he said.

Must be the priest, Solomon thought. Then he answered, "Good afternoon."

"How can I help you?"

"I don't know if you can." Solomon smiled. "It's my mother's birthday. And she's been very ill. My father is afraid she is dying. She sold her gold cross to buy food for our family, and now she doesn't have one anymore. And I want her to have one in case . . ."

"You mean her rosary?"

"Yes," Solomon said, not sure what a rosary was. But he hoped this was what he was looking for.

"Maybe I can help. Wait here."

The priest returned a few minutes later, carrying a small necklace of beads with a cross hanging from the end.

"How much do I owe you, sir?"

"Take it as a gift. Perhaps it will give your mother peace in her time of need."

"Many thanks to you, sir."

"God be with you, my son," the priest said as Solomon left the church.

A rosary, he called it. *I'll wear it as a necklace. I'll use it to identify me as a Catholic. Now I just have to find out what this thing is actually used for.*

When Solomon returned to the alley where he'd left Sarah, he found her huddled under the stairs red eyed and sucking her thumb. "Hi there," he whispered to her softly. "Are you all right?"

"I was scared. I didn't know if you'd ever come back. I wanted to run back to Mama, but I didn't remember how to get back, and even if I could find the way, I was afraid to go through that crack in the wall that you pushed me through last night." She was mad at him. He could see it in her eyes, which were so bloodshot from crying that it made him feel sick with guilt to look at her.

"I'm glad you didn't leave." He wanted to reassure her. "I promised you I'd be back, and here I am. Now I know you think of me as your older brother, and you don't always like to obey me, but it's important that you do as I ask at least for right now. You can't ever go back through that crack in the wall. Do you understand me?" His voice was tender and caring.

She nodded. He gently put his hands on her shoulders and looked into her eyes, then he continued to speak. "Sarah, I will always take care of you if you will only let me. But you must listen to me carefully and do whatever I say."

"I don't have to." She struggled to get away from him. He held her shoulders gently but firmly.

"Sarah. I love you. I know that you think I am being bossy. But I'm not. I'm trying to protect us. Please, promise me you will do as I ask."

She scoffed but she nodded.

"Good." He smiled. "So did you have something to eat?"

"No." She shook her head. "I couldn't eat."

"Let's have a little bread now. Would you like that?"

She nodded.

He'd eaten the apple he stole, but it had hardly made a dent in his empty stomach. Solomon was growing fast and because of this he was always hungry. Most nights he dreamed of food. And there were times he wanted to throw caution to the wind and gobble every last morsel they had. But he knew he was on his own. No one was going to help them. So even as his stomach growled, he knew he had to make the food last as long as possible. Saliva generated in his mouth as he ripped off a nice-sized piece of bread for Sarah and then a small one for himself. "Eat this," he said.

"You should take the bigger one," she said.

He kissed the top of her head. "I had an apple. That one is for you."

"Are you sure?"

"Absolutely sure." He smiled at her. She smiled back.

"Don't ever leave me alone. Don't ever go away on a transport. Promise me you'll always come back and get me. Promise me," she said.

"I won't leave you."

"Do you promise?"

"I promise," he said, taking a deep breath hoping it was true, hoping he wouldn't be arrested and taken away leaving her alone. But he said nothing. Instead, he forced a reassuring smile. "Here, take these clothes and put them on."

"Where did you get these?" she asked.

"I worked for them."

"Today?"

"Yes, today, Sarah. Please stop asking so many questions. I'm tired. Just put them on . . . please?"

"Turn around and don't look, all right?" she said.

"Of course. I promise not to look. Just put on the clothes."

CHAPTER 5

THAT NIGHT SOLOMON TOOK SARAH WITH HIM WHEN HE WENT TO meet with Wiktor. It was an inconvenience to have her tagging along that made negotiating deals tougher, but he dared not leave her alone under the stairwell at night. Anything could happen. When they arrived at the meeting spot, Solomon let out his bird call, but there was no answer. A full hour passed before Solomon heard the bird call returned. Cautiously, he answered with the same call.

"Sol?"

"Yes."

"I got everything you asked for." It was Wiktor.

"Good," Solomon said, then he turned to Sarah and said, "Stay here and wait." Then he stepped out of the shadows.

"Do you know how to use this gun?" Wiktor asked.

"Show me once. I'll remember."

"How is a nine-year-old child so sure of himself?" Wiktor asked, shaking his head.

"Because I've had to be. Now show me."

Wiktor showed Solomon how to use the gun, but they did not fire it because of the noise, and they also wanted to conserve bullets.

"I also got you some bread. And here's the doll you wanted."

"How much for all of it?" Solomon asked. "The ring. I thought we agreed on the ring," Wiktor said as he cast his eyes on Solomon.

"The ring is worth so much more than this," Solomon said.

"It's your decision. But you'll have a hard time getting your hands on a gun. If you want the gun, I want the ring in exchange."

"All right," Solomon moaned, stuffing the gun and ammunition into his pocket.

"It's none of my business, of course, but why do you need a gun?" Wiktor asked suddenly.

"It's strange that you would ask so many questions. Why do you want to know?"

"Because yesterday I heard a rumor. I heard they were taking all the children out of the ghetto and sending them away to some kind of prison camp. Is it true?"

"It's true."

"Are you going back there? With the gun?"

"What's it to you?"

"I don't think you should go back, even with a gun," Wiktor said. "Listen to me. I have a place for you to go. I happen to know of a farmer who needs workers. His place is way out in the country. He wouldn't need to know you were Jewish. I'd tell him you and your sister are the children of friends of mine. I'll say your parents can't afford to keep you and that's why you need to go out and work."

"What's in it for you, Wiktor? I know you're not doing this out of the kindness of your heart." Solomon stood there in the shadow holding the doll by one arm and wishing he could see the older man's eyes. He trusted no one.

"I'll get paid from the farmer for bringing him help, workers who will work for him."

"He'll give you money?"

"Not money, but extra food."

"And Sarah and me? Do we get paid anything?"

"You get a place to sleep and food to fill your belly. What more do you want? You could end up in a prison camp. It wouldn't

21

surprise me to find out the Nazi bastards killed those children. They are heartless."

"Yeah, you're right." Solomon nodded, raising one eyebrow as he considered the proposal. "A farm wouldn't be bad."

"It's hard work; I won't lie to you. But you'll have a fighting chance at survival."

"We'll take it."

"I have a truck I can use to drive the two of you out to the farm tomorrow night. Meet me here at the same time."

"We'll be here," Solomon said as he watched Wiktor walk away. He had no reason not to trust this man, but even so, Solomon had learned that anyone could have an agenda. After all, there was a reward for turning in Jews. Solomon had a price tag on his head. That made him very cautious. So he trusted no one except Sarah.

Sarah had been waiting quietly in the alley. When Solomon returned, he heard her sigh with relief. Then he handed her the doll.

"Solomon!" she exclaimed and wrapped her small arms around his neck and hugged him. "Is she mine?"

"Yes, of course she's yours."

"She's beautiful," Sarah said.

They could hardly see the doll in the darkness, but Solomon could tell the doll was far from new. She was a doll made from rags, very similar to the one Sarah lost, but probably dirtier and older. They would be able to see her better in the morning light. Still, Solomon could tell how happy Sarah was by the way she held the doll close to her chest, and he was glad that he'd spent the extra money even though they needed every penny they could get their hands on for food.

"Come on," he said. "We have to get back under the stairwell for the night." Taking Sarah's hand, he led her away from his meeting spot near the ghetto wall where he always met with Wiktor or Majec.

That night, Solomon was dog tired but he couldn't sleep. Watching Sarah as she snored softly, he felt a strange mixture of protective love and resentment. If he were alone, he could take risks more easily. He'd always been fast on his feet and able to escape when necessary, but with Sarah at his side, he was encumbered. She might not be able to keep up, and he would never leave her behind. Solomon sighed, and his thoughts shifted to his parents, especially his mother. He'd never cared for his father who had beaten him more times than he could count. But his mother, he loved his mother, and he wondered if he would ever see her again. He felt his eyes well up, but he dared not cry. *I must be the grown-up, and if Sarah awakens and sees me crying she will be afraid. No, I must not cry. Not now, not ever.*

Taking a deep breath, he thought about Wiktor and the Polish underground. So far, they'd been fair with him. They'd over-charged him sometimes, but that was to be expected. At least they had not turned him in to the Nazis. But Solomon believed that he'd only survived for this long because of his instincts. And right now, his instincts were flashing a warning. Wiktor had proven to him that he was truly a hater of Nazis, but Solomon knew that Wiktor was also a lover of money. Could he put his life and Sarah's life in Wiktor's hands? What if he was planning to sell them to the Nazis? How was it that he knew that all the Jewish children were being removed from the ghetto? Would he be so cunning as to lure Solomon and his sister so as to claim a reward? Solomon bit his lower lip and assessed his situation. If he didn't go with Wiktor, he and Sarah could escape to the forests and wander until they found a farm on their own then ask for work. If they did this, there would be no risk because no one would know they were really Jews. If they went with Wiktor, he could always hold the truth over their heads.

Glancing over at Sarah as she slept, he looked at her trusting face and wished someone other than he were making the decisions. Feeling the cold steel of the gun in his pocket, he felt a little more secure. Next to the gun was the cross he bought. He felt the beads and sighed. Tomorrow he would make his way to the cobbler and see if he could find a way to get his hands on a leather cord to attach to the cross instead of the beads. Then he would wear it around his neck. At least neither he nor Sarah wore the yellow star on their clothing anymore, so they appeared to be regular Polish children.

Again, Solomon glanced over at Sarah. She was bathed in moonlight as she held the doll tightly in her little arms. A smile came over his face. Some people might think the doll was a waste of money, but he didn't. He was glad about how happy it made her. It gave her comfort. And God knows, he thought, the poor child needs some comfort.

CHAPTER 6

IN THE MORNING BEFORE SOLOMON TOOK SARAH INTO TOWN WITH him, he warned her several times not to tell anyone that they were Jewish.

"Now we are going to have to use different names."

"Why?"

"Because our names are Jewish names."

"I don't understand," she said.

"You don't have to understand everything. Just do what I tell you. I am going to give you a new name, and you are going to use that name."

"You always boss me around, Solomon. Just because you're older doesn't mean you can lord it over me."

"Sarah"—he sighed exasperated—"please, just do as I ask. Will you? I am saying please. I'm not lording it over you."

She looked down at the ground and nodded.

"All right," he said, fluffing her hair. "How do you like the name Maria? It's pretty, isn't it?"

Sarah shrugged. "Yes, I suppose it is."

"And my name will be Artur."

"Maria and Artur Rabinowitz?"

"No, not Rabinowitz." He smiled. "How do you like the surname Zajec?"

"I don't know. But Mama says it's wrong to lie. And this is like lying."

"No, it's like playing pretend."

"It is?"

"Yes, but you must be sure that no one ever finds out the truth. It's very important. Very important."

"So if anyone asks, my name is Maria Zajec?"

"Exactly. We are strict Catholics. We go to church on Sunday."

"I don't think Mama would like this. This is really lying."

"Sarah . . . do as I tell you. I am doing this for your own good. And I can't keep begging you. Please, Sarah? Please?"

She nodded.

"My name is Maria, and your name is Artur; our last name is Zajec, and we are Catholics."

"Right. Our parents were killed in a fire. We are looking for work."

"We're orphans? Isn't it bad luck to say that? Our parents might get killed because we said it."

"We're just playing pretend, remember?"

"Yes. I remember."

"Good." He smiled. "It's all right. You'll see. You can play pretend, and nothing bad will happen."

"And Solomon . . . thank you for the doll."

He smiled.

CHAPTER 7

THE FOLLOWING NIGHT THEY DIDN'T SHOW UP TO MEET WITH Wiktor. Solomon decided he and Sarah would make a go of it on their own. He felt it was safer than putting his trust in Wiktor. For five nights they took shelter under the stairwell, but with each passing day, their food supply was dwindling more and more, and the weather was growing colder. Solomon knew he could steal food from the carts of vendors, which would keep them alive at least for now, but once the upcoming winter set in they would need shelter.

In the afternoons when the sun was shining it was not nearly as chilly as it was at night. Sarah shivered as she tried to sleep. And even though Solomon told her many times that he was trying to steal blankets for them, she continued to complain about how cold she was. So in order to keep her quiet, he gave her the use of his jacket, which left him freezing and angry.

By the end of the week, all of their food was gone, and Solomon was stealing food from the carts of the street vendors. He'd leave Sarah for a few hours in the morning and go off to see what he could find. Once, he returned with an apple and several small raw potatoes, which Sarah had complained tasted funny. He considered trying to find work of some sort. Because of his height and heavy bone structure, it would be easy to lie about his age. But he was afraid that a potential employer would ask for papers. When Solomon had no papers, the employer might suspect he was Jewish and have him arrested. He was terrified of being arrested because he'd seen the cruelty of the Nazis firsthand when they'd beaten an old woman to death in the ghetto. And he was certain they would do even worse to a Jewish child who had evaded the transport in the Lodz ghetto. Those chilling facts were always lingering in the back of his mind. But there was even more to consider: if Solomon were arrested and taken away, that would leave Sarah waiting for him under the stairwell. She would be there all alone waiting for a brother who would not return.

Solomon bit his lower lip as he allowed himself to consider Sarah. The poor thing was just a child. She was much more of a child than he'd ever been, and he knew she would never be able to fend for herself. She would starve or turn herself in, hoping to find sympathy from the local people. A sympathy that he was convinced did not exist. *They would turn her right in to the Nazis and collect whatever reward was offered,* he thought. *To make matters even worse, Sarah and I are not blonde-haired, blue-eyed children which the Nazis love. No, both of us have dark hair and dark eyes. Both of us look Jewish.*

"Sol, is this all we have to eat?" Sarah asked, shivering as the sun began to set. She bit into a potato that had begun sprouting eyes.

"Yes, for now it is."

"Why can't we get some bread?"

"Because there is no bread," he said. "How am I supposed to get us bread?"

"Don't you have any money left?"

"No, I spent it all on food and this gun."

"And my dolly, right? My dolly cost us money, and now we are going to starve. It's all my fault." She looked down, and there were tears in her eyes.

"Don't cry, Sarah. It's not your fault. I'll do what I can to get us some bread tomorrow," he said, trying to soothe her. But he was thinking that she was driving him crazy. She needed constant reassurance, and she was always crying. It was hard enough on him to try and find food and keep them safe, but he had to comfort her too.

She laid her head on his lap. "I wish we could go back to Mama," she said.

"I know. But we can't."

"Why not?"

"Because its not safe. We can't go back there," he said, trying to keep his voice kind and gentle, but his patience was waning. *She asks me the same questions over and over.*

"I want to . . ." she said, ready to throw a fit. "I don't care what happens; I want to go back to Mama."

"I know, but stop asking me about it, will you, please? Because we can't go back."

CHAPTER 8

THE FOLLOWING MORNING, SOLOMON LEFT EARLY AND WENT OUT TO see what food he might steal. The market had been busy which made it easy for him to lift two apples and a small loaf of bread. He hummed softly to himself as he returned to the stairwell where he'd left Sarah. *This will make a wonderful meal for Sarah and I. She'll be so happy. I know how hard it is for her to eat the raw potatoes. Things sure went well this morning. I'll have to go out earlier from now on when the market is busy and the vendors are distracted.*

As Solomon swung his body over the railing that hid the deep stairwell where he'd left his little sister, he heard her saying something. It was a muffled cry, but it sounded like she was calling for him. *Something's wrong.* Taking the stairs two at a time he reached the bottom quickly. There he saw an old man with greasy gray hair and a filthy white shirt. The man's pants were around his knees. His bare buttocks were pale and wrinkled, and his hand covered Sarah's mouth. She was trapped in the corner. Her face was filled with tears; her eyes were wide with horror.

His breath caught in his throat. This terrible man was about to do something unspeakable to his little sister. Not even a second passed before Solomon pulled the gun out of his pocket and started walking toward the man. Instinctively, he knew to stay far enough away from the old bastard just in case he might try to take the gun away and use it on him or Sarah. His heart raced, but there was no time to think. Moving quickly, within seconds he was within firing distance. Without allowing himself to think, Solomon pulled the trigger. The man fell on Sarah like a giant rag doll. She let out a scream. Blood flew into Solomon's face. He wiped it away with his hand and then with all of his strength, he pulled the man off his sister. It was only once Sarah was free that he realized the smell of alcohol that permeated the room. He recognized it from the days when his father would drink too much and beat him or his mother.

"Sarah? Are you all right?" he asked.

She didn't answer. Instead, she ran into his arms. Her face was wet with tears and the man's splattered blood. "Are you all right?" he asked again, falling to his knees. How could he let this happen? He blamed himself. He should never have left her alone. Solomon held his sister tightly. "Did he hurt you?" he asked again.

"He hit me," she said.

"Come over here where there is some light and let me see," Solomon said.

Sarah's face was red and already starting to bruise, but there was only a little blood around her nose and lip.

"What happened?" he asked.

Between heart-wrenching sobs, she said, "It was my fault. I went outside. I didn't want to stay down here; it was so dark, and I was scared because I was all alone. I wanted to see if I could find a little girl to play with. There was no one out there, so I just sat outside under a tree for a little while. I'm sorry. I'm so sorry." She was choking on her tears. "Then I saw this man looking at me and I got a bad feeling. So I ran back down here. But he followed me, and he tried to put his hands under my dress. I told him no. But he got mad, and I was so scared, Solomon. Then he hit me. I fell down, and I hurt my knee, but he still kept trying to touch me in my private place. Mama said I should never let anyone do that to me. But when I said no, he put his hand over my mouth. I was so scared. It was horrible. He was like a monster.

31

Please, Solomon, I want to go home to Mama. I want to go home."

Solomon hugged his sister tightly.

"Did he touch you in your private place?"

"He tried, but I kept moving around, and he couldn't touch me there. He said that he was going to kill me. He was so angry, and his eyes were red like a demon. But then you came . . ."

"Let's get out of here," Solomon said. He wanted to vomit. Bile rose into his mouth. Fighting to keep it down, he looked away from her.

Solomon was shaking. He'd killed a man today. He was glad he'd come in time, and he was glad he'd been able to help his sister before that bastard had really hurt her. But he couldn't get over the fact that he'd killed another human being. Before this he'd never so much as hurt another living thing.

As they emerged out into the light, Solomon saw the blood on his jacket and on his sister's face and dress. Both her knees were skinned. So he decided if anyone stopped them and asked questions, he would tell them Sarah had taken a fall and that was where the blood came from.

She was gripping his hand so tightly that it hurt. He never realized she had that much strength in her little hand. Solomon didn't say anything or move his hand. He just let her. He knew how terrified she was. In her other hand she held the doll tightly. They walked for a long while before she spoke. "Are you angry with me?" she said in a small voice.

"Why?"

"Because I went outside when you told me not to. And . . ." Looking down, she saw the blood on her dress. "I ruined my new dress. Oh, Solomon, look at my dress." She was crying again.

"I'm not angry," he said, stopping and kneeling down so that his face was at the same level as hers. "But you must listen to me from now on. Please. This is not a game, Sarah. We don't have Mama to rely on. It's all on me. I am responsible to take care of you, and the only way I can do that is if you listen to me, all right?"

"Yes, I promise. I will try to listen to everything you tell me from now on. But please, don't leave me alone again. It was terrible. So horrible. That man . . . I can still see his eyes . . ."

"I know," Solomon said. "I know." Then he hugged her tightly. "And don't feel bad. I'll find a way to get you another dress very soon. I promise, all right?" He put his thumb under her chin so she would lift her face and look into his eyes. "Don't cry."

She shrugged.

"Come on, please don't cry."

She looked so small holding the old doll he'd gotten for her. "I hate to see you cry."

She tried to muster a smile.

"There you go. You look so pretty when you smile."

"Mama always used to say that."

"I know," he said. "I remember."

That night, Solomon found an area in the park where there was a patch of trees and bushes. "Why don't we sit here and have our meal. We can stay here until morning."

"It's dark and it's cold. I want to go home," Sarah said.

"We talk about this everyday, Sarah. And every day I tell you that we can't go home. Here," Solomon said, handing his sister an apple, "you love apples."

Sarah shook her head. "I can't eat. I feel sick. And I won't even try until you take me back to Mama," she demanded.

He didn't force her to eat; he couldn't even bring himself to try. Instead, he wrapped her portion of the food he had stolen in the cloth his mother had given them and hoped she would be hungry enough to eat it in the morning. But she wasn't. And by the following night, Sarah still had not eaten. Solomon stayed by her side. His stomach growled with hunger, but he dared not leave her to go out and forage for food. Instead, he sat beside her patting her head the way their mother did when they were small. Finally, Sarah insisted he eat the bread and the apple that he'd saved for her. He wanted to be noble and say no. But his hunger won out, and he finally gobbled it down. As he watched her lay next to him without speaking, he tried to make-believe that everything would be all right. But a nagging voice in the back of his mind told him that nothing would ever be all right again. Little Sarah had been harmed, if not physically, certainly emotionally, and the change in her once feisty, argumentative personality worried him. She just lay still; she seemed to have lost all fight. And Solomon knew that if she didn't eat, she would become physically weak and then susceptible to diseases. He'd seen it happen to plenty of children who were starving when they were in the ghetto.

"Sarah," he whispered, "do you ever want to see Mama again?"

"I want to see Mama and Papa again," she said.

His father had been taken out of the ghetto on a transport, and he couldn't be sure where he was. But even though he didn't know if they would ever see their parents again, he promised anyway. "If you want to see them again, you have to eat. Because if you don't eat, you'll get very sick, and you might even die."

"Die?" She looked at him, her eyes wide. "Do you think I could really die?"

"Yes," he said somberly.

"But we don't have any more food," she argued.

"I'll go out and get some."

"You can't leave me here alone again. Please, Solomon. Please take me with you," she begged.

How am I going to steal food with her hanging on to me? I won't be able to get away fast enough if I'm spotted. "I can't take you, Sarah. I don't think you will be able to keep up."

"Don't leave me here alone. I would rather die than be here all alone. Please, Solomon."

Solomon looked at his sister and shook his head. "All right," he said, "come on. Let's go and see what we can get for you to eat. But if I take you with me . . . I'm going to need a promise from you."

"All right. I'll promise you anything, only don't leave me here."

"You have to promise me that you'll eat the food I get. Will you?"

She nodded. "I will."

"And that you'll do whatever I tell you to do without questioning me?"

"I promise."

"Come on, then."

Solomon took Sarah's hand, and they walked toward the village square where the merchants sold their goods. "Keep up with me. Don't slow down," he warned her. But he could see she was moving her short little legs as fast as she could.

He easily stole two potatoes and a bunch of carrots from the cart of a vendor who was busy flirting with a pretty young house-wife. Then came the baker. They walked inside the bakery shop. It was crowded, but there were loaves of bread on a shelf. Solomon's eyes darted around the room. He felt his heart pound in his throat. No one seemed to be looking. He glanced down at Sarah. *She is slow,* he thought. Then grasping Sarah's hand tighter, he grabbed a loaf of bread and shoved it into his jacket. A middle-aged woman with a red, wind-burned face and a wart on her chin, yelled out, "Thief! Stop him!" and pointed at Solomon.

Pulling Sarah through the crowd, Solomon felt as if there were a thousand hands reaching out to grab him. "Run," he told Sarah. "Run as fast as you can."

She tripped on a stone and almost fell on her face, but Solomon's grip on her arm was so tight that he held her upright. Sarah winced but Solomon kept going. They raced through the streets. People stopped what they were doing to stare as the baker yelled, pointing at the children. "Get the boy! Stop him! He's a thief!"

A woman who had been standing outside a beauty shop shouted in a voice loud enough for Solomon to hear as he and Sarah ran by. "I think that boy stole a woman's handbag. He's a criminal. Who knows what else he is capable of . . ."

Solomon didn't know where they came from, but he saw that two Gestapo agents had joined the chase. They were yelling at him in German, telling him to stop or they would shoot. He didn't stop. He pulled Sarah and ran as fast as he could. Even as he ran, he could hear her crying. *This mistake could cost us our lives. She's far too slow,* he thought as he stopped for a single moment and lifted her. Already out of breath from running he found Sarah too heavy to carry, and they both fell down. Sarah skinned her knee ripping the old scab off. She began weeping even louder now, but Solomon knew there was no time to comfort her. He pulled her to her feet. Then he pushed her inside an apartment building, and pulling her arm he led her down the hall.

"You hurt me," she said.

"I'm sorry." He was leaning against a wall struggling to catch his breath. *We are still not safe*, he thought. *We can't stay here. The Gestapo could come in and find us any minute. I have to find somewhere that is safer. But where?* The sweat from his brow stung as it ran into his eyes. He'd never paid much attention to God or religion. It had been something that his parents had tried to force on him on high holidays. He'd gone to the synagogue with them because his father demanded it, but he didn't pay attention. Instead, when his father wasn't looking, he played practical jokes on his friends or made faces at the boys who were sitting across the aisle. That was a more innocent time. But now as he stood in the dimly lit hallway of an apartment building far away from his parents' protection, holding his sister's hand, he was desperate. Solomon Lipman needed help, so he turned to God. Solomon began to pray silently. He begged God to help him, to ensure that no one would find them. Closing his eyes, he prayed as he had never prayed before. Sarah watched him silently, still holding the arm of her rag doll in her hand, her face stained with tears and her eyes wide with fear. The crowd was outside. Terrifying sounds of the angry Gestapo agents shouting in their guttural German penetrated the thin walls of the building.

If we are caught, they will see that we have no papers. Then they'll know we're Jews. They could easily shoot us on the spot.

But something in the prayers of the frightened nine-year-old attracted God's attention.

A young woman wearing a brown wool coat and carrying a toddler in her arms came out of one of the apartments. She glanced over at Solomon and Sarah. Her eyes met Solomon's and held his gaze for a moment.

"Are you two the reason for all the commotion in the street?" she asked.

Solomon wanted to run, but he dared not go outside. "Yes." He nodded, feeling his heart drop into his belly, but not knowing what else to do.

She looked at him and then at Sarah and said, "Hurry up. Come inside before they find you."

Sarah squeezed Solomon's hand. He looked at her and could see she wasn't sure that they should go inside. "It's all right," Solomon told his sister, hoping it was. "Let's do what the nice lady tells us to do."

Sarah followed Solomon inside.

"Both of you, quickly, get under the bed, and stay there until this blows over," she said.

Solomon did as the woman asked. He listened to Sarah's heavy breathing as they lay beneath the bed. His heart was racing. This woman had them captive. She could easily go outside and alert the Gestapo. But he had to trust her. He had no other option. Then he heard a knock on the door.

"Yes?" he heard the woman say.

"Have you seen two young hooligans come through here?" the man said in a mixture of German with a little Polish. This led Solomon to believe that it might be the Gestapo agent.

"Hooligans?" she said. "No, I haven't seen anyone."

"Well, you'd better keep your door locked," the man said. His tone was almost flirtatious.

"Thank you. I will."

Solomon heard the door close and the lock turn. *This woman who didn't know them at all had protected them. Why?* he thought.

"Don't come out yet," she whispered. "Wait for a few minutes. I want to be sure they are gone."

Solomon didn't answer, but he did as she instructed.

After several minutes of silence outside, the woman came into the bedroom. "You can come out. I think it's safe. I think they are gone."

Solomon helped Sarah out.

"What happened?" the woman asked.

Solomon considered making up a story, but he couldn't think

straight, so he blurted out the truth. He even told this kind stranger that they were Jewish.

She listened quietly. He couldn't help but think she was very pretty with her soft and gentle eyes. When he'd finished, she said, "You can stay here until nightfall. My husband comes home from work right after dark. I am afraid he would not approve of what I did today. He would think it was reckless and that it put the baby and I in danger. I hope you understand. So you'll have to be gone before he arrives. I'm sorry. I wish I could offer you more time here, but I can't. I have a little boy, and I must protect him too. And I know that if I am caught harboring Jews, my child will be in danger. I don't know what else to say."

"I understand. Of course, I understand," Solomon said. "And . . . thank you for helping us. May God bless you." *This was God. God sent this woman to help us. I never understood before today, but now I think I do.* His body tingled as he realized the miracle he'd just experienced.

CHAPTER 9

LUDWIG HADN'T HEARD ANYTHING ABOUT ESCAPED CHILDREN;
however, the quota had been short. Each day, as Hedy had
suggested, he watched the hole in the wall to see if any of the children returned to their parents, but no one ever came back. He'd
almost given up when one of the other Grüne Polizei officers told
him about two children who had robbed the bakery shop that day.

"They got away with all of the old baker's money. I heard they
held a knife to his neck," the other officer said. "They were a couple
of cunning children who took everything he had. They sound like
dirty little Jews, don't they?"

Ludwig listened carefully. *He used the word cunning. Wasn't that the
same word Hedy had used?* "Did anyone check the neighborhood to see
if they were hiding somewhere?"

"Yes, these two children, a boy and a girl, were seen going into
an apartment just a few blocks away from the bakery."

"Who owns the apartment?" Ludwig asked.

"Helmut and Irma Reinhardt."

"You have an address?"

"Why, are you going to talk to them?"

"If you'll watch the ghetto for me, I'd like to," Ludwig said.

"I could do that for you, but I need a favor," the other officer said.

"Of course. A favor for a favor. What do you need?" Ludwig said, trying to hide the bit of sarcasm in his voice.

"I need Saturday night off. I have a date. Will you cover for me?"

"Yes, of course." Ludwig nodded, relieved that the favor was not something that could cause him any problems.

CHAPTER 10

THAT EVENING AT AROUND SEVEN, LUDWIG MADE HIS WAY TO THE Reinhardts' apartment. He knocked on the door and waited several minutes until a man in a white sleeveless T-shirt, with thick tufts of hair spraying out from under his arms, opened the door.

"Helmut Reinhardt?" Ludwig asked in the most authoritative voice he could muster.

Irma came up behind her husband with the baby in her arms. When she saw Ludwig in his police uniform, she gasped and almost lost her grip on the baby.

Helmut heard her gasp and turned to see that her face had lost all of its color. A quick glance at her hand told him she was trembling. He turned back to the officer. "I am Helmut Reinhardt. I am the man of this house. What is it you want?" he said, walking outside and closing the door behind him.

Irma lay the baby down in his bassinet, which was really no more than an empty dresser drawer filled with blankets, then she put his pacifier in his mouth. Once he began to suck on the pacifier, she ran to the bedroom and got down on her knees to look under the bed. She had to be sure there was no evidence that the children had been there. She saw a spot of blood on the floor. There was no time to get a rag. Quickly, she took the bottom of her dress and wiped it. Once she was sure there was no other trace of the children to be found, she ran back to the door and leaned against it to listen. The speech between her husband and the police officer was muffled, but she made out enough to know that the Lodz ghetto police were still hunting for the children. As she felt the doorknob turn, she moved away from the door. Then officer Ludwig Beck came rushing inside with her husband at his heels. The baby felt the tension in the room and began to scream in a high-pitched voice. Irma picked him up and cradled him, but he was still howling. She rocked him until he was quiet, and all she could hear were Ludwig's bootheels on the floor and her own terrified heartbeat.

Ludwig went through the apartment searching like a bloodhound. He found nothing. Defeated and embarrassed, he apologized to Helmut and proceeded to make his way to the door. Then just as Ludwig opened the door to leave, the baby let out a loud wail. The sound startled him, and he turned. When he did, he saw the blood on the skirt of Irma's dress. "It looks like you're bleeding?" he asked.

Irma thought she might faint. The words caught in her throat. She could not speak.

"Oh, I didn't realize that I'd gotten blood on your dress when I handed the baby to you earlier," Helmut said to Irma. Then shaking his head he added, "How clumsy of me." He continued now addressing his conversation to Ludwig. "Our son is teething. I'm afraid my wife is better at taking care of this problem than I. So earlier when his tooth was coming through and he started bleeding, I handed him to her. It seems I've ruined her dress."

Ludwig didn't know much about children so he smiled and left the apartment, but something didn't seem quite right to him. His gut told him they were lying. But he had no proof.

If these children were here, they did a very good job of hiding the fact. Hedy was right when she called them cunning little beasts. I will keep an eye out and contact all my informants to see what I can find out.

42

CHAPTER 11

WHILE SARAH AND HER BROTHER WAITED FOR NIGHTFALL, SOLOMON gave Sarah a hunk of the bread and two carrots they'd stolen. "Eat this," he demanded. He was hungry but not hungry enough to eat. Instead, he tried to hold on to the food as long as possible. This time she didn't argue with him. The young woman who was hiding them had given them water. And while Sarah ate, Solomon chewed on his lower lip and began to think. *We can't go on this way. It's only a matter of time before we are arrested for something. Sarah is too slow to keep up. The only thing we can do is go back and find Wiktor. I am going to have to take him up on his offer to take us out to a farm. I am going to have to trust him. I know things could go badly because he has every reason to turn us in. After all, we are worth money to him, but he's always seemed to be a decent man. I have to believe that he is not the kind of man who would put two children in danger. But then again, money does things to people. I've seen this firsthand. I've seen people turn their families in for money in order to buy food . . . to stay alive for one more day. And I know Wiktor is always looking for ways to earn money. Still, I am forced to trust him. I must. What else can I do?* Solomon argued with himself.

Finally, they arrived at the familiar place where Solomon and Wiktor always met. "We have to wait here until it's totally dark outside," Solomon told Sarah.

"Do you think he'll come here?"

"I don't know. He expected me days ago, and I never came."

"He might not come. If he doesn't, what are we going to do?"

"I don't know. I will have plenty of time to worry about that if it happens," Solomon said, and then he ripped off a piece from the loaf of bread and handed it to Sarah. "Eat this." Then ripping a smaller piece for himself, he sat down and waited. The trees shifted in the gentle but chilly autumn breeze. Sarah shivered from the cold as Solomon broke the silence of the night with the call of the night bird.

There was no answer. In desperation he tried again, this time louder. Then he waited for several seconds. When he heard the coo-coo echo through the darkness, his stomach lurched with fear but also with relief.

"Wiktor?" he said.

"No, it's me Majec. Is that you, Sol?"

"Yes, it's me."

Majec stepped out of the shadows. Then another bird call came from somewhere in the area. Majec answered it with a call of his own. A man Solomon recognized from the ghetto appeared. He was a small, slender fellow, short enough and thin enough to be able to get through the crack in the ghetto wall. Solomon assumed that since there were no more children in the ghetto, this man had taken over the business of buying goods from the Polish for the black market.

"Is that you, Heimy Blumenthal?" Solomon asked.

"Solomon Lipman? Zelda's boy?"

"Yes, it's me."

"It's good to see you," Heimy said. "The children are all gone from the ghetto."

"I know. My sister and I ran away the night before that Judenrat, Rumkowski, sent the children on the transport."

Heimy just nodded and shuffled his feet.

"Do you happen to know how my mother is doing?" Solomon asked.

Heimy hesitated. "Yes. I know."

"Well, Nu? Tell me?" Solomon was anxious, but he needed to know.

"Oy, Sol. She was sent away on the transfer with the children. Except for the real old folks, she was the only adult on the transport. I'm sorry to be the one to tell you this."

"Are you sure?" Solomon asked, his heart in his throat.

"I'm sure. I saw it with my own eyes. I couldn't help her. No one could."

Until now, Sarah had been silent. But when she heard the news about her mother, she let out a small cry of pain. Solomon turned to look at her. His heart ached for his mother, and for himself, but most of all for little Sarah who looked so small and helpless holding the dirty rag doll as she sat on the pavement in the darkness.

"Does anyone know where they sent the transport?"

"No, no one knows. People speculate, but no one really knows," Solomon answered, but he had to turn away. Even in the darkness he couldn't hide the tears that had begun to form in his eyes. *Mama?* he thought. *My mother is gone. They've taken her away. They might even have killed her.* The idea was so painful that he pushed it out of his mind.

"I'm sorry, Sol," Majec said. "I really am." He patted Solomon's shoulder. Solomon just nodded. Then Majec turned to the other man and took out a potato sack with a few items inside. "Here are the things you wanted me to get for you. Do you have the money?"

Heimy nodded and took a bunch of coins out of his pocket. He placed them in Majec's hand. Then he turned to Solomon. "If I hear anything else about your mother or the transport she was on, I'll let Majec know." He nodded at Majec who responded with a nod.

"Go in peace and good luck to you," Majec said.

Solomon nodded again, but his shoulders were slumped. At nine years old he felt like an old man. There were things he wanted to say, but his throat was closed, and he found that he was unable to speak.

Heimy took the sack that Majec had given him and ran off toward the ghetto wall.

Majec turned to Solomon. "Bring your sister and follow me."

"Where are we going?"

"To my home, of course. I'll explain everything to you there."

Solomon was still unsure if he was making the right choice, but he motioned for Sarah to come, and together, hand in hand, they followed Majec through the shadows to an apartment building on the poor side of town.

Once they were inside, Solomon saw two young boys playing on the floor, and although the place was small and sparsely furnished, there was a warm glow.

"Irena, I've brought some company home with me," Majec called out.

A pretty, slender blonde woman came out of the kitchen. She wore a simple yellow cotton housedress. Her hair was finger waved around her face. Majec leaned down to kiss her quickly.

"I was just straightening things up. Your dinner is on the stove," she said. Then she looked at Sarah and Solomon. "What have we here? Two children?" Her eyes opened wide as she looked at her husband.

"Yes, two Jewish children."

Irena frowned and shook her head. "Oh, Majec, it's not safe for us to have them here. Think of our own children. If we are caught . . ."

"They'll be gone in the morning. I am going to help them."

"I don't know. I am afraid."

"Look at them, Irena. Look at their faces. They are only children. The Nazis have it in for them. If we throw them out, will you be able to live with yourself if we find out that they are murdered?"

"How can you ask me that?"

"I ask you that because I know your heart. What if our boys were wandering around alone without us to protect them? Can you imagine something so terrible? These children are hungry. So although we don't have much, let's do what is right. We'll give them something to eat. The poor things have been out sleeping on the street for a week at least."

Irena's face softened. "I'm sorry. I agree with you; we should help them. But I am scared."

"Do you trust me?" he asked.

She nodded. "I do."

"Then don't you worry about anything."

"I am constantly worried," she said, "with you being in the Resistance . . ."

"Shhh . . . enough. I'm starving, and let's scrounge up some food for these two."

Irena obediently went into the kitchen. There was some noise, then she called all of them. "Come on into the kitchen. I have some food ready for you," she said.

It had been a long time since Solomon and his sister had eaten anything that was hot. So when Irena placed the bowls of soup in front of them, they ate quickly and sloppily. Irena and her husband watched them eat with pity in their eyes. But once they'd finished, Solomon saw Irena look at Sarah's torn stockings and the dried blood on her thighs.

"What happened to this little girl?" she asked Solomon accusingly.

"We were hiding from the Nazis. I had to leave her under a stairwell so I could go out and find us some food. While I was gone a man came and . . ."

Sarah looked away.

"Is this true?" Irena asked her.

"Yes, ma'am," she managed to say.

"Well then, let's go and get you cleaned up." Irena tried to sound cheerful, but her voice was filled with sympathy.

Once Sarah and Irena left the room, Majec pounded his fist on the table. "I am sick to death of the Nazis and what they have done to our beloved Poland."

"Yes, so am I," Solomon said.

"Wiktor told you that he wanted you to go to work on a farm that is out in the country. Is that right?"

"That's what he said."

"It's only partially true. He and I have discussed this. We want you to join us in the Resistance. You're a savvy, smart boy. You are quick and agile, but you are also mature for your age. We could use your help."

"The Polish Resistance?"

"Yes, of course."

"And you want me to do this while I am working on a farm?" Solomon asked.

"Exactly. You and Sarah would work on the farm. Both you and your sister would receive food and a place to sleep. In return, you would help the Resistance by delivering messages between groups of partisans who are hiding in the forests. If the Nazis come to the farm, we will make sure that you have papers that claim you are a gentile. But if you can, you should try to hide when they come. Better if they don't see you at all. Take your sister and run into the forest. Watch from there. Wait until they've gone before you return."

Solomon listened closely. He was feeling better about this meeting. He was starting to trust Majec and Wiktor. Not because he believed that they were necessarily helping him and Sarah as an act of pure kindness but because he could see how keeping him alive might be of help to the Resistance.

"Are you interested?" Majec asked.

"Yes, of course I am."

"Then I'll go to Wiktor's flat tonight and tell him to have our forger make your papers. You can sleep here in my children's room tonight. If all goes well, we can leave in the morning."

"I don't know if this matters at all, but I've already given my sister a false name to use, and she has started to get used to it. Since she is only five, I think it would be very difficult for her to get used to changing our names again. So I don't know if it is possible, but if it is, then perhaps we can use the names we have been using. I have been going by Artur and she by Maria. Our alias surname is Zajec."

"I'll see what can be done," Majec said. "I can't promise anything."

"Thank you," Solomon said.

CHAPTER 12

MAJEC WOKE SOLOMON IN THE MIDDLE OF THE NIGHT TO GIVE HIM the papers.

"I was able to use the names you gave me. So, from today on, you are Artur Zajec, and Sarah will be Maria Zajec. Never, under any circumstances, are you to use your real names. Do you understand me?"

"Yes."

"And you must be sure to stress the importance of this to little Sarah. Because one mistake, just one mistake, could cost all of us our lives. Do you understand?"

Again Solomon answered, "Yes."

"Good, now wake your sister so that we can get out of here and on the road."

They left before sunrise, heading right out of the city. Irena packed them each a small bag of food to take with them. Sarah whispered into Solomon's ear. "I wish we could have stayed there. The lady was nice. She reminded me of our mother."

Solomon was exasperated with Sarah. He knew she was just a child, but it was hard for him to make her understand anything. She held her doll close to her chest. He remained quiet, but he patted her hand.

Sarah fell asleep with her head on Solomon's shoulder as they rode for over an hour through wooded areas. Then just as the sun began to rise they came to a clearing where they saw several farms lined up. Majec drove another twenty minutes until they found themselves in front of a well-maintained farmhouse with two horses and three cows grazing in an open field and crops growing in neat rows.

"This is it," Majec said.

"Does the farmer know we are Jews?" Solomon asked.

"No, he knows only that you are a part of the Polish Resistance. Make sure to use the names on your papers. You don't want to draw any suspicions. Trust no one, Solomon. Tell no one the truth. Keep wearing that cross you have around your neck. Remember that you and Sarah are Catholic children who were living in a Catholic orphanage because your parents died. Don't forget that, and make sure you never drop your guard. No one can be trusted to be a friend to Jews these days."

"Is there anything else I should know?"

"Probably, but I don't have time to go over things with you. Just keep to yourself. Be quiet. Keep your sister quiet. The less you say the better. You'll get more instructions from the partisans as time goes by. They will find you and tell you what they want you to do."

"Will I see you or Wiktor again?"

"Perhaps. Who knows? We are in the city most of the time, but things could change. For now, may God be with you and just be careful."

"Thank you, Majec."

"Good luck, Solomon."

Before they went inside to meet the farmer, Solomon held Sarah's shoulders and looked into her eyes. "Do you remember your name?"

"Sarah . . . oh no . . . Maria, right?"

"Yes, but you must never use the name Sarah again."

"All right. Maria Zajec. And your name is Artur."

"Yes. That's good. You remembered." He mustered a smile. "Now you must never forget this. You must never use your real name again. If you do, something terrible might happen."

"I'm scared, Solomon."

"Call me Artur." He tried to keep his voice calm and have patience.

She started crying. "I don't want to play this game anymore. I want to go back to Mama."

"Maria!" he said. "You must do what I tell you."

Sarah nodded, but she put her thumb in her mouth.

CHAPTER 13

THE FARMER WAS A MIDDLE-AGED ROBUST MAN WITH A SUN-wrinkled red face. There wasn't much of an introduction. But from the conversation between Majec and the farmer, Solomon learned the farmer's name was Hubert Borkowski. His wife was Aldona, and they had a teenage daughter named Jula, who stood in the doorway of the room staring at him and Sarah.

"All right." Majec finally turned to Solomon. "He accepts the two of you to work here for him. Every morning you and a group of other children will go out before sunrise and dig shallow pits where you will bury potatoes. You must never tell anyone what you are doing. Ever! Is that understood?"

"Yes."

"In the afternoon, the horses must be groomed and fed. You'll have to shovel the path clean of manure. Things like that. You understand? Yes?"

"Yes."

"I know you are a smart boy. I have seen you work your magic negotiating with the underground. Keep to yourself. Remember, like I said before, don't talk too much. I don't know when it will happen, but you will be asked to deliver messages between partisan groups.

Do as you're told. And with God's help, you should be all right. By the way, my wife likes your sister. Would you two consider separating? My sister recently died, God rest her soul. She had a daughter who also passed away from typhoid. None of my neighbors know anything about this. I could easily say that my sister passed and Sarah was her daughter. I could tell them that the child lived and that Sarah was the child she left behind."

"Separating?" Solomon said. "I don't know. I made a promise to my mother that I would take care of Sarah."

"She would be safer with us. She's a little girl, Sol. It's a dangerous world out there for anyone, but it's worse for a little girl."

Solomon thought about what happened to Sarah when he'd left her alone. What the stranger had almost done to her. "Let me think about it. I can't agree to this without giving it lots of thought."

"Of course."

"I can't always come out here to the country. But I'll try to drop in on you. In the past when I came out here, the farmer gave me some extra potatoes. I sold them on the black market. If all goes well, I'll see you again. You can tell me your decision about separating from Sarah then."

Solomon nodded. "Thank you for helping us."

"You're helping us too. We have a fancy name. People call us the underground, but we are really just Polish men and women who hate the Nazis. We hate what they have done to our beloved country and we want them out. We want Poland back the way it was before they invaded us."

"I feel the same way."

"Come on, let me show you where the workers sleep. It's in the barn, but it's clean and comfortable. I know it will still be cold in the winter, but it will be better than being outside, and the farmer will make sure you have plenty of blankets. He's a good person, but it's still best that he doesn't know you're Jews. It's hard to tell how people will respond if they find out that you are Jews."

CHAPTER 14

THERE WERE FIVE BOYS, INCLUDING SOLOMON, WHO LIVED IN THE barn behind the farmer's home. They ranged in age from nine to sixteen, Solomon being the youngest. The two oldest were brothers; their names were Peter and John, and they had run away from an orphanage. They were working their way back to their hometown somewhere near Krakow. Vadik, a painfully skinny fourteen-year-old with blond hair and a huge nose, had lost his parents when his father was arrested for being part of the Resistance. In order to keep him safe, his mother had traded his labor for room and board with the farmer. Kade, a twelve-year-old had left home to find work when his widowed mother died, leaving him to fend for himself. Little Sarah was the only girl. And even though she was just five years old, Solomon watched her like a hawk at least at first. Until he got to know the other boys, he wasn't sure if they might be a danger to Sarah. Once he got to know them, he allowed himself to relax if only a little.

The barn was drafty, and the work that was expected of the children was physically demanding. But as Majec promised, they were fed enough to get by and given plenty of blankets to keep warm. If the farmer or his wife came across any used clothing at the church, they brought it home for the children. During the day, the children were doing regular chores, but at night they were aiding the farmer and his wife in the act of stealing food from the farm which would technically have belonged to the Germans. If they were caught, the farmer, his family, and all of the children would face certain death.

In one corner of the barn was an old horse and an equally old cow in the other. Piles of hay filled the area where the children slept. At night, after a long day of work, Sarah curled her small body into her brother's and fell asleep. He often watched her and wondered if she would not be better off if he sent her away to live with Majec and his family. After all, Majec's wife, Irena, liked Sarah. And to prove it, over the past two months since Sarah and Solomon had arrived at the farm, Irena had sent a dress she'd made for Sarah with a matching dress for Sarah's doll. Sarah told Solomon that she would like to see Irena again, but whenever he asked her if she wanted to stay and live with Irena and Majec for a while, Sarah's answer never wavered: "Only if you are coming too," she said.

"You know I can't," was always Solomon's response.

"Then I want to stay with you."

She was a pain in the neck most of the time. He had to admit that his life would have been much easier without her. But he'd promised their mother that he would take care of her, and he intended to keep that promise. Besides, the honest truth was, he loved that precious little monster. She was a handful, but she was also a joy. When he was at work, sweating from the intensity of the labor during the day, sometimes he would catch a glimpse of her watching him, and he would see the admiration in her eyes. Or when he went out at night and broke through the cold, hard ground to bury the potatoes, he would glance back at the barn thinking she was asleep, only to find her watching him and smiling. It was at times like those when he swore he could feel his heart swell. And if someone would have asked him what he wanted more than anything else in the world, he would have told them "I want to protect my sister. I want my sister to survive."

Solomon put thoughts of his mother out of his mind. It wasn't that he didn't miss her, he did, but his tragic life had made him a realist. The horrors he'd witnessed had jaded him. From what he'd seen of the Nazis, he felt certain his mother was dead. If he were to allow himself the luxury of tears he felt he might weep and never be able to stop. However, Solomon was a self-proclaimed survivor, and he refused to indulge in self-pity. He would force himself to put every tender moment from his past out of his mind. Instead, he got up every morning and forced himself to forge on, to provide for Sarah and himself. Once this was all over, and he did believe the day would come when the Nazis' reign would end, he and his sister would search for his mother. Then they would be forced to accept whatever they found. But until that time arrived, he knew he must not think about his mother.

Solomon was friendly and always helpful to the other boys. He could be counted on to carry more than his share of the work. He did it to make up for the fact that Sarah was not capable of being much help. And he never asked for any favors from anyone. The others liked him well enough, but he remembered Majec's warning, and he did not make friends. He never sat with the others while they told jokes during their meals. Except for Sarah, he kept to himself.

One afternoon Majec arrived. Taking Solomon aside, Majec stuffed a small folded piece of yellowed paper into his pocket.

"Read this after I go, yes?" Majec said.

"Yes," Solomon replied.

"And about Sarah?"

"I decided that no matter what happens, she and I must stay together."

"I understand, and I'll tell Irena. She'll be disappointed. She always wanted a daughter."

"I'm sorry."

"Ehh, I don't blame you. Anyway, what I have to say now is about the letter I gave you, so listen good. Tonight, as soon as it gets dark, leave here and go south. You will find a group of partisans. The truth is they will probably find you. Tell them your name is Artur Zajec and you have brought them important information. Then give them the note I gave you, and get back here to the farm as quickly as you can."

Solomon nodded, his fingers squeezing the paper in the pocket of his jacket.

"Can I count on you?"

"Yes."

"If you find the partisans before they find you, be careful not to get shot when you approach the camp. There are always scouts watching."

"I'll be careful," Solomon answered.

"By the way, are you still burying potatoes at night?"

"We stopped last week. There is little left of the last crop. I suppose the farmer is expecting the Nazis to come and get their share of that. But at least he will have what we have already buried."

"He shares what he can with us, with the Resistance. Borkowski's a good man."

"He still hates Jews."

"Yes, and so do many others. But he hates the Nazis more."

"I suppose that should be a comfort to me, yes?" Solomon said cynically.

"I don't hate the Jews," Majec said. "Neither does Wiktor. But I am sorry to tell you that I have no control of how others feel. All I can do is help you and your sister as much as possible."

"Thank you for all of your help. I don't blame you or Wiktor for the hatred of my people. How could I? It's not your fault. Besides, I feel fortunate to have your friendship . . . and Wiktor's too. Anyway, don't worry about anything. I'll take care of this tonight."

CHAPTER 15

JULA BORKOWSKI, THE FARMER'S ONLY CHILD, WHO HAD YEARNED for a younger sister, took a special liking to Sarah. And in turn, Sarah relished every bit of attention that Jula paid her. Each of them had individual jobs: Sarah was expected to collect the eggs and milk the cow, and Jula did the cooking and helped her mother keep house. But when they had free time, Jula would go to the barn and find Sarah. They took walks together, and they played with Sarah's doll. Perhaps it was because Jula could feel that Sarah worshiped her in the way a child worships an older sibling that made Jula feel comfortable enough with Sarah to tell her things she might not have told anyone else.

"You have to promise not to tell anyone what I am going to tell you," Jula warned.

"I promise," Sarah said, her voice very serious.

"You have to keep your promise . . ." Jula loved the way Sarah hung on her every word.

"I promise. You can tell me anything. I will never tell anyone your secrets." Sarah's face lit up. She was excited to be a confidante to this older, pretty, and popular girl.

"All right, then. I'll tell you," Jula said, her bright azure eyes sparkling. "You know Kade, don't you? He's the handsome boy who lives with you and the others in the barn."

"Yes, I know who he is."

"He's my boyfriend. No one knows it, but he kissed me—on the lips!"

"Oh!" Sarah exclaimed.

"He did. We have been flirting with each other for months. But last week, I was coming out of the chicken coop and no one was around. Kade saw me and I saw him. Then he walked over to me and asked me how my day was going."

"So what did you say?"

"I told him it was fine, silly." Jula winked and Sarah giggled.

"Then he just kissed you?"

"No, not yet."

"So what happened? Come on, tell me . . ."

Jula laughed at how filled with anticipation Sarah was. "Well, he asked me to sit down and talk. He gave me this hair ribbon as a gift." Jula showed Sarah the royal-blue ribbon she had used to tie the braid in her hair.

"How did he get it?"

"I have no idea. I didn't ask. I was so surprised that he was giving me a gift that I could hardly speak. I've never received a gift from a boy before."

"Then what happened? Hurry up and tell me; I can hardly stand it," Sarah said.

"Well," Jula said, then she giggled as she watched Sarah's face. "Well . . ."

"Come on, already . . . please . . ."

"All right. So he told me that I was pretty and that he thought I was the prettiest girl he'd ever met."

"No, he didn't!" Sarah said.

"Yes, he did. Why, don't you think I'm pretty?"

"Of course I do. I think you are the prettiest girl I've ever seen. But it's very bold of him to say."

"Bold but charming." Jula laughed, then Sarah chuckled too.

"Then guess what he did."

"He kissed you."

"Not yet, silly, not yet."

"So go on and tell me . . ."

"He tied the ribbon around my hair. My whole body was shivering. Then he touched my cheek and I closed my eyes. And then . . . and then . . . he kissed me."

"Oh my!" Sarah covered her mouth with her hand. "Are you going to get married?"

"Someday, I hope so. I don't think we can right now. I mean, my father would throw him off the farm if he knew that he dared to kiss me. My goodness, but my father would be very angry. He's made me swear that I would never have anything to do with any of those boys."

"But you really like Kade, don't you?"

"I think I am falling in love with him. Of course, my mother would say that I am only fourteen and I don't know what love is. But what does she know. I know what I feel and it's definitely love."

"What does it feel like?"

"Every time I think of him, my whole body gets warm all over. And when I see him, I get all nervous and giddy inside. When he looks at me, all I can think of is that I hope someday he'll kiss me again."

"I'm sure he will."

"I believe he will too. But I can hardly wait."

"I hope someday I'll know what it feels like to be in love. Sometimes I am afraid that I'll die first."

"How can you say such a terrible thing. You're so young. How old are you?"

"I'm going to be six in the spring."

"You have your whole life ahead of you."

"I hear the boys talking about the war and the future and how if we are caught burying potatoes we will all be killed by the Nazis, and all that talk makes me wonder if I will live to grow up."

"Is that all they say?"

"No, they say lots of things that make me afraid. Terrible things. Scary things. I can't repeat them."

CHAPTER 16

Later that evening when Solomon told Sarah that he was going to have to leave her for a few hours to do some work for Majec that night, she grabbed on to the sleeve of his shirt and said, "Take me with you."

"I can't. It's too dangerous. You'll be too slow. We've talked about this a hundred times. You will be safer here waiting for me."

"I don't want to be here alone without you. The other night I had a dream about that bad man who tried to touch me in my private place. You must remember that? Do you? Do you remember? I want to go with you. Can I please?"

He couldn't look into her eyes. How could he forget ? He blamed himself everyday for how she'd suffered that night. And the very thought of her agony left him cold and terrified. Perhaps he'd made the wrong decision not sending her to live with Majec. There was no guarantee that she would be safe there, but at least Majec and his family would do their best for her.

"Sarah . . ."

She looked up at him and he wanted to cry. It was times like these that he wished with all his heart he could just be a child again without responsibilities. But that was not an option. Regardless of his age, Solomon was a man, and he was in charge of his sister's safety. The weight of this was heavy on his heart.

"Would you like to stay with Majec and his family for a while? You liked his wife, didn't you?"

"I would love to! She would take very good care of us. She was so nice to me . . ."

"Not us, Sarah. Just you. I must work. I have responsibilities. Someone must earn our keep, whether it is through delivering messages for the underground or working on the farm. Someone must pay the price for our needs to be fulfilled."

"That means that you wouldn't come with me to live with Irena and Majec. Would you stay here?"

"Yes, I'm afraid I would have to. But at least when I went out at night like . . . tonight . . . you would be safe in your bed with Majec's wife looking after you."

"No," she said firmly. "No, no no. I don't want to go, anyway, because then I would have to leave my friend Jula. Why is everyone and everything I love taken away from me?" Then she started to cry. If only he could break down and cry like that when things didn't go his way. Instead, he took her into his arms.

"The boys here don't bother you, do they? They don't do anything bad to you, do they?"

"No, they don't bother me. Or do anything bad," Sarah admitted.

"Besides, when I go out tonight they'll already be asleep. You'll be all right. Just go to sleep, and by the time you wake up, I'll be back here."

"What if a man like that bad man who was under the stairs comes and tries to do bad things to me?"

"The other boys wouldn't let it happen."

"Are you going to tell them to watch out for me?"

"I can't. I can't even tell them I'm going."

"But Solomon . . . what if I wake up and the bad man is here? What will I do then?"

He was irritated. He wanted to yell at her, to tell her that all of this was as hard for him as it was for her. He wanted to tell her that he was afraid of going out into the woods alone in the middle of the night looking for a group of partisans who might not recognize him as a friend. But he couldn't tell her. She was too young, and he couldn't blame her for being afraid. Solomon looked into Sarah's eyes and reminded himself that she'd been through so much.

"Listen to me, will you?" He gently turned her chin upward so his eyes met hers. "I promise you'll be all right. Will you trust me?" *How can I make this promise? There are no guarantees. Not anymore, not since the Nazis came to Poland.* But he had to promise, or she would follow him into the darkness, and that would be a disaster. The only way to ensure he and Sarah would be able to stay on the farm was to deliver the note. And although the barn wasn't perfect, so far they had been safe and were blessed to have a warm place to sleep and food in their bellies. All he could do was pray that she would be all right while he was gone.

She nodded. "I trust you." Sarah squeezed her brother's hand with her small one. Her eyes were glassy with tears, and it made his heart ache with pity for her. Sometimes he wanted to holler at her, to tell her not to depend on him so much. He wanted to let her know that he wasn't perfect, and he could no more protect her than he could protect himself. Solomon wanted to say "You expect too much from me. I am not an adult. I am just a child too, and I am scared. I am scared all the time." But he didn't say it. In fact, he forced a reassuring smile and ruffled her hair the same way their mother used to do.

"It'll be all right," he said, mustering up a voice of confidence he didn't feel.

She nodded. "I'll wait up for you."

"Sleep. It will be better for you if you sleep."

"I'll try."

CHAPTER 17

SHE WAS FAST ASLEEP WHEN THE DARKNESS FELL LIKE A VEIL OF spilled black ink over the little farm. Solomon kissed Sarah's head the way his mother had always kissed their heads when she put them to bed in a time that seemed like a thousand years ago. Then without turning around, he snuck quietly out of the barn and walked for less than a mile until he was in the deep woods. Night sounds from the throats of nocturnal creatures filled the forest. In the shadows of night, the arms of the gnarled trees seemed to reach up and out to him in terrifying gestures. A shiver ran down Solomon's spine, but he forced himself to go on. An owl let out a loud hoot and a wolf howled, startling Solomon who tripped on the roots of a tree that had grown out of the ground resembling large, thick vein-like fingers. Falling facedown into the dirt, he began to weep. For several minutes he lay there crying. Then he got up, shook himself off, wiped the dirt from his tear-stained face, and forced himself to keep walking forward.

The partisans found Solomon before he saw them. Two men came out of the trees and grabbed both of his arms.

"Who are you?" one of them said.

"My name is Artur Zajec. I have a note for you from a friend from the Polish underground."

"Where is it?"

"In my pocket. Let go of my arm, and I'll get it for you."

"I'll get it myself," the man said. Then finding the gun in Solomon's pocket, he took it and stuffed it into his own pocket. "A gun?"

"The note is right there too," Solomon said, trembling.

The man rifled through Solomon's pocket and brought out the note. He held it up to the moon. "I can hardly see in this light," he said to his friend.

"Give it to me. I can see it," the other man offered.

"Nazis coming to collect harvest from neighboring farms tomorrow. Get out of the area before dawn. Majec."

"You know Majec?" one of the partisans asked.

"Of course," Solomon said. "The gun was for protection from the Nazis, not from you. I am one of you."

The man let out a laugh. "So you are, young fellow. Come on, follow me."

Solomon followed the man for several minutes until they came to a small clearing in the middle of a cluster of trees. Two other men, who had been sitting on the ground, got up to meet them.

"What is this?" one of the men asked.

"A boy. Majec sent him with a note. The note said that a small group of Nazis are coming to collect the harvest at the local farms."

"Hmmm."

"Stay in the forest. Stay away from the farm for the next day or so," the first man said to Solomon.

"I have to go back. My sister is there."

"Your sister?"

"My little sister."

"How old are you?"

"Sixteen," Solomon lied.

"You're sixteen like I am the king of England," the man said, then all the others laughed. "How old are you really?"

"Nine. My sister is five."

"Good God, you're just children. You should be in school. Where is your mother?"

"It doesn't matter," Solomon said, afraid to tell him the truth.

"It does to me."

"I don't know. Probably dead." Solomon choked the words out.

"You're a Jew, aren't you?"

Solomon didn't answer, but he stared at the man with wide eyes. He was about to run when the man grabbed the sleeve of his jacket.

"It's all right," he said, indicating the other two men. "Samuel and Issac are Jewish. I'm not, but some of the others with our group are Jews. Some are Gypsies too. It seems we're all united against a common enemy, huh?"

"Yes," Solomon said, nodding.

"Is Artur your real name?"

"No, I'm Solomon. My sister is Sarah."

"Bible names. I grew up a Catholic in a small town in the outskirts of Warsaw. I was even a choirboy when I was your age. I thought about becoming a priest. Does that surprise you? By the way, my name is Luke."

Solomon nodded a greeting. "Well, now that you have the letter, I have to go. I must get back to my sister. Can I please have my gun back," he said.

"Listen to me. Go back and get your sister, and bring her back here with you. You can stay with us until things settle down, then you can go back to work on the farm. Believe me, you don't want to be on the farm when we attack the Nazis there."

Solomon was skeptical. But for some odd reason, even though he'd just met him, he found that he believed Luke. "I'll go and get Sarah. We'll come back here tonight.

CHAPTER 18

"Sarah," Solomon whispered, "wake up."

She was sleeping so lightly that she woke easily. "What is it? Is everything all right? Is Mama here? I thought I heard her voice."

"No," he said. "I'm sorry, but Mama's not here. You must have been dreaming."

"Oh," she said. He could hear the disappointment in her voice.

"Come on, you have to wake up and follow me. We have to leave here before dawn."

"Solomon, where are we going?"

"I'll explain later. Just get up."

"I have to pee."

"Hurry up. Go outside and pee. I'll wait for you. But hurry. We have to go as soon as possible."

She nodded and got up.

"Be quiet," he said, "very quiet."

"I'm scared. I hate to go to the outhouse at night all alone. That's why I was holding it until morning."

"Fine. I'll follow you and wait right outside while you go."

"Thank you, Solomon."

He shook his head. Sometimes she drove him crazy with frustration, but she was all he had in the world.

While he was waiting for Sarah, Solomon filled his pockets with potatoes from the bags that the farmer had packed for the Nazis who would come to collect their share the following day. He was careful to take only a few from each bag so no one would know they were missing. Then he turned around to see Sarah as she ran toward him.

"Ready?"

"Yes," she said.

"Where's your doll?"

"Oh no!" She let out a loud shriek.

"Shhh, it's all right. We haven't left yet. Let's go back to the barn and I'll get her."

"Oh, Solomon, thank you. I would have been so sad if I left her behind."

"I know," he said, ruffling her hair. "Come on, follow me. We'll go and get her right now."

Once he had the doll, Solomon led his sister by the hand back to the clearing where he'd met the partisans. They were welcomed by a young woman of about twenty years, with long auburn hair. She introduced herself as Ewa and then gave Sarah and Solomon each a heel of hard bread and a cup of water. Once they'd finished eating, she gave each of them a blanket and showed them where to sleep.

"It's dark out here," Sarah said, "and there are wild animals."

"You'll be all right," the woman called Ewa said.

"I'm scared," Sarah said as she glanced at Solomon.

"Why don't you set your blanket up right next to mine?" Ewa offered.

Sarah nodded. "All right, I'd like that."

"And don't be afraid. Look over there. Do you see that man hiding in the shadows?"

"I don't see anyone."

"That's because he is very good at hiding," Ewa said, and she winked at Sarah. "But he is on watch tonight. Do you know what that means?"

Sarah shook her head.

"It means that he is watching out for all of us. Protecting us. He has a gun, so if any Nazis or wild animals come near here he can shoot them."

"But what if he falls asleep?"

"You don't have to worry. You see, we thought about that possibility, and so there are two men over there; they keep each other awake." Ewa smiled at Sarah and Sarah smiled back. Then Ewa continued, "Come on, now. I think it's best if you get some rest." She took the blanket she'd given Sarah and spread it out on the ground. Then she lay down and motioned for Sarah to lay beside her. Sarah did as she asked. Ewa took her own blanket and covered them both with it.

"Now we will both stay warm through the night," she said.

Sarah looked at Solomon. "Where are you going?" she asked.

"I'll be right here," he answered, laying down on the cold, hard ground and pulling the blanket over him.

Solomon lay awake long after Sarah and Ewa had fallen asleep. He glanced over at them to find his sister wrapped in the arms of this beautiful and gentle stranger. As he gazed up at the sliver of a silver moon that hung overhead, he began to think about what the future might hold for him. He wondered if life would ever go back to the way it was before Hitler invaded Poland. *Will I have a chance to grow up and get married to a girl like Ewa? Or will I die at nine or ten years old?* When Solomon looked at Ewa he was smitten. This was the first time in his life that he'd actually found himself truly infatuated with a female.

When he was dealing on the black market, he'd been propositioned by plenty of prostitutes. They wanted the food he was selling and were more than willing to trade their services for a hunk of bread or a bag of potatoes. He understood, even at nine years old. He understood everyone had to find a way to survive. But when they had shown him their bare breasts, although he was curious about sex, he found them repugnant. But not this woman, Ewa, with her sweet, gentle smile. She made him think of home.

As he lay beneath the dark sky unable to sleep, his mind began to wander. *Will I have children and a wife someday? Will I ever be a man, or will Sarah and I die here in these dark woods? I wonder what it feels like to die. I wonder if it hurts much worse than it hurt when I cut myself on the barbed wire in the ghetto last spring. That cut stung so badly, and Mama was so afraid it would get infected. Mama. I miss her so much. I miss her gentle hands and the way she made me feel that everything would be all right. I sure don't miss my father though. He didn't care about any of us. He never cared. All he cared about was drinking. Dear God, how I miss my mother. When I think that she might be gone forever and that I'll never see her again I can't believe it.*

I wish Sarah wasn't such a baby. If only I could talk to her and tell her how I am feeling. I need someone to talk to, but I can't talk to her. She would get so upset and she would cry, and that would only make things worse. Right now, I'm not sure she realizes that we might never see our mother again. The truth is, as hard as I try, I somehow don't believe it. Sometimes I think this is all just a nightmare and I'll wake up and I'll be back in my own bed. Not the one in the ghetto, but the one in our old house. The house we lived in before the Nazis. I'd even be willing to see Papa again if it meant that this would all have been a dream. Truth is, I wish Ben had been our father. He was always so kind and easy to talk to, and once Papa was gone, I could tell that Mama started to love Ben a lot. So if I could make just one wish, it would be that Sarah, Mama, and me were back in our old house and that Ben was our father. Make it two wishes. For the second wish, I would wish the Nazis were not real, that they were only monsters from my imagination. I wish . . . I wish . . . Dear God, if it could only be true.

It was a chilly night, but once he saw that Sarah and Ewa were fast asleep, Solomon took the blanket he'd been given and covered Sarah and Ewa. Then he lay back down and rested his head on his arm like a pillow. For several minutes he watched his sister sleep, and he didn't realize he was crying until a tear fell from his cheek landing on his hand.

CHAPTER 19

THE FOLLOWING DAY, THE PARTISANS' CAMP WAS ALIVE WITH excitement. Guns were distributed to the members. Solomon and Sarah were told to stay out of the way and not to follow when the others went out to attack the Nazis.

"Stay here. Keep your sister close. You should be safe here. Can you fire a gun?" Luke asked Solomon.

"Yes, can I have my gun back? The one that was taken from me by your group?"

"Of course. I'll get it for you."

"Thanks. I promise you I know how to shoot."

"I must say that is impressive for a boy your age." Luke smiled. "I don't think that any Nazis will find you here, but one can never be too careful."

"My brother killed a bad man with a gun," Sarah offered. "I saw it happen. It was very scary, but he had to do it."

"I see." Luke nodded.

Solomon gave Sarah an angry look. "Nobody asked you to say anything," he said.

She turned away and sat down on the ground. Then she curled up with her doll.

"I have to go now. Keep your eyes open, and when I return, we'll talk about your future missions."

Solomon nodded.

Ewa walked over holding a rifle. A man who was tall and slender with deep-set dark eyes and a long, thick nose had his arm across her shoulders. "It's a shame that our children have to learn about war and hatred at such young ages," Ewa said.

"It is," Luke said, "but these are bad times. And they must if they are to survive."

Ewa nodded. "Be safe, you two," she said as she walked away with the others.

Solomon watched Ewa and his heart swelled. He wondered if that man who had his arm around her was her husband. *I know I am too young, and she would never be interested in me as a boyfriend, but I think I am in love with her*, he thought.

It was almost nightfall when the partisans returned. Solomon had been anxious all day, worried about Ewa. At first the men dribbled into the camp slowly, and as each one arrived Solomon became a little more anxious, and his heart sank a little further because he didn't see Ewa. Sarah, he noticed, was watching for her too. Finally, about an hour after the sun had set, Ewa arrived. Her face was dirty and her hair was matted. She looked very tired, but she mustered a smile for Sarah and Solomon.

"How are you two?" she asked with a look of genuine concern on her face.

"We're all right. We were worried about you," Solomon said.

"I'm fine. It was a difficult mission, but we didn't lose anyone. So I can't complain."

"That fellow you were with earlier?" Solomon asked. "Is that your husband?"

"Oh no, he and I have been friends for a long time. I knew him from the village where I grew up. I used to be a teacher for young children."

"You did?" Sarah said.

"Yes, I did." Ewa smiled.

"Perhaps you might be willing to teach Sarah and I. We went to school until we were sent to the ghetto. Then our mother tried to keep up with our lessons, but she had to work and then things happened. Anyway, it's a long story, but we had to run away from the ghetto and . . ."

"Never mind about all of that. I know the story of what happened to the children in the Lodz ghetto. The way they were all sent away on transports. Thank God you two got out in time," Ewa said, sighing. "And, of course, I would be happy to give you lessons, but I don't know when there will be time. I am sure you have to return to Borkowski's farm, don't you?"

Solomon couldn't hold back his smile. He didn't really care much for school, but the idea of spending more time with Ewa, even if it was to study, made him want to shout with joy from a mountaintop.

"Do we have to go back to the farm, or can we stay here with Ewa?" Sarah asked. "But then when would I see Jula? If I stay here I'd never see her again."

"We can't worry about Jula. We have to do what's best for you," Solomon said.

"But maybe I could stay here with Ewa and go and visit Jula every few days."

Solomon bit his lower lip. Sarah was trying his patience again. He didn't answer her. Instead, he turned and spoke to Ewa. "I have a job to do. I've promised to work for the Resistance, so I figure I am going to have to go back to the farm. But do you think it's best if Sarah stays here?"

"I am not sure. She is so young, and it's very dangerous. But let me see what I can arrange," Ewa said. "Come with me," she said to Solomon. "You wait for us, Sarah. All right?"

Sarah nodded.

Ewa took Solomon and went to talk to the man who was the leader of the group. He was middle aged but surprisingly handsome with a thick gray beard and a head of heavy gray hair.

"Cereck," she said, "I know you have seen this boy. His name is

Solomon. He is the one who brought us the information about the Nazis for the last raid."

"Yes, I know all about it. Nice to meet you, Solomon. Don't you also have a little sister? I've seen her in the camp."

"That's right," Ewa said. "His sister's name is Sarah, and I have a request for you. I would like to teach them to read and write. If they survive, they will need to be literate."

Cereck let out a laugh. "Read and write. Spoken like a teacher. We're in the middle of a war, and you want to teach two children to read?"

"Yes, I do. Education is important. This nightmare we are living can't last forever."

Cereck smiled. "From your mouth to God's ears," he said. "All right, I suppose you can you teach them when they are here, but they can only stay with us for a few days at a time."

"I was hoping that the little girl could stay permanently. Solomon has to return to the farm so he can get more orders from the Resistance. But the girl . . ."

"Ewa, I would love to let you have your way. However, in order for us to stay hidden, we must keep moving. And I am sorry, but we can't have children tagging along. So when Solomon brings us a message, they can stay for a day or two, and then you have my permission to give them lessons. Of course, time permitting."

"Of course." She nodded, then she added, "Perhaps it would be all right with you if they came every night for an hour or two? They could come when everyone is asleep and be back at the farm before daylight."

"Let me think about it," Cereck said.

Then Cereck took Ewa's elbow and led her away from Solomon. "Do they know?" Cereck asked.

"Know what?"

"That we are Jews?"

"I've never told them. I would assume they don't know, but his name is Solomon. That's a Jewish name," Ewa said.

They walked back to where Solomon waited. Then Cereck said, "Are you a Jew?"

Solomon cast a glance at Ewa, then he looked into Cereck's eyes to see if he could detect any malice or trickery. But he saw none. "Yes, I am a Jew," he answered.

"Good, so am I," Cereck said.

CHAPTER 20

The next time one of the Resistance brought a message to Solomon to deliver, he didn't bring anything written down.

"You will have to memorize everything I tell you. The first time we sent you to meet up with the band of partisans, I needed to send you with some form of document, so they would believe that you were with us. But from now on there will be nothing written down. Do you understand?"

"Yes." Solomon nodded.

"I will tell you how many Nazis they can expect to find, where they will find them, and how they are armed. You will deliver the message exactly as I give it to you. Can you do this?"

"I can," Solomon said with confidence.

"Good. Get ready to memorize."

CHAPTER 21

ONE EVENING, SOLOMON BROUGHT A MESSAGE FOR CERECK FROM Wiktor. As he walked through the camp, Ewa came over to him. She looked sad.

"What's wrong?" he asked.

Ewa told him that she was not going to be able to give lessons to Solomon and Sarah.

"I tried, Solomon. I really did. I talked to Cereck for over an hour yesterday. He said he gave the matter a lot of thought, but Cereck is afraid you'll be followed when you come here at night," she said. "It is already enough of a risk when you come to deliver messages to us, but he doesn't want you to come nightly. I am truly sorry. I was looking forward to teaching you and Sarah. I miss my profession. I really loved working with children."

Ewa didn't know that calling Solomon a child had wounded him deeply. She was his first crush, and even though he knew that he was far too young for her to take him seriously, he hated being confronted with that knowledge. So instead of answering, he just nodded.

"I really am sorry," she repeated. He knew she thought he felt bad about not being able to better his skills in reading and writing, but that was not it at all.

"It's all right. I understand." He forced the words out. The truth was he'd been looking forward to spending more time with her. And now that fantasy had been thwarted.

CHAPTER 22

Ludwig Beck had spoken to the townspeople, and from them he gathered several physical descriptions of the children who had robbed the baker. He felt sure they were the same children who had escaped the Lodz ghetto, but he could not imagine where they might be hiding. One of the women who he spoke with told him that she saw a very scrappy-looking boy and a little girl riding by in a truck with a man who she believed was a part of the Polish underground. He asked her if she had anything more to say. She smiled and told him that she could give him a little more information in exchange for a loaf of bread. He obliged her, and she told him that she heard this same man from the underground was known to have sold children to work on the farms. Ludwig knew that several of the farms in the countryside used child labor, but there were so many that he could not begin to determine which one the two Jewish children had been taken to.

Ludwig bit his lower lip and considered the information he had received from the woman as he rode to Hedy's apartment on the bus. He had enjoyed working during the day for a change instead of his usual night shift. A smile crossed his face as he glanced out the window. It was nice to have the opportunity to share dinner with

Hedy. This was a rarity. As he walked into Hedy's apartment, Ludwig was greeted by the aroma of grilled sausage and sauerkraut. Hedy wore her hair in braids wrapped around her head, and for a moment he was taken in by how well she fit the role of hausfrau.

"Hello, my love," she said. "You must be famished."

"I am, but I want to clean up first. The smell from that place lingers in my hair and in my skin. Give me a few minutes."

"Of course. Take your time." She smiled.

As he sat down at the table, Hedy said, "Isn't it lovely to spend evenings together? Wouldn't it be just wonderful if you worked days from now on instead of midnights?"

"Actually, I liked it very much. And I am still hunting for those children. I think I might just have an idea of where they have gone. Let me explain."

She poured him a beer and sat beside him as he told her what the woman informant had told him.

"She could just be working me over to get extra food. But I have a feeling about this, and I was wondering if you could ask your father if I might ride along with the Gestapo when they collect their rations from the local farms. Tell him that I would go during the day, and so it would not interfere with my job."

"What a good idea. Perhaps you might even get a little extra money for it. Who knows what my vater can arrange. After all, he got this job for you, didn't he?"

It was two weeks before Solomon was required to deliver another message to the partisan camp where Ewa was staying. Two days prior to receiving the message for that camp, he'd been instructed to deliver a message to another group of partisans that was located several miles to the north.

The message he relayed to both camps was the same. He was told to tell them the Nazis were not coming through the area where the Borkowski farm was located. This time the Nazis were headed to several farms that were located north of the Borkowski farm where they would pick up their share of the annual crops. Solomon was glad. He hated it when the Nazis came around, but there was also a disappointing side to this. Because the Borkowski farm was not in any danger, it was not necessary for Sarah and Solomon to leave the farm and stay with the partisans even for a few hours. Solomon did his best to hide his displeasure at this news when he saw Ewa.

He arrived at the camp to find her leaning against a tree. She was talking with a new man, a handsome young man Solomon had never seen before. Solomon scrutinized the man's looks. He was tall with a slender build and dark hair that needed to be cut. Ewa saw Solomon and waved but did not come over to speak. He'd already delivered the message to Cereck. He didn't want to meet this new man. Instead, he turned away pretending he didn't see Ewa. Dejected, Solomon left the camp and made his way back to the farm. Over the next several days, he forced himself not to think about Ewa because when he thought of her he envisioned the handsome man with the dark hair. It seemed that this man had crushed all his dreams, and this made him feel sad and lonely. So to keep her out of his thoughts, he worked even harder than usual.

Then one afternoon in late autumn, just before the first snowfall, Solomon was working in the field trying to ready the farm for winter when Sarah came running toward him. She was growing out of her shoes, and there was no money for a new pair. This made her even clumsier than normal. As she ran, she tripped on her short legs and fell flat on her face, but instead of crying, she got up and ran even faster. Solomon stopped and ran toward his sister.

"The Nazis are coming. I saw a black car down the road. They're headed this way."

Solomon dropped the hoe and grabbed Sarah's hand. Together they began to run toward the forest, but she couldn't run fast enough. Solomon had inherited his thick muscular body structure from his father. And the physical work he'd been doing on the farm had helped him to develop it even further. He lifted his sister into his arms, and carrying her, he ran as fast as he could. They entered the forest just as the black car stopped in front of the farm. Breathing heavily, the two children took refuge behind a cluster of trees as they watched three Gestapo agents walk up to the door of the farmhouse. One of the agents stayed by the side of the automobile, with his arms wrapped around his chest, just watching.

Solomon glanced at Sarah whose face had gone pale. She looked back at him.

"You did a good job. You got us out of there just in time," he said, trying to reassure her. But his heart was racing as he watched the scene unfold.

Sarah leaned against Solomon who kept his eyes glued to the farmhouse. He saw one of the men from the Gestapo pull the farmer outside. One of the others was speaking, his face red, and from the way he was standing, he looked angry as he waved his arms wildly. A shiver ran up Solomon's spine when the agent pushed Borkowski forward, and Borkowski fell face down in the dirt. Then one of the other Gestapo agents lifted Borkowski by his shirt collar and delivered a kick to Borkowski's buttocks. Again, Borkowski fell on his face.

The Nazi stood over him and pointed to the area where Solomon and the other boys had planted the potatoes. Borkowski shrugged his shoulders and shook his head, but the Gestapo agent hit him across the face then picked Borkowski up by the shirt again. This time he forced him to walk over to the area where the potatoes were hidden and pointed to the ground. Solomon felt like he was watching a nightmare come to life right in front of him.

Borkowski fell to his knees and began digging with his bare hands. One of the agents kicked him, and Borkowski dug more frantically. As he dug, one of the other Nazis led the boys who had worked with Solomon outside at gunpoint and lined them up. Borkowski's wife burst through the door with her hands gripping the hair at her temples. She ran over to her husband and pulled at the Gestapo agent's arm. He gave her a hard push, and she flew out of the way falling to the ground. But she didn't back off. Instead, she crawled back to the agent who kicked her in the face with his boot. She tried to get up, but she was unable to rise and fell back to the ground. Even from far away, Solomon could tell she was badly hurt.

Next, one of the Gestapo agents came outside holding Jula's arm. She was wriggling to get away, screaming and crying. The blue ribbon that had been so precious to her had fallen out of her hair and lay on the ground. Sarah gasped when she saw it. Even though they were too far away to be heard by the Germans, Solomon put his hand over his sister's mouth. "Shhhh," he whispered in her ear. Sarah was trembling.

The Gestapo agent pulled Jula's dress up to reveal her white underwear. She was fighting to pull her dress back down, but the Germans were teasing her and laughing. Then Kade rushed over and punched one of the Nazis in the face. Solomon and Sarah were too far away to make out what was said, but from the Germans' gestures, they knew he was very angry. He tossed Jula away like a rag doll. She fell. Kade went to help her get back on her feet, but a shot rang out and Kade collapsed where he stood. Jula's hands covered her mouth, and Sarah was sure she was screaming. But then another shot rang out and Jula lay beside Kade bleeding out onto the dirt of the farm, dirt that had sustained generations of her family.

Two young lives, gone in an instant.

When Borkowski still hadn't uncovered the stolen treasure, the agent pointed to two of the boys. Solomon couldn't hear what was said, but the next thing he knew the boys were digging up the area. They unearthed the potatoes. The Nazi took one of the potatoes and held it in his hand. Then he raised it up to the sky. He tossed it in the air and quickly drew his gun. The breath caught in Solomon's throat. The Gestapo agent pointed the gun at Borkowski, and a moment later a shot rang out. Before Solomon could catch his breath the other two Gestapo agents shot the boys. Then all three of the Nazis began to walk away. The Gestapo agents were almost at their automobile when the first one turned around and walked back. He drew a pistol from his belt and shot the farmer's wife. Then he walked back to the automobile and got in. The car roared to life, and within seconds it was gone.

"Should we go and see if anyone is still alive?" Sarah asked, her voice small and filled with terror.

"They aren't. I'm sure they're all dead," Solomon said. "Come on, we can't take the risk of going down there. We are lucky we got out when we did. Now let's go back to the partisans' camp and tell them what we saw."

CHAPTER 23

LUDWIG WONDERED WHY HE COULD NOT BECOME DESENSITIZED TO the sight of blood. He'd certainly seen plenty of it in the ghetto. He'd watched the whole scene unfold, and he'd been able to distance himself from it. But now as he walked over to look at the carnage, he felt a nervous laugh bubbling up in his throat. A burst of wild laughter came from his lips as sweat formed on his brow. *Why do I want to laugh when in fact I would like to fall on my knees and puke?* He would have preferred to get back into the automobile, but he couldn't. He needed to see the faces of those who'd been killed. It was important to see if any of the children who were now dead were the two he'd been searching for. He hoped not. Not because he cared about any of them, but because if they were, then he couldn't claim credit. After all, the Gestapo had taken care of this, not him.

Bile rose in his throat, and he coughed as he surveyed the scene. He felt sexual arousal and disgust at the same time as his gaze fell upon the young, pretty farmer's daughter, with her white thighs exposed and smeared with blood. *She looks like a German girl. She looks a little like my sister.* Ludwig shuddered, and the momentary arousal was gone. Now he wished he could go over to the girl and pull her skirt over her exposed thighs to protect her modesty but dared not do such a thing. If he did, the three Gestapo agents would most assuredly laugh at him. He turned his face away from the girl. *She's not a German girl. She's not my sister. She is not real, not human.*

He walked a little farther to look at the faces of the children. *None of these children look like the ones I am searching for, but I can't be sure. How can I? I've never seen the Jewish children I'm hunting. I only know what I've been told by informants who saw the burglary in the city. I know for certain the little girl isn't here because she was described as very young, perhaps two or three years old. There is no child of that age here at this farm. But the boy? He was described as a tall, big-boned, young man of about fifteen. He could be any one of these boys.* Ludwig felt the bile rise again, and then it was followed by another bout of laughter. One of the Gestapo officers laughed too then offered Ludwig a cigarette. Ludwig took it and lit it with trembling hands. Taking a deep puff to steady himself, he walked back toward the car with the others. *It's strange how the deep inhaling of cigarette smoke is satisfying after sex and after an experience like this.*

"We'll have to have a group of Jews from the ghetto brought out here to dig up all these potatoes," one of the Gestapo agents said to the others. "It looks like the farmer has buried quite a stash. Can you arrange for a group of laborers for tomorrow? Jews from the ghetto?" the Gestapo agent asked Ludwig.

"Of course. I'll take care of it first thing in the morning," Ludwig said.

"By the way, good work, Ludwig. You were right. It seems that you got a good tip. You must have good informants in that ghetto, yes? How did you ever find out that the Borkowskis were stealing from the Reich at this farm?"

"One of my informants in the ghetto told me he'd gotten the information from someone in the underground."

"You allow them to associate with the underground?"

"Only if I can keep a close eye on them. And . . . of course, only the informants. I allow them to buy a few things that they sell on the black market. In turn they tell me everything I need to know."

"And he told you this?"

"Yes," Ludwig said.

"Just like that, he told you?" the Gestapo agent said, shaking his head as they all got back into the automobile. "Do you ever wonder if those Jews are keeping things from you? I wouldn't trust them."

"I watch them closely," Ludwig said. But he was wondering how much he knew and how much slipped by him. "I have ways of making the Jews talk."

The other agent laughed, and the car sped away back toward the city.

CHAPTER 24

THE FOLLOWING DAY, LUDWIG WENT ALONG WITH ANOTHER GROUP of Gestapo agents to collect the rations from several farms. It was, for the most part, a long and boring day. They rode in the back of an open-air truck where they loaded all the barrels of crops they collected. The frightened farmers were very cooperative. They knew they were required to give most of their harvest to the Germans for the war effort. But as the day wore on and Ludwig and his group rode from farm to farm, Ludwig became more discouraged about finding the Jewish runaways.

The Gestapo searched each of the farms for any illegal activities, but they found none. Ludwig was glad. He hadn't slept well the previous night. He'd had a nightmare of the girl with the bloody thighs. In his dream she'd been dancing, and her skirt was torn off to reveal her thighs. But when she turned to look at Ludwig, her eyes were weeping blood, and she was not the girl who he'd seen. Her face was the face of his sister, Helene.

The Gestapo were relentless. At each farm they searched the barns and sheds like bloodhounds, but they found no Jews hiding and no stolen bounty. It was getting late. They had one more farm to stop at before heading back to the city. And Ludwig couldn't wait.

His back hurt from the bouncing of the truck, and his eyes burned from the relentless sunshine. Besides all of that, his bladder was near bursting.

While the others went down to the farm to collect their goods, Ludwig excused himself and walked up a hill and behind a cluster of trees to relieve himself. Relief spread over him, and he moaned as he began to urinate. Then he heard a commotion below. Shots were fired. He ran forward to see what was going on. Perhaps the Gestapo had found another farmer stealing. But as he walked closer, he saw two of the Gestapo agents lying on the ground. Fear gripped him. Were the Nazis being attacked? He ran back to hide behind the trees and fell to the ground into the puddle of his own urine, but he didn't move.

Ludwig trembled as he watched a band of partisans, men and women in shabby clothes, come running back toward the forest. They began to disappear into the clusters of trees. He stayed down listening to the unsteady rhythm of his own breath and rapid heart-beat until he was sure they were gone. Then he looked down. This time it was not the farmer but the Gestapo agents who lay on the ground bleeding. Ludwig was curious. He wanted to know more. *Be careful*, he warned himself as he began to follow the partisans, but not too closely.

CHAPTER 25

Darkness hung over the woods like a hangman's noose hangs over the head of a condemned man. Sarah clung to her brother's hand as he led her back toward the partisans' camp.

"I'm cold," she whispered.

"I know. So am I."

When they arrived at the clearing where the partisan camp had been, it was empty. No one was there. Sarah squeezed her brother's hand. "What are we going to do?" she asked. He heard the fear and desperation in her voice, but he didn't know what to say to comfort her.

"Something went wrong. Someone must have informed them about what the Borkowskis were doing." Solomon shook his head. *This was too close for comfort,* he thought. *Sarah and I escaped within minutes of the arrival of the Gestapo. If we had been at the farm instead of hiding in the woods, the two of us would be dead.* The hair on the back of his neck stood up. The responsibilities of the last several months were weighing heavily on him. And now as he looked down at Sarah, he saw she was crying.

"What do you want me to do? What can I do?" he said, his voice filled with rage caused by desperation. He shook his hand away from hers and squeezed his temples. "I don't know where Ewa and the rest of them went."

"How will we survive without them? Everyone at the farm is dead. Did you see that, Solomon? Did you see what happened? There was blood everywhere." Her body was still trembling.

"Of course I saw it. I was right there beside you, wasn't I?"

"What are we going to do? We have nowhere to go now." She began weeping. "And . . . I forgot my doll. I want to go back to the farm and get my doll."

"Are you crazy?" His face was red. He'd had all he could take. His voice was hard and cruel, and it was obvious that he'd lost all patience with her. "We can't go back there, you dummy. This time you're just going to have to grow up and forget about your damn doll."

She would normally have whined and begged him to go back, and if he hadn't been so unnerved and overwhelmed, she might have convinced him. But today she didn't even ask. She had never seen him so angry, and she dared not mention it again. Plopping down on the ground with her back against a tree, Sarah wiped her eyes and nose with the back of her sleeve.

For a few minutes Solomon was silent. His head was buried in his hands as he listened to his own raspy breathing and his wild heartbeat. He tried to take deep breaths until finally he had calmed down. Then he lifted his face and he turned to his sister. Solomon cleared his throat, and in a soft and kind voice he said, "I'm sorry, I didn't mean to holler at you. I wish we could go back for your dolly, but it's not safe for us to go back there. Do you understand?"

She nodded.

"I'll get you a new doll when I can. It might be a while. But I promise you I will. And I've never broken a promise to you, have I?"

"No," she whispered.

"All right."

She nodded again.

"Now, come on. Give me your hand. We're going to have to try to find Ewa and the rest of the group."

"I hope we can. I would love to find Ewa."

"I know. Come on."

They wandered that entire night and most of the following day.

"I'm hungry," Sarah complained. "And I'm so cold, Solomon."

"I can't help it," he said, "but tonight I'll try to find us a place to sleep."

"Where?"

"I don't know. I don't know," he said in anguish.

And when nightfall came, he tried to find an unlocked barn or cellar but he couldn't. They continued walking until he found an outhouse. The smell was nauseating, but at least it was warmer than being outside. He led Sarah inside. She gagged. "Solomon, I can't stay in here," she said, gagging again.

"We have no place else to stay."

"I'd rather freeze."

"Come on," he said, leading her back outside. "Let's keep looking for a warm place."

They walked for a long time for what seemed like hours. But still the sun had not yet peeked her golden head through the dark of night.

"I'm so cold and so tired. I want Mama so badly . . . and my dolly. I wish I had my dolly," Sarah said, finally plopping down on the cold ground and refusing to walk any farther.

"We have to keep moving," Solomon warned. But even as he watched his sister, he knew that this was nothing. The worst was yet to come. They had to find shelter before the winter fell upon them, or they would freeze to death.

"I can't walk anymore. My shoes hurt. They are too small and they pinch my toes. I want to go home. I don't care what happens to me. All I know is I just want Mama."

"I know. I know. I do too. But you have to try and get up and walk."

"I want to sleep at least for a while, Solomon. Please."

She was so scared, and so young, that it hurt his heart to look at her. "All right, come here," he said, holding her tightly in his arms to ward off as much of the chill as was possible. She shivered, but within minutes she fell into a deep sleep. Solomon remained awake.

He tried reciting the prayers he'd learned in the temple before his family had been taken to the ghetto. But when he recited prayers from a book, he found that he felt no connection with God. So he began to talk to God, speaking to him as if he were a gentle and caring father, nothing like his real father, more like Ben his mother's good friend.

"God, I am so scared. It's cold, and Sarah and I are very hungry. We can't go back to the ghetto. To be honest I don't even know how we would get back to Lodz if we wanted to. Why do all these adults want to kill us just because we're Jews? Before we had to leave our parents I used to think of myself as a grown-up, but the real truth is Sarah and I are just children. Some of these Nazis must have children of their own. They can't all be evil people. Not all of them. It's just not possible, is it? Don't some of them feel pity for us? Don't some of them realize that we are no different than their own children? And I am sure that a lot of them are fathers.

"Oh God, I don't know what to do next. All I can do is sit here under the moon and watch my sister shiver in her sleep. I thought I was smart and that I could find my way no matter what happened. I thought I was good at stealing and dealing in the black market. I guess I thought it was fun to get away with things. And it did help my family. It got us food when there was none. But I know stealing is bad and it's against your laws. And I sure am sorry now. If I am being punished for what I did, I beg you, God, please just punish me, but not poor little Sarah. She never broke your laws. And I know that I killed that man too, and that was sure a terrible thing to do. And, of course, that's also against your laws." He bowed his head in shame but continued to whisper, "But what else could I do? That man was hurting my sister. He was a bad man with evil ideas. I know it's wrong to kill, but please, you must forgive me. You must. I need you now so badly. My sister is innocent even if I am not, and she really needs you. If you don't help us, she'll die. I know she will."

An owl let out a loud hoot, and Solomon jumped, but Sarah didn't stir. He put his hand under her nose to make sure she was still breathing and let out a sigh of relief when he realized she was. "I probably will die too. I doubt I'll ever live to grow up and have a family of my own. And like I said before, I know I am not a good boy. I suppose I deserve whatever happens to me as punishment for all the bad things I did. But I have to say it again—not Sarah though. She's always been a real good girl. Sure she used to fight with me and turn me in to Mama when I went out at night to work the black market. Even so, I can remember her doing such sweet things, like putting her biscuit on my plate when she knew I was hungry or helping me to wash a cut on my leg when I got hurt on the barbed wire. She did it and promised never to tell Mama. She kept her promise, God. My sister is a real good girl, like I said. She deserves more than this. She's lost everything, everything. I'm begging you to save her life, God, even if you won't help me . . ."

After he finished praying, Solomon drifted off to sleep and didn't open his eyes again until the sun was rising, and the forest was filling with light.

CHAPTER 26

THAT DAY, SOLOMON OFFERED A FARMER A DAY OF LABOR IN exchange for food and a place to sleep. He never told the farmer about Sarah who he left hidden in the forest while he mended a broken fence. He'd been afraid to leave Sarah alone but he knew if he brought her with him, a small child, to the farm, it was more likely that the farmer would ask questions and want to know who he was and where he'd come from. So he was forced to leave her behind. It was hard work. His hands bled, and at one point he felt like running away, running away from everything, from the responsibility of caring for his sister, running away from the hard work and the harsh treatment of his people. If he were alone, he could travel faster; he could lie more easily and find a way to fit in as a gentile. In fact, had Sarah not been dependent on him, he would have taken the risk and run down to the murder scene at the Borkowski farm and stolen the papers and the identity of one of the older boys. He would also have taken any food or valuables he could find. Anything he might use or sell. But he didn't return because he knew if he were caught, his sister would have to fend for herself. And he wouldn't do that to her. Just like he would not run away and leave her now. He would wrap his bleeding hand in a rag and continue to work on the fence.

Once he finished, the farmer's wife gave him a bowl of boiled potatoes and told him he could sleep in the barn. He gobbled half the potatoes and wrapped the rest in a piece of fabric he tore off his shirt. Then Solomon waited until dusk when he ran up the hill into the trees to find Sarah. Relieved to see her, he told her to quickly come with him to the barn. She ran as fast as she could, slipping and falling, but she no longer cried when she fell. Instead, she just brushed off her dress and began to run again. Once inside the barn, Solomon gave her the potatoes. She ate them quickly.

"We can stay in here, but you must be very quiet."

"I will," she said, her voice very serious. "I was scared today and cold too when you left me."

"I know, but I had to leave you. We needed food."

"It's all right. I'm glad you came back."

"Let's get some sleep. I think it's best if we get out of this barn before dawn."

"But, Solomon, why can't we just stay here forever? It's warm and it's safe. I don't want to go back out."

"I know that. Of course I know that. But how do you expect me to make that happen? I have to sleep with one eye open because you're not even supposed to be in here. My life would be a lot easier without you." He was frustrated with her again. His voice was curt, and he was a lot meaner than he'd meant to be. *Take a deep breath*, he thought as he reminded himself that she was only a child. She had endured more than any small child should ever endure, and she understood more than she should have had to at that age. But he knew she didn't understand everything. Not even close. Sometimes she just wanted to be a willful little girl. She wanted to be warm and safe and cuddled, and he couldn't blame her. But he also knew that what she wanted was impossible.

She lay on the straw with her lower lip puckered as if she might burst into tears at any moment. He walked over to her and sat down beside her. "I'm sorry, Sarah. I didn't mean to hurt your feelings."

"But you wish you could get rid of me, don't you?"

"No, you're my sister and my best friend. Fact is, you and me are all we've got, right?"

"You're all I've got."

"And you're all I have too. So let's not fight. I don't want to ever be without you. Someday, I want to dance at your wedding."

She giggled. "Mama always used to say that. She would say, 'Someday, my little girl, I am going to dance at your wedding.' Do you remember?"

"Of course, I do," he said, turning away from her so she wouldn't see the sadness in his face.

"Do you think Mama is really dead?" she asked earnestly.

"I don't know." He shrugged, and a pang of terror shot through him whenever he thought about the possibility.

"Do you think Papa is dead too?"

"I can't say."

"You never liked Papa anyway. He was too mean."

"He was mean."

"But you loved Mama, didn't you?"

"I'll always love Mama."

"I love her too. I want to see her soon." She hesitated then she asked, "What does it mean to be dead?"

She doesn't understand, he thought. "It's getting late, and we have to leave here early in the morning. Let's go to sleep. We can talk about this another time." There were two horse blankets hanging from a hook on the wall. Solomon took them down and covered Sarah with one. Then he wrapped himself in the other. But when he looked over at her, she was shivering from the cold. He smiled at her. Then he removed the blanket from his own shoulders and covered her with it.

"Don't you need your blanket? It's very cold in here."

"I'm not cold. You use it."

"Are you sure?"

"I'm sure," he said, then he kissed the top of her head the way their mother had always done when she put them to bed. "Sleep now, Sarah."

She put her thumb in her mouth. He noted that she still did that sometimes, and he wondered if she would ever stop. He watched her as she began to breathe heavily and her eyes closed.

Before a quarter of an hour passed, Sarah and Solomon had fallen into a deep sleep. They lay curled up together shivering like two kittens trying to stay warm. Solomon tried to force himself to stay awake so that he could keep watch, but his young eyes would not remain open, so he finally succumbed to sleep, and putting his trust in God to protect him and his sister, the two children lay huddled on a pile of hay in a barn, similar, I would guess, to the one where Jesus was born. But this one was far away from Bethlehem; this barn was located somewhere on the outskirts of a dark forest deep in the Polish countryside.

CHAPTER 27

IT WAS ALREADY MORNING WHEN SOLOMON WAS AWAKENED BY THE opening of the barn door. His heart beat fast as he looked around frantic for somewhere to hide. There was nowhere. He was afraid to hide behind the horse in its stall. It could very well kick them. Sarah was still asleep. He nudged her shoulder. The farmer walked in.

"You're still here?"

Solomon nodded.

"What's this?" the farmer asked as he glanced at Sarah.

"My sister," Solomon admitted, not knowing what else to do.

"You're in some kind of trouble, aren't you?" the farmer asked, shaking his head knowingly.

"No, no trouble. Just trying to earn extra money to bring back to my mother who is badly in need of money since my father died."

"You're lying. You're Jews. You two are Jews," he said, shaking his head.

Solomon felt for the gun in his pocket. He would shoot and kill this man if he had to. The very thought of killing another person made him feel sick and terrified. But he would do it before he would let the man turn him and Sarah in to the authorities.

"We want to leave," Solomon said with as much conviction as he could muster. "Just let us go, and there won't be any trouble."

"Hmmm," the farmer said, "you two don't have to be afraid. I'm not going to turn you in. I would like the reward money but not enough to send two innocent children to the Gestapo. I have a grandchild your sister's age. I couldn't do it with a good conscience. But I do want you to leave. I wish I could help you more, but I can't. I can't risk being caught with the two of you in here. They'd say I was hiding Jews, and I'm an old man. I don't think I'd survive prison. Go on, take the blankets with you—and go."

"Thank you," Solomon said. He felt a tear fall from his eye and immediately brushed it away. Then he took the blankets, and with his other hand, he grabbed Sarah's arm and led her out the barn door.

"Wait," the farmer said.

Has he changed his mind? Solomon wanted to run, but the farmer was too close.

"Here." The old man handed Solomon three potatoes from a bag he had on a shelf. "Good luck," he said, and then he walked back into his barn as Solomon took the potatoes.

"Thank you again," he said, then he pulled Sarah away.

"I wish we could stay here," she said. "He's nice like an old grandpa."

"We can't. That's for sure, and I think we should get out of here before he changes his mind. We're worth money to him. He might decide to turn us in. Let's go. Come on, and besides, what if someone else comes along and sees us? We can't trust anyone."

They ran as fast as they could back into the safety of the forest.

Later that day, Solomon was offering Sarah an insect to eat. He'd forced himself to eat them on occasion, but she still refused. Regardless of how hungry she was, she could not put the tiny wriggling thing into her mouth.

"I hate this," Sarah said as she sat with her back against a tree while Solomon made a futile attempt to catch a fish from a pond a few feet away. "I want to go home. I want to eat Mama's chicken soup for lunch. I am tired of eating things that make me want to throw up, like raw potatoes and bugs." She shivered. "Do you know what Mama would say if she knew we were eating worms and stuff like that? She would be furious."

"I think she'd want us to eat whatever we had to eat to survive. And right now, I'm doing my best just to keep us alive." He frowned at her as he took a tree branch and made a fishing pole using a thick thread from the horse blanket and a hook he made from thick wire that he found in the barn the night before. He took the insect he had tried to give to Sarah and shoved the hook through it. "I'm going to try to catch a fish."

"Last time you got a fish, you made me it eat raw. It was so slimy."

"We can't risk making a fire, Sarah. Fire could bring the Nazis right to us."

She pursed her lips. "You just go on and fish. If you catch one, I'm not going to eat it anyway."

"Please stop this. I know you're tired and crabby, but just stop fighting me. I'm tired too."

"What about the doll you promised me? You said you'd get me another doll." She crossed her arms over her chest.

He looked at her exasperated. He wanted to slap her across her face. *She's only five*, he reminded himself. *She doesn't understand.* "I'll get you a doll when I can," he said, then he felt a tug on the pole. He was careful not to break the thread as he pulled. It was a small fish. But it was better, he decided, than a big one. A big fish might have broken the threads. He pulled it out of the water and grabbed it. It squirmed, but he held it tightly until it stopped.

"We have a fish," he said.

"I'm still not going to eat it." She crossed her arms over her chest.

"All right. You have to eat, so I'll make a fire."

"You can?"

"Yes, I can. I stole these matches from Borkowski's farm. I didn't want to make a fire, but I will."

"They were really nice to us, and you stole from them? Solomon, you know better."

"Sarah, please. Just let me do what I have to do to take care of us."

She turned away.

"If I cook the fish, will you eat it?"

She nodded.

"Does that mean yes?"

"Yes," she answered.

"Then I'll take the risk of making a fire."

It was late afternoon by the time they finished eating.

"I'm tired," Sarah said.

"Let's get some rest." Solomon patted the ground next to him. Sarah came over slowly and lay down on her side using her hand as a pillow. He lay beside her and covered his sister with the blankets. Then they huddled close so they could weather the cold with their body heat. Solomon marveled at how quickly Sarah fell into a deep sleep. A smile came over his face as he listened to the gentle rhythm of her slow, even breathing.

She sleeps so soundly because she doesn't understand how bad things really are. I wish I didn't understand. I can't help but worry that the entire group of partisans was arrested. If they'd been killed we would have found their remains. So either they were taken away, or they are hiding somewhere else. And I have no idea where to look. I keep trying to figure it all out, but I am lost, and I'm tired. Still, I can't give up. I have to keep fighting to stay alive, to keep Sarah alive. Every day I say to myself, fight for one more day, Sol. Just one more day, and something good will happen; someone will find us. Papa hated me for my stubbornness, but right now that's all Sarah and I have left to count on. Papa called me scrappy. He said I was a streetwise punk. Maybe he was right. And maybe, just maybe, that's what's saving our lives. I hope our luck holds out.

He finally fell asleep just as the sun set.

CHAPTER 28

WHEN SOLOMON OPENED HIS EYES, IT WAS EARLY MORNING. SARAH was not beside him. He jumped to his feet, his heart pounding. "Sarah, Sarah!" he called out. He was so distressed he forgot the danger of making noise in the forest. There were enemies lurking everywhere. He spun around searching frantically in every direction not knowing what to do. *Was she taken by a wild animal in the night?* He felt the bile rise into his throat. *Sarah, my baby sister, she could be dead, killed by a wild animal. Or who knows what? She would be too afraid to leave my side when it was dark. Even if she had to pee, she would have woken me up.* He didn't realize it, but he was tearing at the hair over his temples.

Then he saw her walking hand in hand with a man in his midtwenties. The man was a stranger. He was tall, very tall. Solomon assumed he was over six feet. His light brown hair was wavy, and although he looked weathered, he was handsome in a rugged way. But the most shocking and unnerving part of it all was that he wore the uniform of a German soldier. Solomon pretended to be asleep as he watched his sister talking animatedly with the soldier. *I have no doubt that he plans to turn us in and get the reward money,* Solomon thought. As quietly as he could, Solomon reached under the blanket and found his gun. The metal felt cold in his hand as his fingers wrapped around the trigger.

"Solomon, are you awake? I want you to meet our new friend. His name is Gunther."

Solomon felt his arm twitch. *I must be quick, very quick. He's a soldier, so I'm sure he has a gun too. Even worse, he's been trained to use it and use it well. He'll be faster and a far better shot than I. I have to wait until he gets real close, so I can be sure that I'll hit him with the first shot. It's so hard to have patience. I'm so afraid that I'll miss, and Sarah is right next to him.* Solomon swallowed hard. His chest hurt, and it was hard to breathe. His throat was dry and scratchy.

They were approaching quickly, his sister and the Nazi she called Gunther. "Solomon, it's late. You never sleep this late. I want you to meet someone."

Solomon sat up quickly with the gun in his trembling hand pointing directly at Gunther. Gunther put one hand in the air. But he still held Sarah's hand with the other one. "Be careful with that thing," he said.

"I know how to use it. I've used it before. Let go of my sister."

Gunther took his hand away from Sarah's and raised it in the air.

"Come over here, now, Sarah."

"He's nice, Solomon. Don't shoot him," Sarah said.

"I said get over here."

"Go on and do what he says," Gunther told Sarah. Then in a calm voice he said to Solomon, "Please put the gun down. No one needs to get hurt here. I am not the enemy."

"Your uniform tells me you are my enemy," Solomon said.

"I was a German soldier. I am now a deserter. I know you're Jews. Your sister told me."

Solomon glared at Sarah.

But Gunther continued to speak. "Please listen to me," he said. "I recently found out how the Nazis are treating the Jews. That's a big part of the reason I am deserting."

"You're worried about Jews? You expect me to believe that?"

"You can believe what you want. It's one of the reasons I no longer chose to fight for the German army. The biggest reason is that Hitler is insane. He has gone mad with his need for power. He'll destroy Germany and every German if he has the chance."

Solomon studied Gunther. He certainly seemed sincere, but this could be a trick.

"What do you mean destroy Germany?"

"He doesn't care about the German people. He only cares about power. He sent German soldiers to Russia without adequate clothing to weather the bitter cold of the Russian winter. I was among them. We lacked adequate food and weapons. In short, Hitler sent his own men to die, and for what? For his lust for power? I am no follower of this man."

"And you don't hate Jews?"

"Why would I? I grew up with Jewish friends. I had a Jewish dentist, for heaven's sake. I don't hate Jews. I don't hate anyone. Except maybe Hitler."

Something in the man's voice made Solomon believe he was sincere. "Sit down," Solomon said.

Gunther sat.

"We are hungry. I want to know if you think you can help me steal food for all of us?" Solomon asked, his eyes fixed on Gunther's face. He was searching for any indication that Gunther could not be trusted. But what he saw was a man with clear eyes who was not afraid to look directly at him.

"I'll help you, but I think it's best if we wait until nightfall. Someone must stay with Sarah; I think it should be you. Once the sun sets, I'll go and see what kind of food I can find. Sarah here is too small to be left alone in the woods." Gunther smiled at Sarah. She returned his smile.

"You are going to go alone to look for food? How do I know you aren't going to go and turn us in for reward money?"

"You don't. You're going to have to trust me," Gunther said. Then he continued, "You know, I have a niece Sarah's age. She's my older brother's daughter. Sarah reminds me of her."

"It's hard to put my trust in a stranger. I can't help but think you would want the reward for turning in a couple of Jews."

"Actually, I didn't know there was a reward, but it doesn't surprise me. Not with what I have seen Germany doing. However, you needn't worry. I'm quite certain that there is a pretty substantial reward for turning in deserters, so I would not take the risk."

Solomon studied Gunther, who was calm and confident. A strange sense of relief spread over Solomon. Although he was afraid to trust this man, for some unexplainable reason, he did. And it felt good to have an adult take control of things, at least for a while.

"All right," Solomon said. "I suppose I will have to trust you."

"I suppose you will."

CHAPTER 29

THAT NIGHT, GUNTHER LEFT SOLOMON AND SARAH HIDDEN DEEP within the heart of the forest while he ventured out to find food. As Solomon watched the back of Gunther's frame disappear into the shadows, a moment of doubt and fear set in, and he considered taking Sarah and running away before Gunther returned. But he was cold and tired, and even more importantly, he was hopeful. He longed to believe that Gunther would keep his promise. Sarah lay down beside her brother and fell asleep, but Solomon couldn't sleep. In his mind, he continually replayed the conversation he'd had with Gunther. *I am trying so hard to trust him. I have to believe that he is telling the truth about there being a reward on his head just like there is one on ours. I must believe he will keep his promise.* Several times he glanced over at Sarah and considered waking her up and escaping deeper into the forest. But he didn't.

Gunther returned just as the sun began to rise. He wore different clothes. He'd abandoned his uniform for the simple civilian clothes of a farmer. In his hands he carried a basket brimming with potatoes and carrots and a pile of heavy blankets.

"How did you get all of that stuff?" Sarah asked as she nibbled on a carrot.

"Let's just say I did what I had to do." Gunther smiled at Sarah and pinched her cheek affectionately.

Solomon's eyes caught Gunther's. Gunther smiled an easy smile. He seemed so genuine, but the time Solomon spent on the street buying and trading for the black market had taught him to be cautious of everyone. The older boys always said that a sweet smile could hide an evil heart. And Solomon had learned it was true. In the early days, there were times that he'd trusted someone only to have them run off with his money or goods. Now he stood looking at a man who he knew for certain had been one of them, a Nazi, and he wondered how this man had gotten his hands on the food and blankets. Had he killed a family, or threatened them, in order to steal these things? *I won't ask any questions, but I'll keep my guard up. Right now, Sarah and I need food and warmth, and he has brought us both. So for now, I will keep my mouth shut. We'll eat his food, and I'll cover myself and my sister with his blankets. And because of his generosity, for whatever reason he may have, Sarah and I will live another day.*

Solomon watched Gunther carefully. He scrutinized the German's every move. But, so far, he could not find any fault with him. Gunther was a man of his word. Gunther had promised he was not planning to turn them in, and up until now the Gestapo had not appeared. *Could it really be possible that a man who fought for Hitler turned out to be a good man?*

"I hate eating raw potatoes," Sarah said as she sat beside Gunther. "They taste terrible."

"I know, but it's the best we can do at least for right now."

"We could make a fire and boil them. Solomon and I made a fire yesterday after Solomon caught a fish in a pond that is right near here."

"I know you started a fire," Gunther said. There was a warning tone to his voice. "Fire sends smoke up into the sky. You see, that's how I found you. Lucky for you it was me and not some Jew-hunting Nazis. I don't think we should start another fire."

"I have to agree with him, Sarah," Solomon said.

Sarah shook her head and puckered her lower lip. "I still hate the taste."

"Then we'll make a game of it; what do you say?" Gunther offered.

"What kind of a game?" Sarah perked up.

"Well, let's see." He smiled. "How about we play hide-and-seek."

"What does that mean?"

"Well, it means that we close our eyes, and you go and hide, then your brother and I come looking for you. If we find you, you must take a bite of the potato. If we don't, we must take a bite. But you mustn't go too far away."

"Hmmmm . . . it could be fun."

"It will be! But remember, now, don't go too far away. Do you understand?"

"I understand."

"All right. I am going to close my eyes, and you are going to go and hide. I will count to ten slowly. By the time I finish, you should be hidden." Gunther smiled at her and winked.

Sarah giggled.

"I think I'll sit this one out," Solomon said. He kept his eyes open, watching his sister to be sure he knew where she was at all times.

"All right," Gunther said. Then he closed his eyes and began to count.

Solomon took a bite of a potato. He was glad for the nourishment even if the taste left a lot to be desired.

". . . four . . . five . . . six . . . seven . . . eight," Gunther counted aloud.

Sarah giggled.

Solomon watched his sister playing with Gunther.

It was getting colder every day. A light snow had begun to dust the ground. And even though the idea of winter struck fear into Solomon's heart, it also brought back memories of his family before the ghetto. How he'd delighted in the lighting of the Hanukkah candles for eight wonderful, magical days. And each evening, playing dreidel with his cousins while waiting to eat delicious latkes, which were a mixture of shredded potatoes and chopped onions fried to a golden brown in freshly rendered chicken fat, which the Jewish people called schmaltz. This was a very special treat that his mother made for the entire family during Hanukkah.

Sometimes, when they were able to get apples, his mother made apple sauce, thick and chunky, to spread on the potato pancakes. His heart ached with longing. Oh, how he missed that life. He missed it so badly he could weep. Had he known then how good his life was, or did he just take for granted that it would always be wonderful? It was hard for him to recall. He couldn't remember how he'd felt or what he thought. All he could remember was the food and the warmth and the love . . . and his mother. His poor mother. A tear fell from his eye, and he turned away just in case Sarah or Gunther might see him. But they weren't paying attention. They were busy playing. Sarah was laughing and then Gunther was laughing too.

Just then a man stepped out from behind the trees. "What's going on here? Who is this man?" It was Luke from the partisans' camp. "I've been looking everywhere for you two," he said to Solomon. "We had to move camp. Do you know what happened at Borkowski's farm?"

"Yes, we saw it. Sarah and I. Sarah saw the Nazis coming, and we ran into the forest to hide. They killed everyone."

"Yes, we know. We heard."

"Is everyone at the partisan camp all right? Did you get away in time?" Solomon asked. "Did they find your camp too?"

"They didn't find our camp, but the whole thing was very unexpected. No one had any idea they were coming. We were lucky. We moved the camp as soon as we heard what happened."

Solomon breathed a secret sigh of relief. *Ewa is all right.* "It was terrible Sarah and I saw them kill everyone, even the other children who were working on the farm," Solomon said.

"They killed my friend too," Sarah said as she came closer. "Jula, the farmer's daughter."

"Who are you?" Luke asked, turning to Gunther. He was holding his gun pointed directly at Gunther.

"I'm a deserter from the German army."

"A Nazi?"

"No, not a Nazi. I am a man who sees the Nazis for what they are: a group of fiends bent on destroying our beloved fatherland."

"Hmmm." Luke studied him.

"He knows we're Jewish, and he likes us anyway," Sarah offered, smiling.

Luke didn't look away from Gunther. He didn't acknowledge Sarah or say anything for several minutes. Then he said, "How do I know I can trust you?"

"Because if I were a Nazi, I would have already turned these children in to the Gestapo. Apparently, there is a reward for turning Jews in. Obviously, I haven't done that. That should tell you something about me."

Luke nodded. "All right, go then. Go on your way."

Gunther nodded and turned to leave, but Solomon said, "Wait." Then he turned to Luke. "This fellow is a trained soldier. He knows how to use a gun. He might be of help to us. Perhaps we should bring him back to meet Cereck."

"Do you want to join us?" Luke asked Gunther.

"Yes, I want to join any group that is working against Hitler."

Luke turned to Solomon and shrugged. "All right, let's bring him back to speak to Cereck and see what he says."

They all followed Luke in silence, walking for at least twenty minutes until several people Solomon recognized from the partisan came out from behind the trees. They nodded to Luke.

Solomon watched as Luke motioned with his head for Gunther to follow him.

"Where are you going with this man?" one of the partisans asked.

"We are going to see Cereck," Luke said. But before they could walk away, Ewa came running up. She put her arms around Sarah and lifted her high in the air. She was laughing and crying at the same time. Then she put Sarah down and embraced Solomon. Turning to Luke, she said, "Thank God they are all right. Where did you find them?"

"In the forest, wandering."

"I was afraid you two had been killed during that terrible raid on the Borkowski farm."

"We're all right," Solomon offered.

"I was afraid too, but they are fine. They escaped in time. Thank God," Luke said.

Then Ewa noticed Gunther. Solomon saw a strange look pass between them, and he didn't know why, but he felt a stab of jealousy run through him. "Who's this?" Ewa asked.

"He's a deserter. He's been helping the children," Luke said.

"A Nazi deserter?" Ewa asked.

"Yes," Gunther said. "A man who stands against the Nazis as strongly as you do."

"I highly doubt that. We're Jews," Ewa said.

"Come on, we have to go and speak with Cereck. You can't stay here with us until Cereck approves of you," Luke said. "So follow me. I'll take you to meet him now."

Ewa took Solomon's and Sarah's hands and led them back to the camp.

Solomon smiled up at her. "I was worried about you," he managed to say shyly.

She squeezed his hand. "I was very worried about the two of you," she said. "When I heard that the massacre happened at the farm where the two of you were staying, I was sick with worry."

Is it possible she cares about me like a girlfriend? Could it be possible? Solomon's heart skipped a beat. He managed to smile at her shyly.

"You and Sarah will stay with us from now on. I don't care what Cereck says. I am not going to let you go off on your own."

"He doesn't want us to stay with you?" Sarah asked.

"It's not that, sweetie," Ewa said. "It's just that he is afraid because you two are children that having you stay here with us might put all of us in danger."

"How could we do that?"

"Oh, I don't know. Perhaps by being too slow to keep up when we are forced to hide. It doesn't matter, anyway," she said as she took Sarah's hand. "I am going to talk to him. He'll listen to me. And you and Solomon will stay with us. Would you like that?"

"Yes, very much," Sarah said. "You know Jula? She was Borkowski's daughter. She was my friend and the Nazis killed her. I saw it happen. I saw a lot of blood. I was scared, Ewa."

"I know." Ewa bent down to hug Sarah. "I am sorry you had to see such a terrible thing happen to your friend."

"I don't want to die. I didn't know what it meant to die before but now I do." Sarah was hugging Ewa tightly. "Please, please don't let that happen to Solomon or me. It was horrible, and I think it hurt a lot."

"Shhh, it's all right. I will protect you as best as I can."

"But what if they get us? What if the Nazis get us?" Sarah was shaking.

"You will be all right. You'll be here with me and with the rest of the group. I'll keep you safe. Do you trust me?"

"Yes," Sarah moaned.

"Good, I am glad to hear it. Now don't you worry about anything except learning. We'll start your studies tomorrow."

"All right," Sarah said.

They began walking again. A few minutes later, Ewa turned to Solomon and asked, "Solomon, how do you feel about all of this? Would you like to stay with us?"

"I would," he said, beaming. *She is so pretty*, he thought. *She is the prettiest girl I've ever seen in my entire life.*

"I am glad. It will be good for everyone to have the two of you here. Now, the first thing we must do is to get you both something to eat. Then I'll go and talk to our gracious leader. Don't you worry, I'll make him see reason." She winked at the children and smiled.

CHAPTER 30

Solomon and Sarah were permitted to stay with the partisans. However, Cereck made it clear that they were to be Ewa's responsibility. She didn't mind.

Cereck's meeting with Gunther took over an hour. Gunther offered several substantial reasons why he would be an asset to the group, and finally after much convincing, he was permitted to stay. However, a few hours later when Cereck was alone with Luke, he advised Luke to keep an eye on Gunther.

"We don't know him. Everything he says sounds believable. It seems as if he is just a good German man, if there is such a thing. However, we don't know; he could be a spy."

"He could. You're right. But it's hard for me to believe that all Germans are bad. I knew plenty of German people before the war. Some were good, some bad."

"Yes, but remember, we are Jews. We are worth money. And not only are we worth reward money, but these are hard times. People need any extras they can get their hands on. A couple of Jews are not as important to them as a loaf of bread, which could keep their family alive for another day or two. You understand?"

"Of course. I agree with you. And I will definitely keep an eye on him."

"Don't let him make a move without your knowing about it."

Luke nodded.

CHAPTER 31

Sarah missed Jula. But she was young and soon forgot. In fact, she was thrilled to be with Ewa who gave her plenty of attention. Ewa was like a combination of a big sister and a mother which Sarah craved.

Sarah followed Ewa around all the time. When they weren't studying, Ewa was reading to Sarah or they were fishing together. At first it was difficult to teach the children because there were no supplies. Ewa had to use a tree branch to carve the letters of the alphabet into the dirt. But within a week, two other partisans in the group offered to allow her to use books that they'd brought with them. And when Gunther and Luke raided a nearby farm one night, they were able to steal a single pencil and some paper. Before Solomon and his family were sent to the ghetto, Solomon had never liked school. He'd found it to be a waste of time. When his mother had tried to teach them, Solomon's mind had always drifted off to thoughts of other things that he found more interesting. But now Solomon was infatuated with Ewa. She was his first crush, so he hung on Ewa's every word. And because he wanted to please her, and he didn't want her to think he was stupid, he was learning to read and write. She would smile at him, pleased by his progress, and his heart would melt. These were the happiest days of his life since he'd left his home, and he would have been content had he not noticed the way Ewa and Gunther looked at each other. It upset him to see the glances that passed between them.

"He's a Nazi, you know," Solomon said to Ewa one day as he, Sarah, and Ewa sat together under a tree doing their studies.

"Who?" Sarah asked.

"Mind your own business; I wasn't talking to you," Solomon snapped at his sister, then he turned to Ewa. "Once a Nazi, always a Nazi."

"You mean Gunther?" Ewa looked into Solomon's eyes.

"Of course I do," he said.

"I think he is a German man who went off to fight for his country, but he became disenchanted with the leadership when he saw what Hitler was doing to Germany."

"Disenchanted? What does that mean?" Sarah asked.

"It means that he didn't like the way things were going," Solomon snapped again. "You like him, don't you?" he asked Ewa.

"I don't know him."

"I like him. I think he is nice. When we first met him and we were in the woods, and we were cold and hungry, he tried to help us, didn't he, Solomon?"

"Shut up, Sarah," Solomon said. Then he stood up and walked away.

CHAPTER 32

An hour or so later, Luke and Gunther came into the clearing where the rest of the group were gathered.

"This is Gunther," Luke announced. "For those of you who have not yet met him, I wanted to introduce him to you. I'm sure you have noticed that he has been here at the camp with us for the last week or so. Cereck has made the decision to allow him to join us."

"Who are you, Gunther? Where do you come from?" one of the men asked.

"I think it's only fair that you should know I'm a German. I was in the German army," Gunther answered.

"A Nazi, you mean," someone else said.

"I was, yes. That is until I found out how terrible Hitler is for our country."

"We're Jews. The last thing we need is for some Nazi to infiltrate our camp. You know we're Jews, don't you?"

"Yes, I know," Gunther said. "And this may sound trite, but I've had Jewish friends before the war. I joined the army to fight for my country because I believed it was the right thing to do. I won't lie to you and say I was not aware of anti-Semitism. You wouldn't believe me if I did."

"I don't believe a word you are saying," someone else said. "I don't trust him. I think he's here to spy on us and find out what our plans are."

"Cereck is convinced that he is not here for that reason. He believes that Gunther is here to join us in our crusade against the Nazis."

"Crusade. Is that what we are doing? Crusading?" Ewa scoffed. "I am just trying to survive. Believe me, I would rather be a teacher, teaching children, than a warrior starving in the forest."

"Yes, and we would all like to go back to our old lives. But we can't. At least not until the Nazis are defeated," Luke said.

"May I speak?" Gunther asked. Luke nodded, and then Gunther said, "I would like to go home. I'd love to go back to my family the way things were before the war. I had plans too. I had dreams that were swept away by the Nazis. Do you think I wanted to go to Russia and freeze . . . and starve? But I went because I wanted to do what was right. Now I know that the Nazi Party is not good for Germany. I left my parents to do this for my country. And my parents are no longer young. They needed me. I was the only boy in the family. My sister is of no use to them. I had a girlfriend too. We planned to marry. She left me when I went off to war. But I did all of this with the belief that I was bettering Germany. Now I know that is not the case. Hitler is the worst thing that ever happened to the German people."

"How sad for you that you were disillusioned," Ewa said. "But the rest of us were not asked to help our country. We were forced into ghettos and murdered. The Nazis took both of my parents away. They were older; they needed help, but they were treated like roaches. With my own two eyes I watched as they killed my brother in the street when he tried to resist. I escaped because a childhood friend of mine helped me. She had a diamond that her mother gave her before her mother was taken away. My friend saved our lives by giving that diamond to the bastard who was in charge. She told him he could have it if he let the two of us go. He did, but then later my friend was caught, and she was killed anyway."

"I'm sorry for what happened to you. I don't know all of your stories. I am sure they are terrible, and believe me, I'm sorry. But I want you to know that not all the Germans are in agreement with Hitler. Some of us are just trying to survive, just trying to get enough food to keep ourselves and our families alive. I know the Nazis weren't killing us the way they were killing your families, but believe me, the German people were not exempt from the horrors that the Third Reich brought to our country."

"I suppose you want me to feel sorry for you," Ewa said, crossing her arms over her chest.

"No, I just want you to understand."

"I understand what you're saying, but I must admit, I don't trust you. I don't think it's wise for us to let you stay here. I truly believe you will betray us," Ewa said gravely.

"I won't. I swear it. I won't."

"Hmmm," one of the other women said. "Ewa is right. Should we be taking such chances?"

"I am a good hunter. I can fish, even ice fish. Having me here will be advantageous to all of you."

"I think he will be a big help," Cereck said.

"Who am I to argue? If you want him here, then let him stay," Ewa said as she turned away from the rest of the group.

Cereck looked at Ewa. "As I said, I think we should allow him to stay. But to be fair to everyone, let's take a vote."

"All in favor?" he said. "Now, all opposed?"

It was close, but it was decided that Gunther would be permitted stay.

CHAPTER 33

A LOUD SHRIEK AWAKENED SOLOMON OUT OF A DEAD SLEEP. HE jumped to his feet. It was Sarah's voice. Glancing over, he saw that she was not sleeping beside him. Without a moment's hesitation he ran toward the sound.

Another scream and then, "Solomon! Help me!"

With his heart beating rapidly in his throat, Solomon cried out, "I'm coming. I'm coming. But where are you?"

"I am at the pond. Help me!"

Solomon ran faster. He tripped over a rock and fell, cutting his forehead on a branch. Blood trickled down into his eye, but he got up and began to run again.

"Sarah, I'm coming . . ."

He ran toward the sound not realizing that several of the others were following him.

When Solomon got to the pond he screamed in desperation. "Where are you? I don't see you!"

"Over here . . ."

Skidding across the ice, falling, and getting up again, Solomon followed the sound. Then he saw Sarah. She was hanging on to a broken chunk of ice.

A second later, Gunther came sprinting out from the trees. His long legs navigating the unstable terrain quickly. "Get off the ice," he commanded Solomon. "Do as I say, and I'll get your sister."

Gunther ran toward Sarah. She was holding on to the ice. Most of her body was submerged, but her head, neck, and shoulders were peeking out of the freezing water.

"I'm going to throw you this branch. I'll be holding on tightly to the other side of it. Grab on to it and I'll pull you in," Gunther said to Sarah.

"All right." She gasped. Her lips were already turning blue.

"We have to hurry, Sarah." Gunther's voice was firm but gentle.

"I'm so cold," Sarah said, her shaky voice growing weaker.

"Stay with me," Gunther commanded. "Don't let go of the ice until I tell you. And then only let go with one hand at a time. Grip the branch firmly. Do you understand?"

"Solomon! Help me," Sarah tried to cry out, but her voice was a whisper.

"Pay attention," Gunther said firmly. "Now here is the branch. Grab on, and hold on to it tightly."

"I can't," she said. "I can't. My fingers are slipping. I'm falling in deeper. Help me. Please help me . . ."

Gunther took off his coat, then he turned to Ewa who was standing beside him. "Go quickly and gather all the blankets you can. Bring them back here."

She nodded and went running toward the camp.

"All right, hold on. I'm coming," Gunther assured Sarah.

Solomon stood frozen with fear.

Gunther ran toward Sarah. He fell and slid on his belly across the ice. Using his arms, he pulled himself over to the broken ice where Sarah was sinking. The ice began to crack under him. Ewa returned holding a large pile of stolen horse blankets. She stood watching as the ice moved beneath Gunther's weight. "It will swallow both of them if he isn't careful," Luke said.

Sarah's face was as white as bone china, her lips a shade of purplish blue. Although he didn't realize it, Solomon had begun to cry. Gunther had a single moment where he might have turned back to safety. He felt the ice giving way beneath him, but he refused to go back because if he did he knew Sarah would die. Instead, he held on tightly to the ice on which he lay and used his hands to paddle toward Sarah. She was slowly falling deeper. He knew if he didn't grab her soon, she would succumb to the cold and then fall beneath the ice forever. He paddled harder until he was beside her, then as he reached out he felt the ice that he lay upon start to crack again. He ignored it.

"Give me your hand," he demanded. She looked at him with a blank stare. "Give me your hand." His voice was loud and commanding. She didn't move. He was finally close enough to grab her hands, so he did. She began to fall beneath the water, but he pulled her up. The sheet of ice divided, and his legs were now submerged. Still, he held tightly to the child with one hand and to the remaining piece of floating ice with the other. Kicking his feet as hard as he could, he managed to move the two of them closer to shore. And just as they reached land, the ice cracked. Using every ounce of strength he had left, Gunther hoisted Sarah onto the dry land then pulled himself up and fell down on the ground beside her. Ewa wrapped them both in blankets. Their teeth were chattering.

"You saved her," Ewa said to Gunther, her eyes glowing with admiration.

"I hope so. Time will tell. Right now, keep her warm. I know we don't like to make a fire, but we are going to have to, and get some hot liquid into her if she is going to make it."

"I will do that. And, of course, I will bring you some too," Ewa said. "Unfortunately, if we make a fire, we will have to move the camp very soon, just in case someone sees the smoke."

"Yes, I know, but she needs the hot liquid."

"As do you," Ewa said.

"Yes, I suppose you're right. I do." He smiled.

Gunther held the child tightly in his arms in an effort to use his body heat to warm her. Solomon was standing beside his sister crying and squeezing Sarah's hand.

Then two of the men in the group picked Sarah up and carried her back to camp. Gunther walked beside them still shivering.

They made a quick fire and boiled the snow into hot water which Gunther drank and Ewa spooned into Sarah's mouth.

Then within an hour, they moved the camp north.

CHAPTER 34

FROM THAT DAY FORWARD, SOLOMON NOTICED THAT EWA AND Gunther smiled at each other more often, and when they looked at each other, their gazes held just a moment too long. Ewa could not lift a bucket of water without Gunther running to her side to help. Solomon resented it when he saw Gunther wrap his coat around Ewa's shoulders on an exceptionally cold night.

By mid-February, food was very scarce. There was hardly anything to eat. One morning, without a word to anyone, Gunther disappeared. Several of the men went to Cereck to tell him they were worried that perhaps Gunther had decided to turn them in and take the reward money. They asked him to consider breaking up the camp and moving before he had a chance to bring the Nazis back. Cereck said he would think about it, but before he had the opportunity to give it much thought, Gunther returned. His face was bright red with the cold, and his hair was tipped with tiny icicles where the snow had melted and then refrozen on his head. But in his hand he carried two rabbits and a squirrel. A treasure to this group of starving people.

Ewa smiled at him openly. She had never doubted that he'd

gone off to do something to help the group. The others still doubted him, but she didn't.

"This is worth making a fire. Even if we have to move camp right after we finish eating," Cereck said, smiling, as he took the food and handed it to one of the women.

Everyone nodded. They were glad to have food.

The smell of the meat cooking made Solomon's stomach ache with hunger. He could hardly wait to eat. But as he watched the meat sizzle on the spit, he noticed Ewa and Gunther taking a walk away from the others. He had to know where they were going, so he followed them.

Staying far enough behind to remain unseen, Solomon followed Gunther to a tree stump which was several feet deeper into the forest.

"Sit down, please," Gunther said to Ewa as he stopped and indicated the tree stump.

She did as he asked.

"I got this for you," he said, clumsily handing her a bracelet.

She looked at him puzzled.

"Please . . . put it on."

"It's beautiful. I don't know what to say. And . . . I don't want to ask how you got it."

"Don't ask, then," he said, smiling.

"It was very sweet of you to think of me. But did you steal this?"

"I thought you weren't going to ask," he said, laughing a little.

"I shouldn't ask, but I feel sorry for the woman you took it from."

"I didn't steal it. I traded a rabbit for it."

"How?"

"I met a man who was hunting in the woods. He wasn't having any luck. He offered it in trade. I thought of you and I agreed." He smiled. Then he carefully put it on her wrist. "I wanted to give you something. I wanted to give you something nice."

She smiled. "I should probably say that you should have kept the food. But . . ."

"But?"

125

"But it is lovely. And it's been so long since I've owned anything lovely."

"May I kiss you?" he asked, clearing his throat.

She nodded.

Gently, he took her face in his hands and held it as if it were the most beautiful piece of delicate porcelain. He gazed into her eyes. Then tenderly he placed his lips on hers. She sighed.

Solomon saw the kiss and his heart ached. At that moment he hated Gunther even though he'd saved his sister's life and brought food to the rest of the partisans. But even more, he hated himself because he knew he was too young, and Ewa could never feel the same way about him as he felt about her. His was a silent and heartbreaking crush that felt like earth-shattering love to a boy turning ten. Tears welled in his eyes and froze on his eyelashes. *I hope that someday I'll be a man and marry a girl like Ewa*, he thought. He was jealous, but in truth, Solomon didn't hate Gunther. In fact, if it weren't for Gunther and Ewa falling in love, Solomon would have to admit that he liked and admired the man.

CHAPTER 35

SPRING 1943

By the end of April, the Resistance fighters found that their constant movement during the miserable winter months had landed them in a part of the woods known as the crooked forest. Solomon hid the fact that he hated the crooked forest. It seemed to be the perfect setting for every frightening fairy tale he'd heard as a young child. The branches of the pine trees in the crooked forest did not reach for the heavens. Instead, they were bent, twisted, and gnarled, like the arms of old witches.

Winter was slow at making her long-awaited exit. But each day brought more evidence of spring's arrival—birds chirped, the sun shone, and wildflowers began to bloom, covering the forest with color. Life began to remerge as the forest animals joined in the dance, relieved to have survived the winter. Fish became more plentiful as the icy ponds had begun to melt. Tiny blades of tender grass began to peek their heads out of the once-frozen ground, to smile at the golden rays of the sun. When Ewa wasn't busy teaching Solomon and Sarah to read and write, she and Sarah gathered bouquets of purple liverworts.

Gunther knew Solomon had a crush on Ewa, and he often felt

the boy's resentment toward him because of it. But he knew Solomon was a smart boy, so he hoped that Solomon realized Ewa was too old for him. However, Gunther could still remember his own first crush. It had been a secret love for his teacher that had consumed him when he was just a preteen. He could still remember how it hurt him when he saw the teacher with her husband one day at a soccer game. And even though he'd known at the time that his dream of being his teacher's boyfriend was just that—a dream—it still hurt his feelings. So Gunther understood Solomon. The closer he and Ewa grew, the further Solomon pushed away from Gunther. Gunther knew the boy needed a father image, and he wanted to be Solomon's friend. So one afternoon when Gunther was getting ready to go hunting, he got an idea. Solomon and Sarah were sitting under a tree studying when he approached the boy.

"I was wondering if you would like to go hunting with me. I would like to teach you how to hunt. You know, my father taught me when I was your age," Gunther said.

Solomon, who was falling asleep from sitting still for too long, jumped at the opportunity to do something more physical. "Yes, I would love to learn to hunt," he said, putting aside his mixed emotions toward Gunther.

"Good! Then it's settled. Shall we go?"

Solomon nodded and stood up.

"Be careful," Sarah said.

"Don't you worry, little sister. I'll take care of your big brother," Gunther said, smiling, then he ruffled Sarah's hair. She giggled.

Ewa was watching from a few feet away. She winked and smiled at Gunther. But then she asked, "Are you sure he's old enough?"

Solomon heard her question his age and his back grew rigid. He wrapped his arms around his chest. Gunther saw his reaction, and he smiled at Ewa reassuringly. "He's the perfect age. Why, he's on the brink of being all grown up. It's time he learned to hunt and fish."

Solomon smiled at Gunther. He liked to be thought of as a grown-up . . . at least sometimes.

"Come on, let's go and see what we bring back for dinner," Gunther said, handing Solomon a gun.

As they walked through the woods, Gunther spoke to Solomon in a soft voice. "Of course, as you know, we have to be careful not to attract any Nazis in the woods. If we do, we are going to have to shoot to kill."

"I know."

"Now, let's discuss hunting and what exactly it means to take an innocent life. Because, as hunters, that's what we are doing."

Solomon walked beside Gunther quietly listening.

"Animals are innocent. They do not have any malice. But sometimes we must kill them in order to eat. When I was your age, my father explained to me that we must never kill for sport. We only take as much as we need to live. We never waste the meat of an animal. Have you ever read the Bible?"

"Me? A little. Not really," Solomon admitted.

"In the Bible it explains that God gave us power over the animal kingdom so that when we needed to eat, we could eat the meat of other animals in order to sustain our lives. But we must never abuse this power. Do you understand?"

Solomon nodded. "Yes, I think so."

"It's also very important to have a healthy respect for the game you catch. The larger the animal the more dangerous. So you must be on your guard at all times. You can get hurt."

Again, Solomon nodded.

It was chilly outside but not as cold as it had been. There was only a slight breeze, and in the golden rays of the sun it felt almost hot.

They saw a rabbit feeding on some grass.

"Go on. Take aim. Carefully take aim . . ." Gunther said.

Solomon did as Gunther instructed. Then he fired and missed.

"It's all right," Gunther assured him.

"But we don't have the bullets to waste."

"That's true. However, everyone has to learn." Gunther patted Solomon's shoulder.

"Gunther . . ." Solomon said, hesitating for a moment.

"Yes?"

"When I saw that little rabbit with his sweet brown eyes, I didn't want to kill him. I am ashamed to admit it, but the thought of killing him made me sick."

"I know. Hunting is like that for some people. And I respect that."

"What about you?"

"Me?" Gunther asked.

"Yes, you."

"Well, the truth is that there have been times when I felt worse killing an innocent animal than I did shooting a man. Men can be evil; they can be bad and hurtful. Animals are always innocent, so I understand. But when you must kill in order to eat; it is good to know how to hunt."

They continued walking in silence for several long minutes. Solomon was lost in thought when Gunther pulled hard on the sleeve of Solomon's jacket. Gunther put his finger to his lips to silence the boy, then he pointed into the distance where a wild boar was drinking from a pond.

Slowly and quietly, the man and the boy approached the animal trying to get within shooting distance. Gunther saw something that alarmed him. Quickly, he stretched his arm out and stopped Solomon. "Stay back," Gunther commanded Solomon. Then Gunther moved slowly forward.

But it was too late. The wild boar heard the voices and began to charge. Instead of going after Gunther, the boar headed straight for Solomon. The massive animal breathed heavily through her large, thick, flared nostrils as she hurtled her massive body toward the boy who cowered in fear. The boar was coming so fast that Solomon could not grab his rifle in time; he was paralyzed by fear. Gunther quickly stepped forward putting himself between the boar and Solomon. He raised his gun. The pig was snorting and coming faster directly toward them. Gunther fired just as the boar came within feet of his face. It was so close that he could smell the animal's foul breath. It fell with a thud to the ground. Solomon thought his heart was going to explode out of his chest as his eyes met Gunther's.

"Are you all right?" Gunther asked.

"Yes."

"Well, it certainly looks as if we are going to have a good dinner tonight," Gunther said, wiping his brow on the sleeve of his jacket. He was out of breath.

Then Solomon laughed out of nervousness. Gunther laughed too and patted the boy on the shoulder. "We have all we need for dinner. So I think we've done enough hunting for one day, don't you?" he asked.

"Yes I do," Solomon said as he helped Gunther drag the boar back to camp.

From that day on, Solomon and Gunther were inseparable. And even though Solomon still had a crush on Ewa, he finally accepted that she and Gunther were a couple. What was once jealousy in Solomon's heart was now emulation.

CHAPTER 36

EVEN THROUGH THE COLD MONTHS OF WINTER, LUDWIG FOLLOWED the partisans. After he finished his shifts at the Lodz ghetto, he went to check on his prey. The hunt became a secret pleasure for him. Every time the group of partisans moved, he became like a bloodhound sifting through the snow-covered forest for bits and pieces they'd left behind. He knew he should have reported them when he'd first encountered them, but he had developed a fascination with the woman they called Ewa. He had never seen a woman like her. She was an equal to the men but gentle with the children, like a mother.

The reward would have been better for the arrest of a large group of partisans than it would have been for the return of two Jewish children. However, the thrill of watching them undetected gave Ludwig the power he craved. Knowing their fate was in his hands made him tingle with pleasure, so he kept watch over them, returning to their camp almost every day. He knew everything about them, how many there were and what kind of weapons and ammunition they had. At any time he could bring the Nazis right to them and end their game. It made him feel godlike.

Ludwig no longer hunted for the children. He knew exactly

where they were. When the two children appeared at the camp escorted by the tall man, he was certain these were the ones he had been searching for. *It's all coming together*, he thought. *They are here now too. I will decide when this farce ends. It will be my choice when to have them arrested.*

However, there was more to it than that. Ludwig's personal life had taken a bad turn. He and Hedy weren't getting along very well lately, and he found that he was enjoying her company less and less. She was disenchanted with him. He'd tried to make her happy, but she was never satisfied with the small gifts he brought her. She wanted bigger and better. He brought her two sunflowers for their anniversary, but she told him she'd expected jewelry. If he had been higher in the party he might have been able to ask for some of the spoils that had been confiscated from the Jews. But he wasn't. So he did what he could, but instead of appreciating his efforts, Hedy made a point of letting him know that he was beneath her. Whenever she was angry at him, she would remind him that he would not have his job had it not been for her father.

The worse his relationship with Hedy became the more he immersed himself in the secret role of playing God to the group of partisans. He took time off from work to follow the group because he found he derived great pleasure from watching the attractive woman who they called Ewa. He liked to hear her voice, which was deep and throaty, and he enjoyed her unabashed laughter. She was different than any of the women he knew. Her body was muscular and strong like a man's but curvy like a woman's. She had ample hips and breasts and a small waist. Her legs were long and hard. Once he'd watched her bathe in a pond. It had excited him so much that he had to touch himself right there in the forest. When he thought about having done such a thing he felt ashamed.

Somehow the girl called Ewa had gotten her hands on some soap, and she stood in the pond washing her long, auburn hair. It was cold, very cold outside, and he found it hard to believe that she was bathing. The ponds had only recently melted. But she was bathing and she was beautiful. Her nipples were hard from the cold. There was a soft blush to her skin. As she rinsed her tresses, she flung her head back, and the way the hair fell upon her naked back and breasts filled Ludwig with desire. He enjoyed it so much that he didn't want this to stop. He promised himself he would turn the partisans in soon, but before he did, he was hoping to have his way with this girl. Or at least to see her naked one more time.

CHAPTER 37

Summer 1943

Gunther sat alone under a tree. He was busy whittling a wooden rabbit out of a thick tree branch, which Solomon had asked him to make for Sarah, when Cereck approached him. Solomon had been trying to learn to whittle but he didn't have the patience, and he wanted something he could give to his sister on her birthday, which was coming up in a week.

"How are you?" Cereck asked as he sat down on a tree stump next to Gunther.

"Alive," Gunther said, letting go of a loud laugh. "At least I'm alive, right?"

Cereck laughed too, then he said, "I suppose we have to make a joke or we'll never survive this."

"Yes, I have to agree. If we can laugh, we can survive anything," Gunther said and continued whittling. "In all honesty, I can't complain; hunting is good; fishing has been good. We all sleep with full bellies."

"Yes, that's true. And you are in love with the prettiest girl in our camp. And she likes you too," Cereck said.

"I would have to agree," Gunther admitted.

Then Cereck heaved a heavy sigh. "I wish I had only come here to make small talk, but that is not the case. I have a mission for you, I have to ask you if you're willing to help the Resistance. You are the only person here who speaks German like a German."

"You mean my accent? Of course I speak German like a German. I am one."

"Yes, and that's why we need your help."

"Go on, what do you need? I'm listening," Gunther said.

"I have some information that must reach the French Resistance by the beginning of next month. It's very important and the timing is crucial. But the only way to deliver it is in person. And, of course, that means that someone has to travel through Germany to meet with the Resistance in France. It concerns the arrival of the Allies."

"Hmmm." Gunther laid the piece of branch and his knife down on the ground and looked directly at Cereck.

"I won't lie to you and tell you that this isn't extremely dangerous, because it is. You'll be provided with papers with a new name," Cereck said.

"Yes, that would be necessary because as you know I am a deserter."

"Yes, I know . . ." Cereck hesitated then continued, "And . . ."

"And . . ."

"Well, I think it would be a good disguise for you to travel with the children and Ewa. They would pose as your wife and family. I think it might help you to blend in."

"Oh, I don't know. I don't want to endanger them in any way."

"Neither do I. But this mission is very important. I can't stress it enough, and we think it is best if you look like a farmer on his way into town with his wife and children when you are traveling through Germany. A man alone looks much more suspicious. And then as part of this mission you will be taking a train from Germany to France. I think traveling with a wife and children would be less conspicuous there too."

"I don't mind doing this job. In fact, I relish doing anything that will help rid Germany of the Nazis. But I still don't like the idea of putting Ewa or the children in danger."

"We are all in danger every day, all of us, even here in the forest. But, of course, you know that."

"Yes." Gunther looked down at the ground; his mind was whirling. He wanted to help. He wanted to do whatever he could to defeat the Nazis and get that bastard Hitler out of control. But the children? Ewa? How could he take them through enemy territory right under the nose of the Nazis? "There would be papers for the children and Ewa as well?"

"Of course."

Gunther nodded. "Of course." Then he looked into Cereck's eyes. "I think we should discuss it with Ewa and with Solomon. Sarah is too young. I don't think I should take her on this mission."

"But don't you see? What makes you so above suspicion is that no one would want to take a six-year-old child on a dangerous Resistance mission."

"You're very convincing," Gunther said.

"That's why I've been chosen as leader of this group," Cereck said in a joking voice.

"Let's talk to Ewa and Solomon," Gunther said.

"All right, let's."

Gunther went to speak to Solomon. He addressed the boy as if he were an adult when he told him about the mission that Cereck had proposed. "After all," Gunther said sincerely, "you have been in charge of things concerning yourself and Sarah for a long time. And I think it's only fair that you should decide if you want to join me."

Solomon considered the danger. Then he asked, "Have you asked Ewa yet?"

"I have. She wants to go."

Solomon nodded, biting his lip. "I hate to take Sarah with us on such a dangerous mission, but I couldn't leave her behind. I would go crazy with worry about her, so I guess she will have to come with us."

"We don't have much time, but you can take an hour to think it over if you'd like," Gunther offered.

"No need. Sarah and I will join you," Solomon said.

Gunther observed the boy and was once again taken aback by how mature he was for his age. *War and misery makes babies into men*, he thought. *But shouldn't babies have a chance to be babies before they become grown-ups and are forced to face life-threatening choices? I pity this boy. He never had the chance to be a child*, Gunther thought as he patted Solomon's shoulder.

So it was decided. The papers would be produced as quickly as possible. And if all went according to plan, the four of them would be on their way to France the following Monday.

CHAPTER 38

CERECK GAVE EVERYONE'S NEW PAPERS TO GUNTHER. EACH OF THE family members, including Sarah, was required to learn their new names and a page of facts concerning their new identity.

"Do you think Sarah is old enough to remember all of this? She is only a little girl," Ewa asked Gunther.

"She will have to," he said. "I wanted to leave her here at the camp with the others. I feel that Solomon can manage, but I am not sure about her. But Cereck was so insistent."

"I am afraid she will get confused and forget her fake name and where she is supposed to be from. I am afraid that she will give us away," Ewa said.

"I know. I am concerned as well. But the best thing to do is to make sure you tell her to speak as little as possible."

"All right, I will do my best."

Gunther gathered Sarah, Solomon, and Ewa together, then he turned to Sarah and asked, "Sarah, what is your name?"

"Sarah."

"No! Your name. Your new name: do you remember?"

"Oh yes, that name. I used to be Maria, but now I'm Heidi. Did you know that when Solomon and I first left our mother, my name was Maria for a while? It's hard to remember all of these different names."

"I know, but you must. It's very important!" Gunther said firmly. He was trying to be patient, but he was nervous and on edge. He took a deep breath and then he said, "You must forget the name Maria and the name Sarah. For now only remember the name Heidi. Do you understand? You are Heidi," he said as gently as he could.

"Yes, Gunther," Sarah said, "my name is Heidi."

"That's good," he said. "Now, what's your surname?"

"I don't remember."

"Fleischer, dummy," Solomon said to Sarah, his voice filled with irritation.

"That's not necessary. You don't need to call her names. This is hard for her, Solomon," Ewa scoffed at him.

"Yes, Fleischer. That's right," Sarah said. "I'll remember from now on. I promise."

"Why don't you just let Ewa or Solomon do the talking. All right, dear one?" Gunther said as gently as possible, crouching down to be at eye level with Sarah.

She nodded. "All right."

"Where are we from?" Gunther asked Solomon.

"Frankfurt. You are a cobbler. We are traveling to France to see your brother who is in the army there. And . . . my name is Hans."

"Good, very good, Solomon."

"Do either of you remember my name or Ewa's?" Solomon nodded, but Sarah shook her head. "It's all right, Sarah. Now listen and try to remember," Gunther said. "I'm Albert and Ewa is Helga."

"What do you remember, Sarah?" Solomon asked.

"Our last name is Fleischer. We come from Frankfurt. And Solomon, you are Hans; I am Heidi, and Ewa is Helga, and Gunther is Albert. But what's a cobbler?"

Even though everyone was tense with worry, Gunther had to smile. "I make and repair shoes," he said.

"Oh!"

"But you are doing very well," he told Sarah, breathing a sigh of relief that she remembered.

"Now, who remembers my brother's name?"

The two children stared at him openmouthed.

"Leo. Remember now? My brother's name is Leo. He is in the army. That's why we are going to see him where he is stationed in France. We are making the trip because our mother, who would be your grandmother, passed away."

Solomon nodded.

"I don't know if I can remember all of this," Sarah said.

"Like I told you. Just don't talk," Gunther said. "Now, Solomon, do you remember your grandmother's name?"

Solomon shook his head in defeat. "I'm sorry."

"Mia, her name was Mia. My father's name was Adolf. He was your grandfather. He died two years ago. You must commit all of this to memory. It's very important that you don't forget anything. Now, we have three days until we leave. Make sure you go over these facts until you have burned them into your minds. Do you understand?" Gunther said, but he looked at Ewa who looked worried.

Both children nodded.

"Good, and remember, where do you go to school?"

"At the day school in Frankfurt," Solomon answered.

"And you are very excited and looking forward to next year when you can join the Hitler Youth," Gunther reminded him.

"Yes, yes, that's right. I'll remember," Solomon said.

CHAPTER 39

THE NIGHT BEFORE THEY WERE TO LEAVE, CERECK PRESENTED
Gunther with two suitcases and fresh clothes. "You won't look like
proper travelers without these. If you don't have any luggage, you
will look like what you are: partisans. I'm sorry, I know the last thing
you want is more to carry, but there are blankets and clothing inside
. . ."

"I understand, and I agree it's necessary," Gunther said.

On the day they were to leave to begin their mission, Ewa woke
the children and helped Sarah get dressed. Then they made their
way out of the camp in the wee hours before the sun came up.
There was an eerie darkness as a soft wind blew the leaves on the
trees surrounding them. An owl hooted and some animal cried out.
Sarah looked up at Ewa who nodded at her and whispered, "Everything is fine."

At first Sarah was cooperative, even enthusiastic. She recited all
she'd memorized. But by the middle of the afternoon, she began to
complain that her feet hurt and she was hungry. Then Sarah and
Solomon began to bicker, about everything. Ewa gently reprimanded them and demanded that they keep their voices down.
Finally, Sarah refused to walk anymore. She sat down and began to

cry. There was a time deadline that had to be met, so there was no time for rest. Solomon was tired, and he knew Gunther was tired too, but he did not let on. He could see that Gunther was not only walking beside them, but he was on constant alert, and every part of him was watching and aware like a prey animal. Solomon knew this was Gunther's way because he'd been hunting with Gunther, and Gunther had told him that in order to find prey you have to think like a prey animal. Now they were prey animals.

Sarah didn't understand anything and that grated on Solomon's nerves. He was surprised that Gunther had not slapped her yet. That was what their father would have done. Solomon had been the victim of many of their father's rages. But instead of lashing out at Sarah for her constant complaining, Gunther forced a smile and a gentle encouraging word. Then when he knew Sarah could not walk anymore, he lifted her and put her on his shoulders.

"Can you manage?" Ewa said, her voice filled with concern.

"I'll manage," Gunther said.

They continued to walk.

It was not until well into the night that they finally bedded down for a few quick hours of sleep. By then Solomon could feel a dampness inside his shoe, and he knew his feet were bleeding.

He slept hard that night in spite of the fear of bedding down in the middle of the forest. When he awoke, he found that Gunther had been keeping watch.

And, again, before sunrise, Solomon and Gunther woke everyone up. They ate a bit of the bread that they packed, and then they continued their journey.

When they arrived in Germany, they abandoned their sleeping blankets behind a thick bunch of bushes. Now their suitcases contained only clothing. Only things that a family on a trip would carry. And anyone who saw them would have no trouble believing that they were the Fleischers, just an ordinary German family on their way to see their father's brother. But before they left the safety of the forest, Gunther hesitated for a moment as he questioned the children again as to their assumed names and their family background. They'd spent so much time rehearsing their answers that even Sarah got everything right. Satisfied, Gunther smiled at Ewa, who raised her eyebrow and bit her lower lip but nodded her head.

"Here we go," he said. "May God be with us."

"Yes, may God be with us," she repeated.

And they walked out of the protection of the forest and onto the open road.

CHAPTER 40

WHERE ARE THEY HEADED? LUDWIG WATCHED FROM BEHIND THE
trees. He'd been following them since they left the camp. He saw
them abandon the blankets and wondered what else was in those
suitcases. He was certain that these two children were the two Jewish
children who had escaped from the ghetto and robbed the baker.
And with them was Ewa, the woman who'd become the main
attraction of his shameful dreams. Also was the man, called
Gunther, who Ludwig had heard announce to the others in the
partisan camp that he was a deserter from the German army. He
hated Gunther most of all, for a deserter was nothing but a filthy
coward. And every time he looked at Ludwig he wanted to spit. *That
man should be ashamed of himself,* Ludwig thought as he watched the
four of them walk out onto the road. He followed them along the
edge of the forest for as long as he could. Then he waited until he
was sure he would not be seen, and he emerged like a demon rising
from the depths of hell and continued to follow them.

Ludwig was so obsessed with their plight and with Ewa that he
could not return home that night. He tingled with the knowledge of
his secret power over this little group. And although he knew he
should turn them in and get back to work, he just didn't want to lose

the feeling of being omnipresent. So he did not return to Lodz the next day and he missed work. *It won't matter anyway that I didn't show up for work once I turn them all in. My superiors will thank me for following them. I may find an entire group of Resistance fighters. That would be quite the accomplishment. And no one could fault me then,* he decided. *Unfortunately, soon I will have to end it. And I must admit I will miss this bit of spy work. But for now, I know that they are certainly up to something. And before I bring my superiors in on it and lose any glory that might be had for discovering these traitors and their secrets, I have to find out what it is they are up to.*

CHAPTER 41

In Germany, Gunther and Ewa took the children to a small restaurant where they ate a meager meal of bread and soup. The entire time Gunther was on high alert. He did not speak. His eyes darted about the room. He ate, but he was watching, constantly aware. However, all went well. No one questioned them or seemed to even pay them much attention. By tomorrow they would be at the station where they would board a train that would carry them into France. Here they would be forced to present their papers, and Gunther knew that this was the point in the journey where things could go awry. If Sarah made a questionable remark, everything could go sour in an instant.

At the train station, Gunther presented their papers to a guard, and then they were directed to the correct train. Ewa and Gunther exchanged a quick glance of relief as they all climbed on board.

After three days of walking, the children were tired. And the rocking motion of the train put the children into a sleepy trance. Even Ewa drifted off, but Gunther did not close his eyes for a second. His mind was racing at a thousand miles an hour. He considered all the possible scenarios of things that might go wrong and it made him shiver. If the Nazi bastards were to catch them, they would kill him and Ewa first, but they'd think nothing of killing the children too. He knew firsthand just how cruel they could be and the very idea left him terrified. He glanced at the three innocent faces that depended upon him and he wanted to cry. *I am a man; men don't cry*, he thought. *But if I fail them. If I fail . . .* Forcing these thoughts out of his mind, he tried to stay positive. He looked out the train window at the countryside and reminded himself that if all went as planned, the following night they would be on their way back to Germany and then back to Poland to join the rest of their group in the forest. *Breathe*, he told himself. *Don't look around at the other people on this train. You must not make eye contact with anyone. You don't want them to see the fear in your eyes. Just keep your focus on the job at hand.*

When two Gestapo officers came through the train demanding that everyone have their papers ready, Gunther felt bile rise in his throat.

"They are searching for someone," Gunther heard one of the women passengers say. "This happens all the time."

Gunther looked at Ewa. Her dark eyes looked massive in her white pale face. Gunther forced himself to swallow hard and to push the bile back down, but his throat burned. "Don't say a word," he warned the children in a whisper.

Solomon nodded, but Sarah stared at him with wide, frightened eyes.

"Don't say a word, Sarah. Do you understand me?"

She nodded and climbed into Ewa's arms, putting her thumb in her mouth.

Ewa unbuttoned the top two buttons on her blouse so that a substantial amount of cleavage was now visible.

Two Gestapo agents, one who was taller and clearly in charge, and another who was short and heavyset with a mustache in the fashion of the führer's, were moving through the train, and within minutes they were standing in front of Ewa and Gunther. "Papers," one of them said in a harsh growl.

"Of course." Gunther reached into his back pocket where he felt the security of the cold metal of the gun. He took the papers out and handed them to the officer.

"Hello, sweetheart," the tall Gestapo officer said to Sarah, "and what is your name?"

Gunther held his breath.

Sarah turned her head away from the Gestapo officer and put her other thumb in her mouth.

"Excuse her, Officer." Ewa managed her prettiest smile. "She is shy. Her name is Heidi."

"Heidi, my niece's name is Heidi. Aren't you an adorable child." The officer was talking to Sarah, but his eyes were glued to Ewa's cleavage.

"She'd be prettier if she were blonde." The mustached Gestapo agent chuckled.

"Oh, come now. Don't be so mean. I'm not blonde, and I'm quite attractive," the agent in charge said in a joking tone of voice.

"Yes, well, she is a girl, and girls are more attractive if they're blonde."

"She's just a child," the tall one said.

"That's true. Anyway, come on, we have a Jew to find. Can't waste any more time here looking at the child's mother's tits, can we?"

"Excuse me, but mind your rank. I am your superior. How dare you tell me what we should and should not be doing!" The tall agent's face was red with anger and embarrassment.

Ewa tried to appear shy and reserved as she cast her eyes down at the ground.

"I'm sorry, I shouldn't have said that. I did not mean to be seen as if I were trying to usurp your authority, sir," the mustached officer said.

"Yes, well . . . you're quite right. We don't have time for tits. But . . . they are a nice pair, aren't they?"

Both of the Nazis laughed, and then they went on to the next row of seats.

"Papers?" the one commanded.

Ewa and Gunther caught each other's gaze for just a moment. Ewa buttoned her shirt.

The Nazis made their way up to the front of the train car and then out the door. *We've survived another close call,* Gunther thought.

When the train reached its destination in Paris, Gunther helped the children and Ewa off the train and on to the platform. Then they began walking.

The timing was working out perfectly. The train had arrived in Paris on time leaving them an hour to get to the café where they were to meet their contact, which was located on the Left Bank. As they walked through the streets, Ewa pretended to window shop. Then they stopped at the hotel which was owned by a member of the French Resistance where Cereck had arranged for them to leave their luggage.

Gunther went up to the reservation desk. "I need to see Pierre," he said in broken French.

A pretty young woman smiled at him fetchingly. "Wait here," she said.

Gunther stood at the desk while Ewa and the children sat on a bench in the lobby. Then a tall, slender man with thinning gray hair walked up to Gunther. "I am Pierre. What can I do for you?" he said.

"Do you have the books for Cereck?"

"Ah yes, of course," Pierre said. He reached under the desk, took out a book, and then handed it to Gunther along with a room key. "Cereck has arranged a room for you," he said. The number on the key was 205. "You can take the stairs up. They are right down the hall."

"Thank you," Gunther said.

Then he motioned to Ewa and the children who followed him upstairs. They put their luggage in the room. Gunther opened the book. As he expected, the inside of the book had been carved out. In the hole lay a small pile of bills. Gunther shoved the money into his pocket.

"Let's go," he said to the others.

It was not difficult to find the café, which was located in the middle of a crowded street. Gunther ordered food and wine for Ewa and himself and bread and soup for the children. Then he waited. They were all hungry, but Gunther was not able to eat. *If only this mission were over already. At least we are on time. The contact should arrive in about a half hour.* The minutes seemed never ending. *I feel as if the clock has been struck by lightning and is now moving in slow motion, but not my heart; my heart is going full speed. I must remain calm. I must smile at the passersby who send smiles to the children. Their acknowledgment of the children is a good indication that we don't look suspicious. And as nervous as I am, I must not show any trace of suspicion. Now, Cereck said to look for the man with a red rose in his lapel. Then I must ask him how far I am from the Eiffel Tower. If he answers "I'm sorry, but I am not very good at determining distance," then I can be certain it's him.*

"Why don't you eat something?" Ewa said, "You look very anxious. Eat."

He nodded and picked up a hunk of bread, then absentmindedly, he dipped it into the soup and forced himself to take a bite. It stuck in his throat, and he found that even though he'd wet the bread with soup, it was difficult to swallow. He couldn't taste the food. His thoughts were focused on the danger all around him and on making sure that he had made the correct contact before sharing the secret information.

Gunther put the hunk of bread down beside his soup bowl and took a sip of wine, and as he did someone came up behind him and tapped him on the shoulder. "Gunther Kuhn? Is that you? What are you doing in France, you old devil?"

The last thing Gunther wanted to hear was his real name. He was traveling under an alias. And the only people who knew him as Gunther Kuhn also knew that he'd been in the army. Gunther felt his heart sink as he turned to see a man close to his own age who had grown up in the same neighborhood he had. He knew this man; his name was Otto Shultz. Gunther felt panic rise through his entire body. He didn't know what to do. He dare not try to say that Otto was mistaken and he was not Gunther. It was clear Otto recognized him. His mind raced. If only he could think of a way to get Otto alone in an alley somewhere far away from all these people who would shoot him. Not that he wanted to kill anyone, but Otto was very close to blowing the entire mission and endangering Ewa and the children.

"I'm visiting friends here in France." Gunther tried to smile but he couldn't; the muscles in his face felt frozen.

"I work just a few streets down from here at the Abwehr. I got myself a good position," Otto said proudly.

"Very nice. Good for you! Congratulations!" Gunther tried to sound enthusiastic, but as he spoke he saw the man with the red rose stop across the street. Gunther made eye contact with the man, who stood there for only a moment. He touched the rose on his lapel. Gunther nodded. Otto kept talking but Gunther didn't hear him. He was watching the man who was looking around assessing the situation. Then the man turned and quickly walked away. Gunther felt anger bubbling up in his belly and rising with him. Otto Shultz had blown his entire mission, and there was nothing to be done. All this travel, all this risk . . . and for what?

"If I recall correctly, you joined the army, didn't you? I thought I heard that you were stationed in the east. Russia, wasn't it? At least that was the last I heard."

"Yes, I was. But I got some time off." Gunther tried not to sound as irritated as he felt.

"Well, that's certainly rare, isn't it?"

"Perhaps."

"And . . . who are these lovely children? They can't be yours? The boy has to be at least fourteen, and as I recall you were unmarried when you left for the front."

"You do remember a great deal, don't you?" Gunther said.

"Yes, Gunther was single when I met him," Ewa chimed in quickly. Her smile was bright as she looked Otto directly in the eyes. "When Gunther and I met, I was a devastated widow all alone with two young children. You see, my husband was a soldier in the Wehrmacht. He, like Gunther, was stationed on the Eastern Front. I am proud of his sacrifice, of course, but until Gunther came into our lives my children and I were lost. My son is big for his age, but he is only ten. And when I met Gunther he was at that age when a father figure meant everything to him."

"I see, and it looks like Gunther stepped right in and took over the role, didn't you, my friend?"

"Yes, I suppose you could put it that way." Gunther forced a smile. He was glad that Ewa had come up with that story as quickly as she had.

"Well then, good for you. I'm happy to see that it all worked out. So many widows from this war. It's sad. But at least you two found each other, so there is a happy ending." Otto gave them a quick smile. "It's late, and I must be getting back to work, but it was certainly good seeing you again, and it was very nice to meet your lovely wife. By the way, what is your name, dear?"

"Helga," Ewa said, smiling.

Gunther did not speak until Otto had turned the corner and was completely out of sight. Then in a voice barely above a whisper, he said, "Take the children and get out of France. Get on the first train back to Germany and then don't hesitate. Head straight back to the forest in Poland and back to the group. I saw our contact while Otto was here. He was across the street. He saw me. I think he knew it was me but I can't be sure. All I know is he continued walking because he saw me talking to Otto. I am going to try to find him, but don't wait for me. Get out of France quickly. I don't why, but I have a bad feeling."

"I can't leave you here like this," Ewa said.

"You can and you must. The children . . ."

"So abort the mission and come with us."

"No, I came this far. I am going to try and make the contact," Gunther insisted.

"I don't want to leave you here . . ." Ewa grabbed Gunther's sleeve.

"I insist—now go. There is no time for discussion. I want to get away from this café as soon as possible. I just have a bad feeling. I don't trust Otto. Please, go . . . now." He handed her the falsified papers for herself and the children. Then he took his papers and tucked them back into his pocket.

"I love you," she whispered.

Solomon looked at Ewa and then at Gunther.

"I love you too. No matter what happens to me, I want you to know that these last few months with you have been the best time of my life. You've brought me so much joy."

Tears fell down her cheeks. She looked around to see if anyone noticed. Then she wiped them quickly.

"Please, Ewa. Take the children and go, so I can leave the café and try to find the contact. Trust me, will you?"

Ewa nodded at him. "I do trust you, with all my heart and soul." Then she turned to the children. "Come on, you two. Follow me."

Sarah gave Ewa her hand, but Solomon stood staring at Gunther for a moment. There was a tear in his eye. It ran down his cheek. Then he said to Gunther, "God be with you."

Gunther nodded. "Go quickly, and may God be with the three of you."

CHAPTER 42

As Otto Shultz turned the corner on his way back to work, he was stopped by a man in civilian clothes.

"Excuse me," the man said. "My name is Ludwig Beck. I must speak with you."

CHAPTER 43

Ewa led the children all the way to the train station, but when she arrived she could not purchase tickets. Something told her that she must go back and find Gunther or she would never see him again. He must not be left behind in France. He must leave this country with Ewa and the children. They must all return to Poland together. She looked at the children. A sad smile came over her face. *Solomon does look fourteen. He looks so grown up, and he acts so grown up. But he is really only a boy,* she thought. *These children are so sweet, so young, so innocent. They should be in school or out playing tag with their friends. They should not be in fear for their lives. But right now, if things go sour, Sarah and Solomon are in just as much danger as Gunther and I. I think the best thing to do is to leave them at an orphanage. They will be safe there until I can convince Gunther to leave France with the three of us. I dare not take these children back to the café with me. It's too dangerous. It's best that I go alone.*

"I have to talk to you quickly, Solomon," Ewa said. "As you can see, things have gone haywire with our plan. But even though Gunther insisted on it, I am not going to leave France without Gunther. However, I am not going to take you and Sarah with me to search for him. It is far too dangerous."

"Do you want us to wait here at the train station for you?"

She shook her head. "I don't think it's a good idea. Just in case . . ."

"In case of what?"

"In case something happens to me. If it does, the two of you will be alone here in France and that would leave you very vulnerable. Now, listen to me. I can read and write French. My mother taught me as she lived in France for several years when she was young. So when we first arrived in Paris I was able to read a sign that said Orphanage. It was on a building that was connected to a Catholic church. Can you or Sarah speak any French?"

"A little. Not much. My mother had a friend who was French before the war. She spoke to us in French."

"I am going to take you and Sarah to the orphanage, and I am going to beg the priest to take care of you. I am going to tell him that you are Polish Catholic children and that your father died of typhus. I will say that I cannot afford to care for you until I can get a job and come back for you."

"No! No! We should stay together," Solomon insisted. "Gunther will catch up with us soon."

"I believe this is best. I must go and find Gunther." Ewa said.

"Then we will go with you."

"Please, Solomon. You could come with me. I know you are a child, and you act like a grown man, but I can't take Sarah back to the café with me. If things go bad . . . well, she is still just a baby. I am begging you to stay with Sarah at the orphanage and take care of her. She needs you. And I need your help. Say you will do this for me."

Solomon looked into Ewa's eyes. His old feelings of tenderness made his heart swell. "I'll do it. But please, please be careful. Please, Ewa, come back for us."

She nodded. "I am not going to give them your German papers. It's too confusing. You both speak fluent Polish and you're in France. It is just too contrived. I think we are better off using your real names. They are biblical names, but just to be careful, you still must not tell anyone at the orphanage that you are Jewish. Do you understand?"

157

"Yes," he said, "and I will make sure Sarah doesn't tell them either."

"Good. Now let's hurry. I must drop you two off soon because I want to try to find Gunther before dark."

They walked in silence toward the large cathedral.

"I want to go with you," Sarah said. "I don't want you to leave me here. Every time I have to say goodbye to someone I never see them again."

"I know. I know," Ewa said, gently running her hand over Sarah's hair. "But I promise you I will be back for you and Solomon." She'd said it, but she wasn't sure she could keep her promise. She would try. God knows she would try. But . . .

They stood in front of the large wooden doors to the cathedral. Ewa was intimidated; she had never been inside a church, and she had no idea what to expect. *Will the priest suspect that we are Jews and turn us all in to the Gestapo?* Her heart pounded as she questioned her decision. *Should I just take the children with me to look for Gunther and hope for the best? Is it a bad choice to leave them here?*

Ewa knocked on the door, but no one came. She knocked again and waited. Still no one came. After several uncomfortable minutes she turned to leave. A disheveled-looking man, with a bottle wrapped in a brown paper bag, who had been sleeping on the church steps, turned to her and said, "Just go in. You don't have to knock."

Ewa looked at him. There were red and purple bruises under his eyes, and he was sickly thin, and even though they were outside, a foul odor emanated from him. Her stomach turned over, and she felt like she might vomit from the sight of the man. But she nodded at him and said, "Thank you." Then she turned to Solomon and Sarah. "Come, children."

Once inside the great cathedral, Ewa was awestruck by the beauty of the stained-glass windows, the mahogany floors, and matching pews. A heavyset man wearing a black robe came out of a booth that was situated on the side of the entrance.

"Hello, Mother. Welcome," he said, walking over to her with a limp. His blue, rheumy eyes were kind.

She smiled and swallowed hard. It felt as if a stone had lodged itself in her dry throat. "I am here to see the priest."

"I am he."

"I need help for my children." She choked the words out, then she felt as if she wanted to run. "I'm sorry, I think I made a mistake."

"No, it's all right. Please go on. I have devoted my life to doing God's work. You have come here because God has sent you. Let me help you."

I lost my job. I can't take care of my children. I need somewhere to leave them until I get established."

"I see," he said, nodding. "And what are your names?" he asked the children.

Sarah looked at him blankly. She was confused. Ewa knew she was unsure of whether to tell him her real name or to say she was Heidi.

"This is Sarah, and that's Solomon. They don't speak French. They speak Polish." She was afraid she'd just raised a red flag, but the priest didn't seem at all ruffled by the admission. He just nodded.

The old priest didn't ask any questions about the origins of the names. He didn't even ask Ewa's name. Then he smiled warmly, and in perfect Polish he said, "Welcome, Sarah. Welcome, Solomon. Welcome to this humble house of God. I am Father Dupaul. And on behalf of my staff and myself, may I say that we are honored to have the two of you as guests in our home."

"I will be back for them soon," she said.

"I know you will. And please be assured that your children will be safe here under God's roof."

Ewa kissed Sarah and Solomon and held them both in her arms for several moments. Tears ran like rivulets down Sarah's face. Solomon was fighting to hold back his tears. "Be good. I promise you . . . I'll be back as soon as I can," Ewa said. Then before she changed her mind, Ewa stood up. "Thank you. Thank you from the bottom of my heart," she said and left quickly.

CHAPTER 44

EWA FELT LOST WITHOUT THE CHILDREN AS SHE QUICKLY WALKED
back to café on the Left Bank where she'd last seen Gunther. She
found the priest to be kind and reassuring, but she still felt pangs of
uncertainty about her decision to leave them. *If all goes well and I find
Gunther, I can go back and collect them tonight.*

Even though it was well past lunchtime and too early for
supper, the café was crowded. People might not be eating full
meals, but they were sipping ersatz coffee and socializing. Ewa's
eyes searched the café and the street for Gunther, but she didn't
see him anywhere. She walked up and down the street all the way
to each corner. She didn't know where he might have gone, and
she felt anxious not knowing where to begin to look. She walked
for a mile to the left of the café, then she returned and did the
same to the right. She glanced into alleyways and then store
windows. Ewa bit her nail as her mind began to race. *What was I
thinking? Did I think I would just come back here, and he would be waiting
where I'd left him? I have to think. I have to think . . . where would he go in
search of his contact?* She racked her brain but she had no answers.
Finally, she sunk down onto a bench across the street from the
café. *If I can't find him, I'll have to do as he asked. I'll go back to the*

orphanage and get the children. Then I suppose we'll head back to Poland. That's all I can do.

Tears welled up in the backs of her eyes. She looked at her watch. It was getting late; she had been back at the Left Bank for over four hours. And it was now half past six. *How much longer do I have before dark? How long can I wait here? Where should I go? Where can I search next? When do I give up? I don't know what to do next.* She began to walk again, more frantic this time. It was difficult to breathe. She felt overwhelmed and alone. Her arms and legs were shaking, and her stomach ached with fear. Staring out at the people walking by her but not really seeing them, she sunk down onto a bench shivering. Ewa was so distracted by her own thoughts that she didn't notice the three Gestapo officers approaching her.

"Papers," one of them said.

Ewa looked up. It felt as if this were not real, as if it were a dream. No, not a dream, a nightmare. Her hands trembled as she gave them the papers in her purse.

"Helga Fleischer?" one of them said. He smiled, but his lips only curved on one side.

"Y-yes," she said.

"I see, and your husband is Hans? Hans Fleischer?"

"Yes, Hans Fleischer." Her heart felt like it was going to explode. Bile rose in her throat. *Don't vomit. Dear God, please don't let me vomit.*

"Now that's very strange, isn't it? My friends and I just met with a colleague. His name is Otto Shultz. And do you know what happened? Otto Shultz just had your husband arrested. His real name is Gunther Kuhn, but he was carrying papers that said his name was Hans Fleischer. So, of course, we knew something was not right, didn't we, Alexander?"

The other Nazi nodded, then the first one continued, "And do you know what? Otto said Gunther had been seen here with a wife. So my friend and I came looking for you."

They were toying with her. She knew it. It was terrifying. They knew the truth. They knew the papers were false. Dare she ask them where Gunther was? Dare she ask? Clearing her throat, she said, "My husband? Where is he?"

"Oh, dear lady, our condolences. Your husband is dead. He was, after all, a deserter. Then he was carrying false papers. We knew he was up to no good . . ."

The Nazi was still talking, but Ewa couldn't hear him. All she could do was remember Gunther's gentle smile, his kind heart, and the way he made her feel safe even in the most perilous situations. And now sitting on this bench, unsure of what to say, Ewa felt as if she were sliding down a dark hole into the center of the Earth. Could it possibly be true? Could Gunther really be dead? It had only been a few hours since she'd last looked into his eyes, since she'd last touched his hand, last heard his reassuring voice. "Oh God . . ." The words spilled out of her without her even realizing she'd spoken.

"God isn't going to help you. You are a Jew, aren't you?" he said, his teeth bared like a rabid dog, yet he was smiling. He didn't wait for her answer. "You are going to finally get what's coming to you. It's just a shame that you had to bring a good German man down to your level before we found you. I wonder if you are the reason he deserted." He slapped Ewa hard across the face. Blood spurted from her lips and nose.

She knew he meant to hurt her, and yet her physical body felt numb. *If I am to die, then please, God, let it happen quickly.*

"What do you have to say for yourself?" The Nazi's eyes narrowed as he growled at her.

She shook her head. Tears spilled down her face. *Oh God, oh God. What are they going to do to me? They will probably kill me. And what about the children? What will become of them when I don't return? The priest seemed to be a good, kind man. All I can do is put my trust in God that the priest will take care of them.*

The Nazi slapped her again. He tore open her blouse. Strangely enough she did not feel the slap. Then he said to his fellow officers, "Shall I shoot her?"

"I think it's best that we take her to headquarters. She may have information that could prove valuable to us."

"Maybe we could have a little fun with her first?" the third Nazi said.

Fun with me? They mean to rape me, Ewa thought. *I should be begging them for mercy.* But instead she felt numb and detached. Her stomach churned, and she felt that she might vomit or lose control of her bowels. But for some odd reason she could not speak. Somehow, she seemed to be watching this horrific scene as if it were happening to someone else not her.

"She's a Jew. You don't want to contaminate yourself with that filth."

The first one nodded. But he was staring at Ewa's chest where he'd torn open the buttons of her shirt. "Get in the car," he said, pulling her up from the bench by her arm.

Ewa heard something in her shoulder snap, but she felt nothing —no pain, no fear, only pure detachment. She vomited as the Nazi pushed her into the car. He was appalled to see bits of vomit land on his uniform, and he slapped her until her nose and lips spurted blood. Then he carefully wiped his hands and his uniform on a clean white handkerchief that he took out of his pocket. After shooting a look of pure disgust at his fellow officers, he got into the car and they drove away.

That night, as Ewa lay on the concrete floor of a dirty cell in the police station, she heard footsteps. Her heart jumped into her throat. For a moment she thought perhaps it was Gunther. Perhaps they'd lied and he wasn't dead. Her entire body tingled with hope. But then as the form of a tall young man wearing a Nazi uniform came within her vision, she felt herself drop as if she'd fallen into a dark well.

"Hello, Ewa," the Nazi said, "my name is Ludwig Beck." Even in the dark she could see his eyes. They reminded her of the eyes of a goat she'd once seen on a farm. They stared through her not really seeing her, not acknowledging her suffering. *He is devoid of all human sympathy,* she thought as a sinister smile came over his face. He winked at her, and she felt the hair on the back of her neck rise. "I know you; I know you very well," he said, "but tonight is a special night; it's the night I have been waiting for. Tonight, you shall know me!"

He turned the key in the lock on the iron door that kept Ewa prisoner. She jumped up and tried to fight him to get out. But he was young, healthy, and strong. He threw her across the room like a rag doll. Then he unbuttoned his pants and came toward her. Ewa closed her eyes tightly and began to pray.

CHAPTER 45

Ewa was a prisoner at the Nazi police station for a week following her arrest. Starving and filthy, she lay on the cold concrete floor trying to stop herself from willing her own death. She told herself that she must survive; the children needed her. If she died they would have no one else. But as hard as she tried to fight her longing for death, each night she was defeated because each night Ludwig returned to her cell.

After a week, Ewa was sent to a work camp that was located on the outskirts of Paris. However, the camp was in the process of being liquidated when Ewa arrived. All of the prisoners were being transferred to another camp, a camp called Auschwitz where they were scheduled to be eliminated. Ewa was among them.

If she could have willed herself to die, she might have chosen to do so after her horrific nights at the hands of Ludwig Beck. But she forced herself to not entertain the idea of dying. If she did, she was afraid she might will it so hard that it would happen, and that would leave Sarah and Solomon alone in the world. No, she dared not wish for death. *My mother always said that life is God's greatest gift.* She constantly reminded herself even as she watched the smug Nazis walk through the camp. Her heart ached. She wanted to believe.

She wanted to believe in life and in God. But it was so very hard. It would have been much easier to give up. Ewa had lost the man she loved, and then at the hands of Ludwig she'd lost her dignity. Her own body repulsed her. She was sick with hunger and a terrible rash that itched and burned all over her entire body. But somehow, against all odds, a tiny voice in her head constantly reminded her that she had to get back to the children. They needed her. She was all they had left.

Ewa was loaded into a cattle car along with a large group of prisoners. The foul smell of unwashed bodies, fear, and feces permeated the air. People were crowded in so tightly that it was impossible to sit; they were forced to stand, each keeping the others around them from falling down. A pregnant woman was smashed in beside Ewa.

"You look very familiar to me," Ewa said. "What is your name?"

"Sylwia Gorecki."

"I'm Ewa. You are not a Jew?"

"No, I was a Polish partisan," she said. "I was caught by the Nazis during a raid. My husband was killed. Now I am here and very pregnant."

"I can see that. When are you due?"

"Any minute. I have been feeling labor pains since early this morning even before I boarded the train."

"My God," Ewa said. "You can't give birth here. You have nowhere to lie down. And it's so dirty . . ."

"I can't stop it either," Sylwia said. "If the baby wants to come, it will come."

Ewa nodded and touched Sylwia's shoulder not knowing what to say.

"You are a Jew?" Sylwia asked.

"Yes, and I, too, was a partisan. My fiancé was killed by the Nazis when he was captured while on a mission."

Sylwia nodded. "I am sorry," she said, then she grabbed Ewa's arm and continued, "Listen to me. I will die here in childbirth. Once I am dead you must take my papers. Take them and become me. Put your papers in my pocket. I will die as you. Believe me, they will never know the difference."

"You aren't going to die," Ewa said.

"Don't be a child. I am going to die because this baby is going to try to come, and there is nowhere for me to give birth."

"I will help you."

"I understand that you will try, but just in case, listen to me. It is important."

"All right," Ewa said.

"I can't promise anything, but I believe that life will be easier on you when you get to wherever this train is going if you are Polish instead of being a Jew. The Nazis hate the Jews worse than anyone."

"I know. I know they do. But you won't die . . ." Ewa tried to sound reassuring, but she didn't believe her own words.

"We'll see."

"Why are you doing this for me?" Ewa said.

"Because you are fellow resister. Anyway, just look, my water has already broken. I am in terrible pain. I don't want to bring a baby into the world just to have them kill it."

Sylwia reached over, took Ewa's hand, and squeezed it hard. Her eyes were glazed over, but she stared into Ewa's eyes and said in a deep, throaty voice, "I want you to kill me. I am begging you to do this for me. For me and for my poor, innocent baby."

"You're mad. You've gone mad."

"Perhaps. The Nazis could drive anyone mad. But out of mercy you must do as I ask. Please, I am begging you, Ewa. Don't you see? They will torture my baby. They will eventually kill it and me too. But first they'll make me watch them torture the poor thing."

"Kill you? Murder you?"

"Yes."

"How?"

"Here, take this." Sylwia handed Ewa a spoon that had been sharpened to a point. "First take these papers and put them in your pocket and give me yours."

"I thought you wanted me to wait until after you were dead,"

Ewa said, her hands shaking. "Please, Sylwia, don't make me do this."

"You must do this. Put the papers in your pocket and give me yours."

Ewa did as Sylwia asked.

"Now cut my wrists. I would do it myself. I planned to, but I can't find the courage." She let out a sad and wry laugh. "Cut this way. I will bleed out and be dead by the time the train stops. They will think I did it myself. They will think it's suicide."

The metal spoon felt cold in Ewa's hand. She'd shot a Nazi once, but she'd never killed an innocent woman and an unborn child with a sharp object. She gagged a little holding back the vomit.

"Do it," Sylwia demanded. Her eyes were sharp. "Do it; please hurry. Do it before I change my mind. If you don't, my poor child will suffer. Save a child from suffering, Ewa."

Sylwia presented her wrist. Ewa bit her lower lip. She closed her eyes and pressed the sharp edge against Sylwia's skin. She had to press harder. But once she felt the skin break, she pulled the spoon forward ripping as she went. It was done. Blood poured from the open wound. Ewa dropped the spoon. She felt sick at what she'd done.

"Now, remember, your name is Sylwia Gorecki. Quickly, here is your background. You worked as a secretary in Warsaw, but you were born and raised in Gdansk."

"Yes," Ewa said. "I'm sorry, Sylwia. I'll never forget you."

"You did a mitzva today. Isn't that what you Jews call it when you do something good to help someone else? You see, I had a lot of Jewish friends," Sylwia said. Her voice was weak and growing weaker. A sad smile came across her face.

"A mitzva means a blessing," Ewa said, but Sylwia never heard her. Sylwia was already dead.

The following morning the train came to an abrupt halt throwing the passengers forward. Then the door clanged open, and several armed officers began to yell, "Get out and get in line: mach schnell!"

Ewa's heart was beating in her throat. Nausea overtook her, and she stopped in her tracks and began vomiting. She'd always had a weak stomach even as a child. But a woman who had been on the train beside her pushed her forward. "Don't stop. Even if you have to throw up, keep running. A woman fell down back there and they shot her. I saw it happen." The woman grabbed Ewa's arm and pulled her along. Some of the vomit had spilled onto the front of Ewa's blouse where it was mixed with Sylwia's blood.

A line of SS officers stood on the sidelines holding the leashes of dogs that barked and growled. Ewa trembled, but she allowed the woman to pull her along. The crowd of newcomers who had just disembarked from the train was pushed into a line. From where she stood, Ewa could see women with shaved heads wearing gray-striped uniforms. They were thin, and their skin hung off their bones. Their eyes were dark and sunken in. They moved slowly, and they looked dead. Ewa felt a chill as she observed them.

"I need five Poles. Women. Not Jews. Send them over to the truck that's waiting over there." A tall, handsome man wearing a stunning pressed black uniform with a shiny hat and boots said to the guard.

"Right away, Hauptscharführer. Where are you sending them?"

"That is none of your affair. Do as I tell you," the hauptscharführer commanded.

Ewa was next in line to have her papers checked. Now she wished she had kept her own Jewish papers instead of trading them with Sylwia. These terrible men wanted five Polish women, and right now, according to her papers, she was a Polish woman. What did they plan to do with the Polish women? She felt a pain shoot through her temple. *Why Poles and not Jews?*

"Next," the guard ordered, his voice harsh.

Ewa's mouth was dry, and she felt the bile rise in her throat again as she handed him the only papers she had. *Damn this weak stomach of mine. If I vomit they will probably shoot me right here.* She swallowed the bitter bile.

"Sylwia Gorecki," the guard said. Then without looking up, he pointed to a place on his right side. "Stand here for now," he commanded.

Ewa stood and waited. She watched as the prisoners were sorted by a handsome, dark-haired man only a few feet away. "Left . . . right . . . left . . . right," the man said. Then two little twin girls were in line with their mother. "I'll take these," the dark-haired man said. "Hello." He bent down to be on the same level as the children. "I'm your new uncle. You can call me Uncle." He smiled, handing the two twin girls a piece of candy each. "Gypsies," he said to the mother, "aren't you?"

The mother answered, "Yes, Romani." She smiled. It was obvious to Ewa that she was glad he was being kind to her children.

"These two are twins?" the SS officer asked.

"Yes, twins."

"Well, good. Then this is their lucky day. They will be under my protection."

"Oh, thank you. Thank you." The mother fell to her knees and kissed his shoes.

"Now you will go to the Gypsy camp, and the twins will be sent to my special accommodations."

"No! Please don't separate us. I'm begging you, sir. Please . . ."

"Mother, don't you worry. I can promise you that you will see your children shortly. Now get back into the line. I've been very tolerant with you. But you must behave yourself before I get angry."

"Please, I am begging you. Take me with them. Don't take them away from me . . ."

She was on the ground, kneeling and holding on to one of his lower legs. He tried to shake himself free, but her grip was too tight. Finally, he took his other foot and kicked her. She flew back holding her chest.

"Now get up and do as I tell you. You try my patience."

The Gypsy mother stood up still holding her chest. Her eyes were glued to her two little daughters. Ewa could see she was trembling as she bent over and placed kisses on the tops of each of their heads. Then the handsome, dark-haired SS officer shook his head. He turned to one of the guards and pointed to the Gypsy mother.

"This one goes to the left," he said, smiling at the woman, but his teeth were bared like a rabid dog.

Ewa felt the woman's pain as she was pulled away from the children and shuffled into a line where she soon disappeared. Ewa noted that most of the women in the line where the Gypsy mother had been sent were old and feeble, and the children in that same line were too young to work. Ewa bit her lower lip. She'd heard stories from prisoners who'd escaped these camps. Horrible stories of murder and burning bodies. She'd also heard stories of the two lines; one led to work and the other to death. *Could it be true?* She forced these terrible thoughts out of her mind, the same way she forced herself not to think about Gunther. If she were ever going to get back to Sarah and Solomon, she had to find a way to escape from this place. And the only way to survive minute to minute was to put every horrible possibility out of her mind.

Finally, the Nazi guard had found five Polish women, including Ewa, to fulfill the quota that had been given to him. The five were lined up. Then they were escorted and loaded onto the back of an open truck at gunpoint. Most of the women, Ewa included, were quiet, their faces masks of grief. Only one young, pretty woman wept softly as the truck roared to life.

Where are they taking us? Ewa thought. *And why were they so specific in wanting only Polish women? Sylwia's papers could be my saving grace or they could be the death of me. I won't know until we arrive at our destination.* She shivered as the truck moved forward.

CHAPTER 46

SARAH AND SOLOMON

When Ewa left the children, Sarah wept. Solomon was frightened too, but he tried to stay hopeful that all would go well. However, when Ewa did not return to the orphanage that night to pick up the children, Solomon hid his own rising fears and instead consoled Sarah. "It's late. I'm sure she will come tomorrow," he promised. But although he could not share his feeling with his sister, he was very worried.

Then to make matters worse, Sarah and Solomon were separated and sent to dormitory-type rooms. Solomon was sent to sleep with other the boys, Sarah with other the girls. But Solomon knew his sister, and he knew she needed him. So once the adults closed the door to the boys dormitory room, he snuck out and went to find his sister. She was sitting on a bunk bed looking small and alone.

"Solomon!" she exclaimed, excited to see him. "Is Ewa here?"

"Not yet, but listen to me. I won't be here with you all the time to remind you, but no matter how friendly you become with the other children, you must not forget that you are not Jewish."

"I know. You keep telling me the same thing over and over." She scoffed. "When is Ewa coming back to get us?"

"I don't know. Perhaps tomorrow."

Two more days passed without any word from Ewa. That night when Solomon went to see his sister, she was weeping and inconsolable. "She's dead, isn't she?"

"Why would you say that?"

"Because Mama's dead, and Papa's probably dead. And even Ben might be dead . . . everyone is dead. Maybe Gunther is dead too. I don't understand, Solomon. What does it mean to be dead, and why does everyone I love end up being dead? Did I do something bad? Am I being punished for something?"

"Sarah . . ." He took her in his arms and held her for several moments, too moved by the sadness of her words to speak. *She doesn't understand. And why should she? What five-year-old child should understand such tragedy? She blames herself. And I don't know what to say to her. I feel like I am going to break down and cry. How can I stay strong? It's so hard for me to shoulder the burden of her heartbreak along with my own.*

"Solomon," she said between gulps of air. She'd been crying so hard that now she was coughing. "Promise me you won't be dead soon, or ever. Promise me you won't go away and be dead. Because dead means I'll never see you again. Dead means forever."

"I promise," he managed. But he found that he could no longer control himself. Solomon was crying too.

CHAPTER 47

When Ludwig returned home, after he'd spent a week following Ewa, Gunther, and the children, the ghetto had been liquidated. Hedy was so angry at him for disappearing without any explanation that she almost threw him out when he appeared back at her apartment. She was sorting and folding clothes when he opened the door.

"Where were you?" Hedy snapped at him.

"I had business to attend to."

"Business? What kind of business?" She glared at him. He smiled smugly remembering the power he'd had over Ewa and the praise he'd received for the arrest of her and Gunther. He did not know what she'd done with the children. All he knew was that she had disappeared for a while and then resurfaced. But now that his sexual desire for her was satisfied, and he was to have the promotion he had been hoping for, he no longer wanted to search for the children.

"What's the matter with you? Don't you even have enough respect for me to answer my question?" Hedy's face was crimson. Her hands were shaking. She dropped the blouse she'd been folding and picked up a vase that had been her mother's. Then in anger she threw it at him. He ducked before the vase hit him, and instead it smashed against the wall.

There were tears on her cheeks, and her voice was high pitched and loud. "You are a nobody, Ludwig. Just like my father said. You are a nothing, and you'll always be a nothing. You don't have any secret business that would keep you away from work for over for a week. You think I haven't noticed that you have been coming over less and less. You work at a small-time job. You are not some important SS agent. You're a guard in the ghetto; that's all you are. And at this point you have lost that job too. And let's not forget that you only had that job because my father got it for you. If he hadn't, you'd be a beggar on the street."

"How dare you!" he said, feeling his lips peel back, baring his teeth like an angry dog.

"And, you stupid fool, had you been here in Lodz you would have known that the ghetto was being liquidated. Perhaps my father could have found you other work. But I suspect you were off staying with some low-class piece of trash woman that you got yourself involved with." Her eyes glared at him.

"What do you mean the ghetto has been liquidated?"

"They sent the Jews away."

"Where?"

"Who the hell knows or cares. All I know is that you have been cheating on me, and you are now an out-of-work lout."

"You're wrong. You usually are. You jump to conclusions. You don't even give me a chance to speak. You want to know where I was?"

"Tell me. Go on, Ludwig. Tell me where were you?" She folded her arms over her chest. "Make up some good lie."

"Why would you say that? Why won't you just listen?"

"I've done nothing but try to help you. You were a nobody when I found you. My father said you were not in our class. But I told him I saw something in you. I begged him to help you because I wanted to marry you. My vati loves me. That's why he helped you get that job. He and I both helped you in every way we could. I ignored your station in life. I ignored that you were born a gutter rat, and this is the thanks I get. I want to hear the story that you come up with. Go on . . . tell me . . . where were you, gutter rat?"

He wanted to strike her. At this moment in time he despised her. The red wart on her cheek looked uglier than usual. Her hair looked thinner and greasier than he remembered. And the wrinkle between her brow was even more pronounced. His hands were clenched into fists. He wanted to see that hideous face of hers covered in blood. But he dared not. If her father ever found out that he hit her, there would be hell to pay. And now that he was out of work, he didn't dare burn any bridges. So he took a deep breath and forced himself to speak calmly. "While I was searching for those Jewish children, I found a group of partisans. I followed them for a while to see what they were up to. Then I turned them in to the Gestapo. You see, I found out that they were up to no good. They were on their way to France to meet with the Resistance. I probably saved a lot of German lives. I was even promised a promotion when I turned them in," he snapped back.

"Yes, well, I suppose that's admirable," she said, her anger subsiding. "Of course, you know I can have my father verify if there is any truth to what you are claiming."

"Why do you mistrust me?" he asked. "I would not lie to you."

Her shoulders relaxed, and he saw the rigidness leave her body.

He walked over to her and touched her hand. She pulled her hand away. But when he touched her cheek, she let her eyes meet his.

Even though he still had not forgotten the cruelty of her words, he knew he must solidify the relationship just in case he needed her father's help in the future. He raised her face to his and kissed her. Hedy's body went rigid, but he kissed her again, and she surrendered to his touch. Taking her hand, he led her to the bedroom. But that night in order for his body to perform, he had to think of dominating Ewa.

The following morning he awoke to Hedy preparing his breakfast. She sat beside him.

"It looks good. Thank you," he said, taking her hand.

He saw in her eyes that she melted with his touch.

"Do you think your father can help me find another job?" he said as sweetly as he could. "We are going to need the money when we get married."

"I'll talk to him," she said, but then she added, "but I have heard some very concerning gossip. I've heard that Germany could be losing the war, and soon the other side is going to come marching in, then what are we going to do?"

"What everyone else does, I suppose." He shook his head. "Besides, do you believe it? I don't."

"I am not sure," she said.

CHAPTER 48

THE TRUCK ROCKED AS IT MOVED FORWARD. EWA GLANCED AT THE other women who were seated beside her. Their heads were all bowed. No one said a word. The male guard who held them at gunpoint looked like a child to Ewa. She decided he was probably about sixteen, and from the look in his eyes he was scared. She wondered if he was afraid he would have to shoot one of the women prisoners. Perhaps he had never killed anyone. *Could he do it if he was commanded to? Was he capable?* she asked herself. Perhaps this was a good time to take the risk of jumping out of the truck and trying to run away. He might not have the courage to shoot her. For a single moment, a brief second in time, her eyes met his. He truly was just a child. Her heart raced. As soon as the truck slowed down she was going to jump and attempt to escape. Ewa had made this decision only seconds before the truck pulled into another compound surrounded by a black wrought-iron fence. The metal door shut behind her. The moment to jump was lost. It was too late. Wherever the Nazis had planned to take her, whatever they had planned to do with her, she was at their mercy.

Before her stood a large two-story manor house that looked more like a hospital or school than a concentration camp.

The women were told to get off the truck and form a line.

"Welcome to Harmense. I am SS Rottenführer Xavier Eidenchinkt. I am in charge here," a tall, well-built man with light hair and strong even features said. Then he continued, "Come inside."

The guard with the gun urged the prisoners forward into the house. Ewa was among them. The house was large and looming and had an odor that Ewa did not recognize. The women were surrounded on all sides by armed guards whose guns were pointed at their heads.

The rottenführer turned to face the group of women and said, "You are the fortunate ones among your peers. You see, they have been sent to Auschwitz-Birkenau where they are working at very difficult, very physical jobs. Can you imagine? Think about this for a moment." He smiled as if he were contemplating the score of a football game. "Only a couple of kilometers from here, the others who arrived on the very same transport with you will be struggling to survive. But you, on the other hand, have been chosen for much more important work. Here in this lovely little village that you see all around you, you will spend your days tending to the poultry and caring for a very special breed of rabbit . . . angora rabbits. They are quite beautiful." He smiled. "Each of you will be given a list of jobs that you are to perform. You will be required to keep the coops clean, prepare the chicken feed as well as the rabbits' very special diet. You are required to treat these animals humanely. Should I hear of anyone treating them in a distasteful manner, that person will be immediately executed. If you do as you are told, you will find me to be fair. But if you don't, I am afraid that you will find me to be a cruel and heartless man. Enough said. Now, follow me."

He walked up the stairs. Ewa and the rest of the women followed behind. They were led into a large room set up with bunk beds. Once they were all inside, the rottenführer said, "Find an open bed." Then he left the room. The rest of the guards followed. The door closed softly followed by the sound of a key turning in the lock.

"We're locked in here," one of the women said, running to the door and trying to open it.

Several others tried. Ewa didn't bother. She knew the door was locked. This was no time to try to escape. She planned to wait for a better opportunity.

CHAPTER 49

THE NEXT DAY ONE OF THE PRISONERS, WHO HAD BEEN AT THE CAMP for a while, showed the others around, explaining what would be expected of them. Ewa was shocked to find that there were over two thousand hens, at least a thousand ducks, a hundred geese, and a hundred turkeys. There were endless rows of incubators and coops to clean. And special chicken feed to prepare. The livestock smelled and needed constant care. She didn't mind. The poor creatures were at her mercy, and she did her best to treat them with kindness.

The poultry farm was hard work but not terrible. However, as soon as she was introduced to the angora rabbits everything changed for Ewa. She fell in love with the soft plush gentle creatures whose fur was the color of virgin snow. They were large for rabbits and had adorable little noses that twitched and tufts on the ends of their ears. It gave her a feeling of comfort to hold them in her arms and cuddle them, and in a strange way these tender, gentle beings offered some relief from the painful gap of being separated from the children, and in some small way holding their soft bodies close to her helped ease the pain of her grief at having lost her beloved Gunther.

Ewa preferred working with the rabbits to any of the other

projects she was assigned to at the camp. She loved waking up early and going outside to the neatly arranged pens where the rabbits were kept. She'd been told by a prisoner who called herself Albina, that there were at least three thousand angora rabbits. "That was the last time we took a count. But they are reproducing very quickly," Albina explained as she taught Ewa everything she would need to know to care for the rabbits.

"It certainly looks like there are more than three thousand. Just look at these pens," Ewa exclaimed.

"I know. And the Nazis are having us breed them as fast as we can. At least they are not crammed into those pens. They have plenty of space. So far, that is. But if we keep breeding them as fast as we are, well, who knows. You see, this whole project is the reichsführer's idea: Himmler. You'll meet him soon enough. He comes here to check on the progress we are making with the rabbits. He comes often enough. I have heard that he wants as much angora wool as he can get his hands on. When he is here, be sure that you treat the rabbits very well, or you will be executed. I saw it happen to several girls."

"I would never hurt an animal if I didn't have to."

"Why would you have to?"

"Well, when I was a partisan, we had to hunt to eat. "

"We don't eat the rabbits."

"I'm glad to hear that. I do like them. They are so pretty and soft and sweet." Then she hesitated. "I suppose we are required to kill and skin them."

"Not at all. We just shave them. We don't kill them."

Ewa smiled; she was glad. "By the way, how much wool does each rabbit provide?" Ewa asked.

"Not much. That's the problem. That's why we need so many," Albina said.

At first Ewa tried not to allow herself to become too attached to the sweet creatures because she was certain the Nazis were going to demand that she and the others kill them for one reason or another. The very idea haunted her. Then one evening while she was in the main room dining with the other prisoners, the fate of the rabbits was discussed.

"What happens to the rabbits when they get old? Are they used for rabbit stew?" one of the inmates asked Albina who was sitting at the table.

"These are special rabbits. The Nazis never kill them, you fool. They never eat them because the rabbits never stop producing fur no matter how old they get. In the spring we will shave them. Their cages are heated so that they don't suffer from losing their fur."

"Funny, isn't it? How kind these Nazi bastards are to animals but how cruel they are to humans," one of the other prisoners stated.

"Quiet. If a guard hears you, you'll be shot right here at the table. And I'd rather not have to clean up your blood right during my dinner."

"What do they use the fur for?" Dyta the prisoner, who sat beside Ewa, asked.

"Angora fur is very luxurious. Right now the Nazis are using it to line the coats and boots of the army men, to keep them warm on the Eastern Front. By the way, have you ever seen an angora dress?"

"Not me," Dyta said.

"Me neither," Ewa offered.

"Well, let me tell you, it's heavenly. Very expensive. I've never owned one, but I would love to," Albina said.

Ewa didn't care about owning an angora dress, but she was relieved to know the rabbits were not destined to die horrible deaths. Their existence had taken on a special meaning for her, and she was glad to know they were to be bred and used for their fur. This she could tolerate.

The food at the camp was not plentiful, and although Ewa didn't know this because she was never in any other camp, the rations at Harmense were far superior to those provided at Auschwitz. Sometimes there were even opportunities to get additional food. And if one was very hungry and cunning enough, there was always a bite or two of the food that was reserved for the animals.

When she first arrived at Harmense, Ewa kept to herself, but as the months passed she found she was lonely, and she began to make friends among the other prisoners. Ewa and several of the others grew up in the cities. But a few of the prisoners came from the countryside where they'd lived their entire lives on farms, and a few of them had never attended school. When Ewa learned they were illiterate, she offered to teach them to read and write. These women were excited by the possibility of learning, and although Ewa was tired at the end of her long workdays, she enjoyed teaching. She wanted to do something that made a difference. And so began nights of learning.

Dyta, an attractive young woman prisoner who worked in the office, had become sexually involved with one of the lower-ranking guards. And because of their relationship, he overlooked it when she stole paper and pencils as well as a few candles for light from the office supplies. Each night, once the women were locked into their sleeping area, Ewa began to give her classes. When Dyta asked her boyfriend for a copy of *Mein Kampf*, he gladly obliged. She told him that she wanted to learn more about the Nazi doctrine and about the great führer. He was impressed. She took the book back to her room and gave it to Ewa. "We can use this to help teach the others to read."

"It is a book," Ewa said, raising her eyebrows. "Not the best book, and certainly not my first choice, but we can do our best. It is in German though. I can speak and read German. But how are the other women ever going to learn to read and write in German when they can't even read and write in Polish?"

"I know. I can read in German and in Polish. But teaching the others another language will be very difficult," Dyta said, then she continued, "Besides, I have no desire to read this trash."

Another prisoner, Felicia, who was illiterate and had grown up on a farm, scoffed at Dyta. "We are doing just fine learning our letters from Ewa. We don't need this disgusting Nazi book. And to be quite frank with you, Dyta, I don't know how you have sex with that man. He's one of them. One of the enemy."

"Yes, don't you think I know that. Don't you think I realize it every time he enters my body? You criticize me, but when I bring extra food you are happy to have it, aren't you?" Dyta said. "Besides, it's not like I have a choice now, is it?"

"Ladies, please, fighting won't do any of us any good. Stop acting like this. We all are here against our will. And anything that any of us can do to make our stay a little less horrible is greatly appreciated. So thank you, Dyta, for bringing the extra food when you can. And also thank you for bringing the book. It was a very kind gesture, and even if we can't use it, I appreciate your trying to help," Ewa said.

Felicia pouted, but she didn't say another word.

CHAPTER 50

ONE MORNING WHEN EWA WENT TO CARE FOR THE RABBITS SHE found that one of the mother rabbits had died giving birth. There were several tiny dead bodies in the cage with her. Ewa sighed and shook her head. This happened sometimes. The other women who cared for the rabbits told her that it was often because of a mistake in breeding. It was important that the rabbits not be bred before they were six months old because their bodies were not developed enough. Ewa looked at the mother rabbit and reminded herself that she must not become emotionally involved with the animals. However, each time there was a death among the rabbits, the tiny dead bodies triggered something in Ewa, and she felt terribly depressed for the rest of the day. Perhaps it was their innocence. Perhaps it was their helplessness, the way they were at the mercy of those who were bigger and stronger than they were. Perhaps they reminded her in a strange way of Sarah and Solomon.

Taking a deep breath, she steeled herself to attack the job of cleaning out the cage to start over. Tears ran down her face as she disposed of the dead rabbits. Tears for the creatures and tears for her lost loved ones. *I should be able to distance myself from this, but the soft fur and the tiny, helpless animals is so unnerving to me.* She wiped her nose with the back of her hand and began to clean out the cage more vigorously, trying to keep her attention on the job at hand and trying to ward off the feeling of hopelessness that was falling upon her like a black veil.

It was then that she found one of the little rabbits who was still alive. He was shaking in the back of the cage. *Oh, little one. You are still fighting. Just look at you.* Her hands trembled as she gently caressed the little white ball of fur. "Shhh, you're all right," she whispered as she took him and gently placed him in the incubator. Every day as soon as she was free to begin her shift, she went to check on him to make sure that he drank his special milk. At first she put the milk on the tip of her finger and he licked it off. But soon he was eating on his own and growing bigger. I promised myself I would not name these rabbits. I promised myself I would not become attached to them, just in case the Germans decided to eat them. But as she looked into the rabbit's sweet, expressive eyes, she couldn't help but give him a name . . . Gunther the Second. *I'll name him for Gunther*, she thought.

CHAPTER 51

JUNE 1944

In December 1941, Japan waged a surprise attack on America. They bombed Pearl Harbor, and the following day the United States of America entered the Second World War.

Japan was a part of the Axis which included Mussolini in Rome, Emperor Hirohito in Japan, and Adolf Hitler in Germany.

The Americans joined Winston Churchill in Great Britain and Joseph Stalin in the USSR who were already engaged in a fight against the Axis. The alliance of these great nations became known as the Allies.

On June 6, 1944 one hundred thirty thousand American, British, and Canadian soldiers landed on five beaches in Normandy in the northern part of France. The Nazis had a stronghold on these beaches and a bloody battle ensued. Many of the ally soldiers arrived seasick because they traveled by boat, and the night before they landed, the seas had been rocky. Still, they advanced bravely.

There was a tremendous loss of life, and the waters ran red with blood. However . . . this was a turning point. The Allies, including the Americans, had arrived, and with them came a long-awaited glimmer of hope.

CHAPTER 52

CHRISTMAS EVE 1944

The priest sat at the head of a long wooden table with the orphaned children surrounding him. As soon as the bread was placed in the center of the table Solomon grabbed for it.

"Solomon," the priest said in a calm but firm voice, "I must have told you a thousand times that we do not start eating before we give thanks to God for our food. And then we do not grab the food first so that we can get the lion's share."

One of the girls giggled. Solomon glared at the priest, but he put the bread back. The priest nodded at Solomon.

As the children joined hands, the priest began his prayer, but Solomon's mind was elsewhere. He resented being treated like a child, being reprimanded and told what to do. He'd been a man, with responsibilities too long. And he wished he could run away from this place and go back to the forest. It was true that here at the orphanage he ate every day even if it was a bowl of hot soup and a heel of bread. But he hated living this lie. He was a Jew, and he hated that he had to hide it because it was considered dirty and undesirable. Besides that, being a Jew was considered so terrible that it could cost him and Sarah their lives.

As the prayers over the food were being said, Solomon glanced around the table. Everyone else's eyes were closed, but he had to look over at Sarah. She'd acclimated far better than he did to this strange place. The nuns who ran the school they attended each day adored her. She was obedient, and although Solomon hated all the rules and structure they had to adhere to, Sarah loved it.

When they'd first arrived, Sarah cried every night. She wouldn't eat, and her tangled hair began to fall out. Then she got a mean-looking rash the color of a lipstick their mother had once owned. It frightened Solomon. He was worried about her. He wished they still lived in Lodz before the ghetto had been built so he could take her to see Dr. Kushman, who was their family doctor. But there was no chance of that. *Who knows what happened to Kushman. He's probably dead,* Solomon thought sadly. *Our whole world is gone. Everyone is scattered or dead.*

Sarah was getting worse until one of the nuns, Sister Mary Joseph, a young, pretty girl with sparkling blue eyes took Sarah under her wing. Sister Mary Joseph put a salve on Sarah's rash that helped with the itching. Then the young nun began to assist Sarah with her schoolwork. And once Sarah began to trust the sister, she spent hours combing Sarah's long hair until all the knots were gone and the hair shined. Sister Mary gave Sarah the attention of an adult, a mother figure, that Sarah so desperately craved. She read Bible stories to Sarah, and in turn, Sarah clung to her.

Solomon was glad his sister was thriving at the orphanage, but he felt constricted, unable to breath. He was a prisoner trapped in the prison of a lie. And now here it was Christmas, and once again, he would be forced to celebrate a holiday he didn't accept as his own. All of the other children, including Sarah, were excited about the small gifts they were going to receive from a silly, imaginary man called Santa Clause who gave children gifts for putting their shoes by the fireplace. *Nonsense,* Solomon thought. He would have much preferred to have his freedom, to be back in the woods with Gunther and Ewa and the others, to a pair of warm socks and a wool hat and perhaps some lame homemade toy that would appear in his shoes in the morning. *I'm sick of this old man,* Solomon thought as he watched the priest smiling and talking to the children. *I'm sick of him and all his rules: No running in the building. Be on time for Mass. You must have proper manners at the table. He knows nothing about me or my family or where I come from . . . or how I've suffered.*

That night, which was Christmas Eve, the children were each given a small slice of cake. They giggled with delight. All of them except Solomon. It had been a long time since they'd eaten anything with sugar. Solomon wondered how the old priest had come by such a treasure. *Black market*, he thought. *Perhaps the priest isn't as perfect as he pretends to be.*

"Has everyone been served their slice of cake?" the priest asked.

The children all answered "yes" in unison.

The priest looked across the table and smiled.

The cake had been cut up carefully, so there was just enough for a very small piece for everyone.

"Then let us thank our friend Monsieur Barbet for thinking of us on this Christmas Eve and bringing us this lovely cake from his bakery."

"Thank you," the happy children cried out. "Thank you, Monsieur Barbet."

Solomon picked up his fork and began to eat. He had to admit, it was delicious. The faces of the children were lit with joy and even Solomon, as bitter as he was, had to smile when he looked at them.

As his eyes searched the room for Sarah, they landed once again on the old priest. The old man's face was almost angelic as he smiled at Solomon. Solomon looked away quickly but not before he noticed that the priest did not have any cake on his plate. Solomon swallowed hard. *The priest didn't take any of the cake. There must not have been enough for him and for all of the children.* A tear formed in the corner of Solomon's eye. He thought about cutting his slice in half and giving half of it to the priest. But he didn't. Instead, he ate it. When they had all finished their treat, Solomon and Sarah, along with the rest of the children, put their shoes by the fireplace, then they went to their respective rooms to go to bed.

The other boys in the large dormitory-like room, where Solomon slept, were filled with anticipation. They talked excitedly about the gifts they would receive in the morning. They talked until one of the nuns came and told them that they must go to sleep or Santa would not come. Solomon was relieved that the room was finally quiet. As the boys slowly drifted off to sleep and he could hear the rhythm of their steady slow breathing, Solomon was left awake with his thoughts. *What's wrong with me? Every child loves to get presents. And we had a decent meal tonight. We even had cake.*

Tomorrow is Christmas. It's not my holiday, but I know that somehow the priest and the nuns will find a way to make it special. So why don't I feel good? Why do I want to run away from this place? It's really not bad here. But I just want to live the only life I know. A life where I make the decisions like a man, not be given rules that don't make sense to me that I am forced to follow, like a child. And as far as my sister is concerned, sometimes I can taste the bitterness in my mouth when I look at her. It's not her fault that she's so easily swayed. She's just a child. Someone has always looked out for her. She's happy here. She would be happy anywhere that she was getting attention. But not me. I have grown up looking after myself. I suppose it's because everyone who was supposed to be looking after me was taken away in one way or another.

I have been fending for myself since I was seven. And I like it that way. While the other seven-year-old children were outside playing, I learned how to distract the vendors so I could steal food. I escaped that filthy apartment in the ghetto at night so I could learn from the older boys. And I sure did. I learned how to weave my way out of the ghetto in order to make deals with the black market. They taught me about sex. Granted, they all laughed at me when they brought me a prostitute, and try as I might, my body wasn't ready to have sex. But the skills I learned were very valuable. I never had the chance to be carefree and foolish like Sarah. So it's hard for me to get excited about gifts and silly things like that. I am angry at losing everything and everyone. And I am angry at God for taking them. I may not be a practicing Jew, but I still hate the fact that I have to be ashamed of what I am.

It was well after midnight before Solomon finally fell asleep.

CHAPTER 53

THE OLD PRIEST FELT THE ACHE IN HIS JOINTS AS HE FILLED EACH OF the children's shoes with a pair of socks and a few candies. The nuns had spent hours making dolls out of thread for the girls, and a few of the local boys had whittled animals out of tree branches for the boys. He carefully placed each gift inside of the shoes remembering little things about each child that made their gifts more special. For instance, Anna Marie loved purple, so he put the doll made from purple thread in her shoe. Michael Jean thought raccoons were funny and cute, so he placed the wooden racoon inside Michael's shoe. When he got to Solomon's shoes he knelt down and took the special gifts from his bag. He spoke softly to God. "This boy is a hard one. He's been through a lot for a child so young. Let this gift soften his heart. Let him know that I understand and I accept him and love him for who he is. And let him know that you love him and that it was you, dear Father, who sent him here to us." Then the priest placed the gifts he'd risked his own life to have specially made for Solomon inside Solomon's shoe.

CHAPTER 54

THE FIRST LIGHT OF MORNING FOUND THE CHILDREN AWAKE AND waiting. They were filled with excitement as they ran down to see what Santa had left for them. Solomon smiled wryly at their innocence, but he felt none of their enthusiasm. He walked slowly behind the other boys.

By the time Solomon had made his way downstairs to the fireplace, Sarah was already sitting with several of the other girls and opening her gifts. She giggled with delight at something one of the other girls said. She was so engrossed that she didn't even notice her brother.

Somehow the old priest had been able to get his hands on enough firewood to build a nice, warm crackling fire for Christmas morning, and the golden glow filled the room. Not wanting to draw attention to himself, Solomon did what the other boys did. He went over to his shoes to see what gifts had been left for him. In one he found a pair of warm socks. *At least they are practical,* he thought. *It's amazing that the priest can get his hands on enough yarn to have the nuns knit socks for all these children.*

Next, Solomon found two small pieces of chocolate. One of

which he immediately popped into his mouth. What a delicious treat. He had not had chocolate since last Christmas. For a moment he closed his eyes and savored the sweetness, then he picked up his shoes not expecting anything else to be inside. And as he did, something fell out. It was small and carefully wrapped in a piece of white fabric that had yellowed with age. Solomon had noticed earlier that all of the boys had received wooden animals, but none of their wooden gifts had been wrapped. He held the small, wrapped package in his hand. He was about to open it when the old priest walked over to him and whispered in his ear, "I think you might want to open that when you are alone. And . . . Solomon . . . I want you to know that I accept you and love you and your sister just as you are. I don't want to change you. God loves you. Jesus loves you. You know Jesus was Jewish, and he suffered while on this earth, just as you have suffered."

Solomon looked into the old man's eyes and saw that they were lit like the flames of two candles.

"When this war is over, I will help you as best I can to find your family." Then the priest walked away.

Solomon tucked the wrapped gift deep into the pocket of his pajama bottoms.

Once they'd all opened their presents, the children were escorted into the large dining room for breakfast. Solomon reached into his pocket and touched the wrapped gift. His curiosity burned. He asked the sister, who was serving the food, if he might be excused to use the bathroom. She smiled and nodded in agreement. He stood up and left the table unnoticed. Then he went upstairs to the bedroom where he slept and quietly closed the door.

All alone in that quiet room, the only sound being the echoes of the children downstairs, Solomon removed the gift from his pocket. He held it in his hand before removing the fabric to reveal a Star of David carved out of wood. Running his fingers over the smooth surface, he felt a tear form in the corner of his eye. Solomon now knew the truth. The priest had known all along that he and Sarah were Jewish. Yet the old man had risked everything, his church, the

195

other children, the nuns, even his life, and he had taken Sarah and Solomon into his church in spite of the danger. A tear fell from Solomon's eyes and landed on the wooden star, then another. And before he realized it, Solomon's shoulders were trembling and he was sobbing.

CHAPTER 55

From that day on Solomon found that he had a new respect for the priest. Before Christmas day Solomon did not know that Jesus was Jewish. After all, he'd had no formal religious training, and this came as a surprise to him. He wanted to know more, and so he would seek the priest out to ask him questions. And the old father, no matter how busy he was, always made time to speak with Solomon.

One day the priest was downstairs outside the classrooms. He was on his way to the library when Solomon was coming out of his morning class.

"Solomon!" The priest smiled.

"Sir, I am glad I found you. I have been meaning to ask you some questions. Do you have a few minutes?"

"Of course, my son. What is it?"

"I want to start by saying that no matter what happens I will never change my religion. You see, I will never turn my back on Judaism, but I would like to learn more about you and your religion," Solomon said to the priest.

"Of course. And I would be glad to tell you anything you want to know. Not because I want to change you, but because you want to know." The priest smiled and sat down on a bench, then he motioned for Solomon to sit beside him.

Solomon had heard Bible stories before, first from his mother, then at the synagogue when he was forced to go. And now from the nuns. He found the Bible stories interesting, even entertaining, but he doubted they were true. However, he never shared his doubts with the priest.

Now he had more important questions for the old man.

"I can see that you are a kind man. You took my sister and me in even though you knew we were Jewish, but you were taking a big risk. Why did you do it?"

"Well, let me explain. You and Sarah are Jewish, but more importantly you are God's children, and I am the keeper here of God's house. Should a child not be welcome in his father's house?"

"Even if that child is not a Catholic?" Solomon asked, puzzled. "This is a Catholic church."

"Yes, no matter what religion you are. You are a child of God. No matter the color of your skin, you are a child of God. All people, in my opinion, should be welcome under God's roof."

"Do all the priests feel the way you do about Jews?"

"I can't speak for others. I can only speak for myself."

"So then, the answer is no. Isn't that right? I know that there are priests who side with the Nazis," Solomon said.

"There are. But I am not, and will never be, one of them. Because I know in my heart that God does not side with Hitler. Jesus would never condone the terrible things the Nazis stand for."

The nuns had created a school in the basement of the church where they held classes. Solomon had never been a good student. He found reading, writing, and arithmetic came too easily to him. And while the other children struggled to learn, he was bored. Instead of paying attention, his mind was busy devising plans to get out of the orphanage and find a way to steal extra food so that no one at the orphanage would ever go to bed hungry. He knew the Germans had a hefty supply, and he wanted to find a way to break into their headquarters at night. However, when he told the priest his plans, the priest shook his head. "No, Solomon. You must not go out of here and steal. It's too dangerous . . . and it's wrong. It's against God's commandments. We have managed thus far. We will continue to manage. God will provide."

Solomon shrugged. He knew that the priest was unyielding when it came to God's commandments. So all he could do was agree.

CHAPTER 56

POLAND, JANUARY 1945

Ewa was busy feeding the rabbits and cleaning their cages early one spring morning when Dyta came into the area where the pens had been set up. The rabbit who she'd named Gunther the Second sat up on his hind legs watching Ewa. It was a bitter-cold winter day, and the sky was ice blue. Ewa shivered, but she was glad that at least the rabbit pens were heated.

"We are being evacuated from here," Dyta blurted out quickly without even saying good morning. "I just heard about it."

"Evacuated? To where?"

"I don't know, butI do know that they think the Allies are going to win, and they don't want us here when the Allies arrive."

Ewa stared at her not knowing what to say.

"I came to find you quickly because the guards have given the girls permission to eat the rabbits. They've been told they can kill them all and make a stew."

Ewa looked over at Gunther the Second and then at Dyta. "Are you sure about this?"

"I'm positive. The Nazis don't want the Allies to get their hands on these rabbits. As you know their fur is valuable."

"Yes, I know." Ewa had sunk down onto her haunches. She loved these creatures. She was hungry too, but she wasn't starving. None of them were starving. She could not let them kill Gunther the Second.

"I came to tell you all of this before the others came to get your rabbits. I know how fond you are of them."

"Thank you," Ewa said.

"Is that all you have to say?" Dyta asked. "Come on, let's hurry up and open the pens, so we can set these animals free. I can't promise they will survive, but at least they'll have a chance if we let them out before the others come and cook them."

"You're right. Let's hurry up and get them out of here," Ewa said. She took Gunther the Second into her arms and held him close, then she whispered softly into his ear, "You've been my salvation while I was here at this prison. I can't do much more for you, my sweet friend. I am no longer able to protect you. So run away, run as fast as you can and don't look back. Don't ever look back," she said. Then she took the large white rabbit out into the yard. He nuzzled her neck, and for a moment she held him close to her. Then she gently pushed him through the fence and out of the camp.

He stood very still at first and looked at her for one long moment. She smiled and nodded, but tears filled her eyes and ran down her cheeks. "Go, little one. Go . . ." she said. Then Gunther the white rabbit looked directly into her eyes. Suddenly he seemed to understand. Ewa could have sworn she saw him nod before he whirled around and hopped away quickly. Ewa watched him until he disappeared into the trees. She sighed and thought of Solomon and Sarah. *Those poor dear children. Have they survived, or have they, God forbid, perished? Solomon, he was such a special boy, always trying to be so strong, so capable. And little tender Sarah, so frightened, so needy. Sometimes I am overwhelmed with guilt for leaving them. They needed me. And my Gunther, my love, he is gone forever. Dear God, please . . . if you must take me, then take me, but let the children survive. I know this sounds silly, but I loved this poor little rabbit, and I know it's a lot to ask, but if you could, please let him survive too.*

"There's no time to stand around. Wake up. You seem to be

asleep standing there. If you want to free the rabbits, there is not much time left," Dyta said.

Ewa nodded at Dyta, and then they began to repeat the steps she'd taken to free Gunther Two with the remaining rabbits. She moved as quickly as she could, and by the time the Nazi guards and the other prisoners came to the rabbit area, they found only empty cages.

Had this happened even six months earlier, Ewa would have been severely punished for releasing the rabbits. But right now, the guards were desperately worried about their own fate. The Allies were at their heels. If they were caught, they knew things would not go well for them. So there was no time for punishing a sentimental girl who loved rabbits. They had to get the prisoners out of the camp and move toward Germany as quickly as possible. So, within hours, the entire group, prisoners and guards, were on their way to Wodzislaw Slaski in the dead of winter. They would make the trip on foot. The snow-and-ice-covered ground made the long walk perilous, but the guards were determined, and because they were so fearful they were even crueler than usual.

CHAPTER 57

JANUARY 1945

The women prisoners marched through the snow-covered landscape at gunpoint. They marched without coats, without hats, and many without shoes. The guards complained to each other about the frigid weather, but at least they had heavy coats and boots.

At first the other women were angry with Ewa and Dyta for releasing the rabbits.

"We could have had a warm, substantial meal," a young Polish prisoner said. "It might have given some of us the strength to survive this miserable walk."

Ewa felt bad for the other women. They had a point. After all, they were hungry, and because of her they'd lost the opportunity to eat a good meal. But although she understood intellectually, Ewa just could never have allowed the rabbits to be killed and eaten. Since she'd been at the camp, she'd spent every day caring for those animals, and in so many ways they had begun to represent more to her than just pens of rabbits. *Perhaps I am going mad,* she thought. *Perhaps all of this has driven me over the edge, and I have lost my mind. I ate plenty of rabbit when I was in the forest, and it never seemed to bother me. But now I can't bear to think of their pure white coats stained red with blood.*

203

She knew the others thought of the rabbits as food, but she couldn't help herself. After she'd rescued Gunther the Second from certain death, she found that she was haunted by parallels that the others clearly could not see. Sometimes she thought about her life before the war and how these sweet animals were at the mercy of the Germans just like the Jewish families in the old neighborhood where she'd grown up. But then she reminded herself that the other prisoners at Harmense were not Jewish. It was easier for them to ignore the Jews as they went like lambs to the slaughter. Or maybe not like lambs, maybe like helpless, white angora rabbits. And so when the opportunity came to set the rabbits free, she felt in a strange way that God had chosen her to deliver them. She didn't care that the others resented her, she had to let them go free. Their freedom felt like a thick umbilical cord that was somehow connected to her own freedom.

After a while the women were too exhausted from the cold and walking to fight. Ewa was fortunate to have wooden clogs, but the blood of the barefoot women stained the snow. Before nightfall, one of the women fell. The guard hollered at her, but she lay shivering, unable to rise. A young handsome guard in his heavy wool coat walked over to her. He wore an expression of annoyance. "Get up. You're holding everyone up."

The woman tried to pull herself up with her arms, but she was too weak. She fell back into the snow. For one brief second Ewa saw a look of sympathy pass over the young Nazi's face. But then one of the other guards, an older more seasoned man, walked over to see what the holdup was.

"Get up!" he yelled at the woman.

But try as she might, she could not move.

"Kill her," he said to the young guard who looked at him frightened. "What's the matter with you? I said kill her so we can go on."

"Why don't we just leave her here. Why waste the bullet? We might need it. She will die anyway," the young one said.

"You coward. Kill her. Kill her," he yelled.

The young guard pulled out his gun. From where Ewa stood she could see that his hand was trembling. Then again the older man hollered, "I said kill her. Do it now. Get on with it, you coward."

The younger Nazi squeezed the trigger. Ewa gasped at the sound of the gunshot. The body of the woman on the ground jumped when the bullet entered her heart. Then she lay completely still. Rich red blood poured like a river staining the white snow.

"Walk!" the older Nazi yelled at the women, and they did as he commanded.

Ewa felt her heart pounding. *How could such a young handsome man have done this? He should not be here murdering women. He should be at home somewhere courting a girl then getting married and having children. But instead, he like so many others, followed Adolf Hitler down the road to hell, and now he is in charge of marching a group of sick and starving women, who must adhere to his commands, or he is forced to leave their dead bodies in the snow to be ravaged by feral animals. What kind of man would he have been? What would fate have had in store for him had Hitler never come to power?*

That night, the women prisoners slept huddled together shivering, coughing, sneezing, and trying to keep warm. Ewa was so tired that every muscle in her body ached. So in spite of the bitter cold that bit at her toes and stung her face, she slept.

At the first light of morning the guards called out, "Get up, you swine. It's time to get moving."

Ewa shook herself awake and stood up. Her head ached. Her eyes burned, and she could no longer feel her little toes, but she was alive. Several of the women lay still that morning. The guards yelled out angry commands. "Get up. Get moving. Are you deaf, you lazy pigs."

The old Nazi guard kicked one of the women who lay on her side in the snow. Except for her deep-blue lips and pale skin, she looked like she was asleep. *So peaceful,* Ewa thought. *She is at peace. And I can hear her laughter in my mind. She is free. She is no longer a prisoner. This Nazi has no control over her because she has no fear. Sleep, sweet soul. They can't hurt you anymore. They can't take anything else away from you. Nothing on this earth will ever hurt you again because you have taken your last breath during the night.*

Ewa tried not to think about anything except putting her foot forward and making the next step. Thinking always seemed to bring on memories. And memories caused sadness. But as time passed and the endless walk caused her entire body to throb with pain, her mind drifted to Gunther. They had only made love once. She wished now that she'd held him longer, that they had made love more often. It was difficult when they were in the forest with all the others to find a time and place to be alone. But she knew, if she'd been willing, he would have found a way. However, at that time she'd been so concerned with her reputation. What would the others in the camp think of her? An unmarried woman sharing her bed with a single man? A German, no less. And . . . she'd allowed that stigma to come between them. But now that he was gone forever, she wished she could bring back those few hours that she had spent wrapped in his arms.

To hell with what people thought. I knew his heart. I knew he was no Nazi. No one decides where they will be born or what nationality they will be. But it was clear to me that Gunther had turned his back on Germany because of Hitler. I was such a fool. I should have realized that I had nothing to prove to the others. I don't know why I cared so much what they thought. He was her first man. She'd never made love before. *How stupid I am. With a world as uncertain as this one is, how could I have denied Gunther and myself those few precious moments? If he could have, he would have married me. I know that. He loved me with all his heart. If I could only go back in time . . .*

Halfway into the fifth day of the march, the group of women from Harmense was joined by a larger group. These women wore the gold Star of David on their sleeves, letting Ewa know they were Jewish. The girls from Harmense were thin and hungry; they were cold and miserable and were barely able to go on. But the Jewish women looked far worse. They were little more than walking corpses. Not one of them had shoes; their feet were all bloody, and their toes had turned black. They were so skinny that their gray-striped uniforms were falling off their bony frames.

Everyone was hungry.

There was no food. None at all. Once the group stopped for the night, Ewa and Dyta sucked on the dirty snow to fill their empty bellies. The snow melted in their mouths, becoming frigid water, which slid down their throats, chilling their bodies from the inside out and making them even colder.

"I'm starting to regret freeing those rabbits," Dyta said, smiling wryly.

"Do you really?"

"Only when I'm hungry." Dyta laughed a little.

"And when is that?" Ewa asked with a little sarcasm in her voice.

"All the time."

Ewa nodded. "Me too," she said. But she was still glad she hadn't eaten the rabbits. However, the ache in her belly from hunger was unbearable.

Dyta and Ewa huddled together through the night shivering in the darkness. In the morning when the guard fired his gun into the air to awaken the prisoners, nearly half the Jewish women did not rise.

"They are dead; let's go," Ewa overheard one of the guards say to another.

"Not until we are sure they aren't faking and just playing dead," the old Nazi said.

"What are you going to do?"

"You'll see." So instead of leaving the broken women behind, the guards walked among them and shot every woman who lay in the snow.

"That was a lot of wasted ammunition," one of the young guards said to the older man.

"Shut up. Don't you dare question me. Remember your rank."

Ewa and Dyta exchanged glances. They were so tired they could hardly lift their feet, but they knew that they must keep on going forward, or their fates would be the same as the poor women who had been left behind to bleed out into the snow.

All the Jewish women were very ill. Their faces and bodies were covered in rashes. Many of them suffered from diarrhea from lack of food or from eating bad food. They were dirty, and they scratched their shaved heads from the lice that had attached to the small regrowth of hair. And even though the women were walking outside, the smell of sickness and filth was still strong enough to make Ewa gag.

The following day, the Nazis led their prisoners through a town. At first people stood staring at the group, their eyes wide and frightened. From the looks of shock on their faces Ewa realized just how terrible the prisoners appeared to outsiders. Some of the children laughed and were cruel, making a motion with their finger across their throat, which was meant to remind the prisoners that they were doomed to die.

However, most of the adults were petrified of the Nazis and to them, this group of half-naked, starving prisoners was horrifying. They tried not to look. They tried to rush away to the safety of their homes, keeping their heads down. No one dared to say a word. The presence of the armed Nazi guards kept them quiet. But then a little girl, perhaps eight years old, with two blonde braids on either side of her head, took a bunch of potatoes out of her skirt pocket and began to throw them to the prisoners. Ewa caught one. It was small and soft, but it was food, and her gratitude toward the child filled her heart. *It would take an innocent child to be so unafraid*, she thought as she took a bite. It hurt her teeth, but it was sweet and starchy, and it had been so long since she'd had any food that she had to force herself not to gobble it down. Ewa took another bite and noticed that Dyta was watching her. Her stomach ached with hunger, but she handed the potato to Dyta.

"Have a bite," she said.

Dyta took a bite of the potato. "My teeth are loose," she said. "It's hard to chew."

"Yes, mine are too. Have another bite though."

Dyta closed her eyes and took another bite. Then she handed the potato back to Ewa. They continued to share until the small potato was gone.

Ewa was so tired that she couldn't speak. Not even to Dyta. All she could feel was pain, and even that was beginning to disappear. Her body seemed to be going numb. Twice she almost fell and would have given up if Dyta hadn't grabbed her arm and held her until she was steady on her feet enough to begin to walk again. Her lungs burned from the cold, and a trail of vapor followed her shallow breath.

The longer they continued to walk, the more women fell. When they did, the guards shot them point-blank without even demanding that they try to get up. The Jewish women who had come from Auschwitz were the weakest. Many of them died without even a sigh of pain. They just fell to the ground in a macabre dance of death. Ewa was certain they were dead even before the guards shot them. Sometimes one of the guards would kick the bodies of the women out of the way so the prisoners could pass; other times the prisoners were forced to walk around the dead.

Ewa tried to avoid looking at their dark, cavernous eyes, which filled her with painful questions. *Every one of these women who are now lying dead in the snow once had a family; they had mothers and fathers. They might have been mothers, wives, sisters. And now their bodies lie lifeless in an open field.* She shivered. *I can't bear to acknowledge what the Nazis have done to them, to all of us. The old woman back there who died with her hands reaching for the heavens, and her eyes asking why could have been my own mother. Dear God, I must wipe these horrific images out of my mind or I will collapse and give up. If I am ever to find my way back to Sarah and Solomon, I must concentrate every ounce of strength on putting one foot in front of the other. And this would be the wrong time to give up. After all, I think it's obvious by how quickly they moved us that the Nazis are scared. The Allies must be close. If only the Allies can get to us before the Nazis kill us all.*

At one point the women reached a clearing located only a few hundred feet from a forest. Ewa's heart leapt as she saw a group of five women run toward the trees. She longed to follow them. Even though every nerve in her feet was on fire with pain, she wished she had the courage to run free. Her body tingled with fear and desire at the same time, but she felt paralyzed. *Run,* she thought. *Just run.* Then shots rang out, and as each of the five women fell to the ground, Ewa felt her courage begin to leave her.

"Should we run?" Dyta said, tugging on Ewa's sleeve.

Ewa thought for a moment. She shivered with fear and anticipation. The truth was she wasn't sure how fast she would be able to run. *I don't want to die in the snow. But this could be our only chance to escape.*

Is it better to die here in the snow than to die in another camp? Dear God, give me the courage. Please give me the courage. Her body was shaking so hard that she felt like she might collapse.

At that moment one of the dogs who belonged to a Nazi guard broke away and began to chase a squirrel. Several of the other guard dogs began to run after him. They were all on leashes but they pulled their masters so hard that the Nazi guards were running and falling behind them. Finally, several of the guards released the leashes, and the dogs rushed toward the woods. Chaos ensued.

Ewa took this as a sign from God. This was their opportunity to run. Sucking in a deep breath, she said, "Let's go."

Dyta nodded.

Hand in hand the women ran across the snow-covered landscape followed by a rain of bullets from the guards who were shooting at them. Between the sound of gun shots were the terrifying voices of the guards as they called after their dogs. A bullet lodged in the tree right next to them. Dyta saw it and turned her head for a second. .

"Keep running." Ewa said breathlessly. "Don't look back."

Then by some wonderful miracle they reached the trees. But just as they were about to enter the protection of the forest, Dyta stepped on a large tree root that was protruding from the ground. She turned her ankle and fell. With two hands she gripped her right foot, wincing in pain. Ewa pulled her to her feet.

"Get up. Get up! We can't stop now. We're almost free."

Dyta forced herself to run. She ran with a limp, but she ran. They entered the trees and kept going until finally, the thick forest closed around them.

"Keep running," Ewa said.

"I can't," Dyta said. "The pain is so terrible."

"You must," Ewa said as she pulled Dyta by the hand. "They will hunt us. Make no mistake. So we have to get as far away from them as we can . . ."

CHAPTER 58

By nightfall, Ewa and Dyta had put miles between themselves and the poor marching women. They were cold and hungry. But they were free.

"What do we do now?" Dyta asked.

"I don't know. I don't even know where we are. I have no idea how far we are from the group of partisans that I was living with."

"Well, we have to find a way to get our hands on some clothes and blankets if we are going to survive." Dyta sat down and rubbed her swollen ankle.

"Let's try to find a farmhouse, and see if we can get into the barn after dark," Ewa said. "Perhaps we can even find some food."

They walked along the edge of the forest until it had grown very dark. Then they began to search for shelter. All of the barns they passed were heavily secured, but after several hours they came upon a tool shed that had been left unlocked. Ewa opened the door. There was no light inside, but if they left the door open they were able to see, not clearly, but at least a little from the light the full moon provided.

A man's jacket hung from a hook on the wall. There was a pile of horse blankets folded neatly on the dirt floor. And there was a gun on a shelf with a small box of ammunition beside it. When they walked farther inside, they found a cow hide drying and two large knives.

"Look at all this," Ewa said.

"We can use all of it," Dyta said.

Ewa nodded and began to wrap the gun and knives in the cow hide. But when she looked up, her heart stopped. She gasped as she saw a tall figure, the shadow of a man, blocking the doorway. He'd entered the shed quietly and he was watching them. There was no way out. Ewa glanced over at Dyta.

"Who are you, and what are you doing here?" he asked.

"We are . . ." Ewa tried to come up with a story of some sort, but she was so tired and hungry that she couldn't think. "I'm sorry," she said. "We are thieves." Then she began to cry.

"I'll have to inform the authorities," he said, but he stood staring at them, unmoving.

"The truth is we are escaping from a work camp. We are partisans, Polish freedom fighters, who love our native country as much as you do," Dyta said, speaking as quickly as she could. "If you bring the police into this, the Nazis will kill us. We were stealing from you because we are cold and hungry. We are not thieves . . ."

"I see," he said, sighing and rubbed his chin with his fingertips. "I see . . ."

"I'm sorry. Please, please don't involve the authorities," Ewa said.

"Come on, follow me," he said.

The women stood motionless in the darkness of the shed. Ewa wondered if she should grab Dyta's hand and try to run. But then the man said in a calm and gentle voice, "My name is Tytus. Come inside. Perhaps I can find you something to eat."

It was too dark to see Dyta's eyes, but something in this man's mannerism made Ewa feel that she could trust him. After all, it was cold, so very cold, and she was tired and hungry, and desperate. Her feet ached, and she could no longer feel her little toe on her left foot. *He told us his name. That means he's not a stranger any longer. His name is Tytus. He is Polish; he speaks our language, and his voice is soft and gentle. I am trusting my instincts,* she thought, *but if I have made the wrong decision, it will probably cost Dyta and me our lives. Should we be running away? Is this a trap?* Dyta was limping beside Ewa. Ewa reached out and took Dyta's hand. Neither of them said a word.

Once inside the farmhouse, Tytus took some logs and began to build a fire in the fireplace. After the fire was burning softly, he cut slices of bread, carrots, and cucumbers, which he placed on a plate. "Sorry, I don't cook much. I'm here alone since my wife's sister took ill, and she went to stay with her in Warsaw."

"Thank you," Dyta said, grabbing the food and stuffing it into her mouth. Ewa was eating so fast that she choked and began coughing.

"Slow down. Slow down. There's no hurry," Tytus said. "If you eat that fast, the food will come right back up." Then he waited a minute until Ewa stopped coughing and continued, "Tell me your names."

"I'm Dyta, and this is Sylwia," Dyta said.

"It's nice to meet you. It gets lonely out here. My wife has been gone for over six months, and unless I go into town I don't see a living soul."

"Did you bake this bread?" Dyta asked.

"I did!" he said, smiling proudly.

"It's pretty good."

"Ehh, perhaps a little doughy, I think, but I'm getting better at it," he said. "However, I would love some hot soup to go with it, but I never get around to preparing any. Like I said, I don't cook much."

"I'd be happy to make soup for you," Dyta offered.

"That would be lovely." He smiled then asked, "Now tell me all about this escape. What happened? What exactly are you escaping?"

And so they told him everything—and he listened.

CHAPTER 59

"YOU CAN STAY HERE WITH ME," TYTUS OFFERED.

"Are you sure?" Ewa asked. "You could be endangering your own life."

"Only if you'll make soup," he said, winking at Dyta.

"It's not funny. If you are caught, you would face a terrible fate."

"I'm not worried. At least you're not Jews. You're Poles, just like me."

"You're a strange man," Dyta said.

"I suppose," he said, "but I am willing to take the risk. So now that you have finished eating, follow me; I have an extra room. You can stay there."

Ewa and Dyta looked at each other.

"Well, come on, then," he said, and they followed him. He carried a kerosene lamp.

When Tytus opened the door, moonlight beamed through the window. The room was small, but it was cheery. There were flowered curtains and a matching quilt on the small bed.

"Look, a real pillow." Ewa gasped. "Do you know how long it's been since I laid my head on a real pillow?"

"Yes, me too," Dyta said.

"Do you like it?" Tytus asked.

"Oh yes," both women agreed.

"Well, good, then. Tomorrow we can draw some water from the well and boil it so you two can have a bath."

"A bath." Dyta sighed.

"Sleep well," Tytus said, smiling, and then he left, softly closing the door behind him.

Immediately, Ewa stood up to check the door. She was so used to being imprisoned that she wanted to be sure he had not locked them in. The door opened easily. Ewa turned to look at Dyta. Dyta smiled. "We are free to go," she said.

"Free!" Ewa said, and a single tear ran down her cheek.

Both women sat on the edge of the bed and took off their shoes and socks. Ewa found that her little toe had fallen off. She gagged when she saw it. Then she glanced over at Dyta.

"I lost my little toes too," Dyta said.

"It makes me want to vomit." Ewa gagged

"Me too," Dyta said, "but what can we do? At least we are alive. Our bellies are full; we are warm, and for now we are safe. What more could we ask for?"

"Yes, that's true. Besides, little toes don't serve much purpose anyway, do they?" Ewa said, and they both laughed with relief.

CHAPTER 60

THE NEXT DAY TYTUS EXPLAINED THAT HE NEEDED TO GO INTO town to purchase a few things.

Dyta made herself at home almost immediately, but Ewa was not so quick to trust the situation. She was concerned that Tytus had gone into town in order to turn them in so he could collect reward money. She discussed her fears with Dyta. It was logical. After all, they were escapees. However, the idea of going out into the cold again without food or shelter seemed a daunting task. And when Ewa suggested it, Dyta said that she was so comfortable in the warm house that she would rather risk her life than leave. Ewa considered leaving the farm on her own, but when she looked out the window at the snow-covered landscape, knowing she had no place to go and no one to turn to, she decided to take her chances and trust Tytus.

With Tytus out of the house, the women found it easy to prepare and take a bath. Ewa went first. They boiled the water so it was warm when she stepped in. She felt the warmth climb up her body and soothe her all the way through. She stayed in the water until it had grown so cold that she was no longer comfortable. Then Ewa and Dyta boiled water for a bath for Dyta.

Once they were clean, Dyta kept her promise to Tytus. She

remembered the bin where Tytus had gotten the vegetables the previous night. She reached in and brought out some carrots, some potatoes, and some onions which she cut. Then she began to boil water to make a soup. Meanwhile, Ewa found a bin of flour, and she baked a fresh loaf of bread.

"I wish I had something clean to wear," Dyta said.

"Yes, and clean, fresh undergarments," Ewa said, knowing they were only fantasizing.

"If you could have a dress of any color, what color would you choose?"

Ewa thought for a moment then she said, "Me? Blue, I think. How about you?"

"Red, definitely red."

Both women laughed.

"And, of course, since we are dreaming, I would like to wear real silk stockings and high-heel pumps."

Dyta got up and stirred the soup pot. "It would be lovely, wouldn't it?"

"Yes," Ewa smiled.

"And suppose we were getting ready to go to a party . . . and for fun, just suppose that Tytus was my boyfriend." Dyta smiled.

"For goodness' sake, Dyta, he's married. Don't start thinking of him in that way. You'll only get your heart broken."

"It's been a long time since I've felt the arms of a man around me. And he's so kind and so generous."

"Do you really find him handsome?" Ewa asked.

"I didn't say handsome." Dyta laughed. "I don't suppose he is the best-looking man I've ever seen, but he is a man . . . and like I said . . . it's been years."

"I understand," Ewa said.

It was late afternoon when Tytus returned. Ewa breathed a sigh of relief when he rode up in his horse-drawn wagon alone. She checked to see if he was being followed, but there was no one following him. And it appeared that he had been honest. Tytus had gone into town for supplies. He came into the house and said hello to the women. Then he went back to the wagon, and one by one he carried two huge sacks of flour into the kitchen. Then he went back outside one more time and got another sack from the back of the wagon, which he poured into a wooden barrel that stood on the kitchen floor.

"I got some flour and some sugar," Tytus said as he removed his coat and shook off the cold.

"How did you ever get sugar?' Dyta asked.

"I made a few good trades in town." Tytus winked.

"Sugar?" Ewa said. A pang of fear shot through her. Had he somehow traded them for a sack of sugar?

"What's wrong?" Tytus asked. Then he sighed. "You think I betrayed you to get the sugar, don't you?"

Ewa shrugged.

"I didn't. I wouldn't. You are fellow Poles. We share a common enemy."

Ewa looked into his eyes. She remembered Gunther saying something very similar, and hearing Tytus express the same convictions comforted her. She wanted to trust him, and so she decided that she would. "May I taste it, please?"

"The sugar?"

"Yes, it's been a very long time since I've tasted sugar," Ewa said.

"Sure," Tytus answered.

Ewa dipped her pinky finger into the sugar and then put it into her mouth. It felt as if her senses had exploded with ecstasy.

"May I taste it too?" Dyta asked.

"Of course."

"I can't believe you were able to get your hands on all of this," Dyta said.

"Well, you know what they say . . . a smart farmer never starves. No matter how bad things get, a farmer won't starve."

"Would you like me to bake a cake?" Dyta asked.

"I would love it." Tytus winked at Dyta and smiled as he added some logs onto the fire. Then he continued, "I was thinking . . . Please don't take offence, but those uniforms are filthy and worn. Besides, they are uniforms. Should the Nazis come here looking for you, I don't want them to see those things. They are a dead give-away. My wife left some clothes. I would like to give each of you a housedress to wear. They aren't fancy things, but at least you'll find that they're clean. And once you change your clothes I suggest that we burn those uniforms."

"Oh!!! Oh!!!" Dyta said breathlessly. "I was daydreaming about how good it would feel to have clean things to wear."

"Well"—he smiled—"why don't you come with me, and you can choose something."

"Don't you think your wife would be angry that you have given her clothes away?" Ewa asked.

For a moment Tytus was silent. Ewa could feel that she'd made him uncomfortable, and she was suddenly sorry she'd asked.

But then Tytus cleared his throat. "My wife is a good Christian woman. She would want to help two women in need."

I don't believe him for a second, Ewa thought. *What woman would want two young women in her home alone with her husband and wearing her clothes? Something is very wrong here.*

Once Ewa and Dyta settled into their new home, they came to realize that the house was in need of a deep cleaning. On the surface it appeared to be well kept up, but there was a lot of dust and dirt behind the furniture. Both women were grateful to have a place to stay, and they immediately set out to make themselves useful by cleaning the house and preparing meals.

CHAPTER 61

PARIS, FEBRUARY 1945

There was a loud and intrusive knock on the door to the priest's living quarters before dawn one Wednesday morning on a frigid February day. The old father got out of bed. His body ached with arthritis, but he wrapped a blanket around his shoulders and opened the door.

"Are you Father Dupaul?"

"Of course! You know who I am, Jacques. How are you? And you, Pierre. You have grown a great deal since I last saw you." The old father smiled, recognizing two former alter boys from his church.

"We are police officers now, with the French police," Jacques said firmly. "And we have been sent by the Germans to make sure that you are not harboring any Jewish children."

"It has come to our attention that you are hiding Jews here." Pierre cleared his throat and coughed self-consciously.

"I see," Father Dupaul said, nodding. "Why don't you boys come on in? It's far too cold outside to stand in the doorway. You can both sit down, and I'll put on a pot of tea. Wouldn't that be nice? I would love to hear about your families. By the way, Pierre, how is your mother feeling? I haven't seen her since I visited your home after your father passed."

"She's doing all right. She gets lonely sometimes," Pierre said, swallowing hard. He lost the authoritative tone of voice that he'd had only moments earlier.

Jacques sat up very straight. "Father, this is very serious. I realize we are old friends. And that's why I am here because we are old friends. I must let you know that if you have any Jewish children living in the church orphanage, you must get rid of them quickly. Your life could depend upon it. I suggest you turn them in to me right now."

The old priest laughed. "Jacques," he said, shaking his head. "Jews? I don't know anything about all of this mad hatred of Jews. All I know is that I only have God's children here in this house. However, you have known me all of your life. So from what you know of me, did you think you were going to come here and scare me with Nazi threats? You should know that I work for a much bigger boss than Adolf Hitler." He let out a small laugh then continued, "You see, boys, I work for God," he said, pouring each of the boys a cup of hot tea. "Now, why don't we just enjoy this tea together, and you can tell me all about your families. How is your sister's new baby, Jacques? He's such a handsome little boy. Just like you were at his age. You see, Jacques, I still remember . . ."

CHAPTER 62

END OF FEBRUARY 1945

Two weeks later in the wee hours of the morning, a group of five young, robust Gestapo officers came to the church. They kicked the door, breaking the stained glass as they entered. Then one of them pulled out his pistol and shot the statue of Jesus that stood above the pulpit. They seemed to know exactly where the priest's sleeping quarters was located, and they headed directly there. Once they arrived, one of the Nazis urinated on the floor outside the door to the priest's sleeping room. The others laughed, then one of them yelled as he pounded on the door, "Open up, right now, old man. I know you are in there, you swine. You are hiding Jews somewhere in this church, which makes you an enemy of the Reich. Open."

Calmly, the priest opened the door. He stared at the puddle of urine on the ground. "Be careful. There seems to be a wet spot on the floor over there. I wouldn't want you boys to fall," he said without any sarcasm in his voice.

"Keep your lousy sense of humor to yourself, old man," the Nazi growled. "Do you have papers for each one of these orphans who you have here in this church?"

"Of course," said Father Dupaul.

"Produce those papers right now or suffer the consequences."

"I would be happy to, but they are not here in my bedroom. They are in my office," the priest said. "Sit down. Make yourselves comfortable, and I will go and get them for you."

"We'll go with you. You aren't going to have a chance to hide those Jews."

Meanwhile, Solomon had seen the Gestapo car arrive. He followed the Nazis, hiding in the shadows and staying far enough behind the group not to be seen. Solomon followed them all to the priest's office. Now he stood outside the door just around the corner where he was able to hear them.

"Come on, then. Follow me to my office, my sons," the priest said.

"I'm not your son," one of the Gestapo agents said. "I want papers for each child! Now! You're wasting my time."

The priest did not speak. He started walking toward his office.

"Move a little faster, or I'll kick you in your ass."

"I'm an old man. I'm going as fast as I can."

The Nazi glared at him, but he didn't kick the old priest. Once they arrived at the priest's office, Father Dupaul opened a cabinet and took out a pile of papers. He placed them in front of the Gestapo agent.

"These are the legitimate papers here for each child?"

"Of course," the priest said. The door to the office was open.

One of the older nuns, Sister Mary Agnus, must have heard the shots when the Gestapo agent shattered the statue of Jesus. And she came walking toward the priest's office, but before she got to the open door, she spotted Solomon hiding. Rushing over to him as fast as she could without running, Sister Mary Agnus grabbed Solomon's arm and put her finger over her lip to warn him to keep silent. She led him quickly away from the priest's office and down a long corridor, then they she removed an old rug and opened a trap-door in the floor. She motioned for him to follow her. He did as she asked. As they walked down a dark hallway, she whispered to Solomon, "I was looking everywhere for you. Thanks be to our Lord that I found you before they did."

At the end of the hallway, Solomon saw a group of children, but it was so dark that he could not see their faces.

"Sarah," Sister Mary Agnus called in a voice barely above a whisper, "I've brought your brother."

"Solomon!" Sarah yelled.

"You must be quiet," the nun said.

Solomon followed the sound of his sister's voice as he ran to her and took her into his arms. Then he sat down beside her. She hugged him tightly.

"The Nazis are in our church," the sister said firmly. "You must all stay down here and be very quiet. Father Dupaul built this secret hallway a little after the Nazi's first came into power. He planned on helping Jewish children as soon as he heard about the way the Nazi's were treating the Jews. He thought that there might come a time when they would need to be hidden. And it seems he was right. But don't you worry. No one else knows that this underground area exists but me and him. So you will all be safe here. There is a chamber pot in the corner of the room. Stay together, and whatever you do, don't leave this room. I will return with food for you later."

Sarah and two of the other little girls started to cry. "But it's dark in here," the other little girl said. "I'm afraid of the dark."

"Don't be afraid," the nun said. "Everything will be all right. God is here with you. I must leave you for now, but I will be back."

At first Sarah wept so hard that her small slender body shook. Solomon gently patted her head and shoulders and continued to reassure her that everything would be all right even though he wasn't confident in his words. Finally, Sarah cried herself to sleep. As Solomon sat with his back against the wall and his sister's head resting peacefully on his lap in the dark room under the church, his mind began to race with thoughts. *I can't believe there were so many other Jewish children at this orphanage. I never knew. But Father Dupaul knew. He knew all along. What a good soul he is. I hope the Nazis haven't taken him. If they have taken him, will he be all right? Will we be all right —Sarah, me, the rest of these children? That's a ridiculous question. Of course, the damn Nazis will kill the old priest, and if they find us they'll kill all of us too. I don't know if the rest of these children realize it, but any minute the Gestapo could find out about where we are and come rushing in here and . . .*

He imagined Sarah being pulled away from him by a Gestapo agent. *She would scream, that was for certain, and it would break my heart that I would be powerless to protect her against the guns.* Solomon bit his lower lip and felt a shiver run up his spine. *But there is also another frightening possibility.* He wondered if any of the other children had even considered this horrific possibility. What if the Germans have taken poor Sister Mary Agnus and Father Dupaul away? *No one else knows that we are here. We will starve to death down here, or we are going have to try to find our way out, and then what? And then Sarah and I will have to find a way back to the forest without papers or money. It's a long way from France to Poland. I don't know what I am going to do . . .*

Solomon could not determine how many hours had passed. He drifted in and out of sleep. Sarah still lay with her head on his lap. His limbs tingled from lack of movement. His fingers and toes were so cold that he felt that they were going to fall off. None of the children had spoken for hours. Although Solomon didn't want to move his sister because he didn't want to risk her crying again, he had to. His body ached so badly. Gently, he stretched his legs out in front of him as Sarah stirred.

"Solomon?"

"Yes, it's me. I'm here with you, Sarah." He stroked her head again damning himself for having to wake her.

"Where are we?" she asked as she awakened in the blackness of that basement room.

"Solomon? Solomon?" she said, her voice filled with fear. "Is that you? Did you say you're here or did I dream it?"

"Yes, it's me, your brother, Sarah. I'm right here. You're not alone. I'm with you."

She grabbed his hand and squeezed it. "Are we still underground?"

"We are. We're waiting for Sister Mary Agnus to return."

"I have a headache. I don't feel good, and I'm hungry too."

"I know. Sister Mary Agnus will be back soon. She'll bring us food. Try to go back to sleep."

"I don't like it here. It's cold and it's dark. And I think there might be monsters . . ."

"If there are any monsters, I'll kill them. I promise. Try to sleep. It's best if you sleep," he said, thinking that the only monsters were the real live Nazis who were living upstairs in the light. His stomach ached with hunger; his eyes had adjusted to the darkness enough for him to see that the other children were huddled together to keep warm.

Sarah cuddled up to him. He could hear her sucking her thumb. Usually he would take her thumb out of her mouth when she started to do this, but he didn't. He knew she needed to do everything possible to comfort herself. And he wished that he could find comfort in something so simple. Gently he rocked his body back and forth to encourage her to fall back to sleep.

"Sing to me," she said. "Sing me the Yiddish lullaby Mama used to sing to us."

"Sarah . . ." he said.

"Please, Sol, please . . ."

He began to sing softly, but the others heard him, and many joined in. Their voices were barely above a whisper. They were the voices of desperate and lonely children who were fighting demons that they were too young to understand.

CHAPTER 63

I<small>T</small> <small>MIGHT HAVE BEEN ANOTHER DAY, IT MIGHT HAVE BEEN TWO,</small>
before Solomon was awakened by the opening of the door. He saw
the figures of Father Dupaul and Sister Mary Agnus enter. They
carried a single lit candle.

"Before we begin to explain everything that is happening, let me
give all of you some food, water, and blankets," the priest said.

Sister Mary Agnus distributed all that they had brought. Sarah
began to eat. But even though he was starving, Solomon couldn't eat
or drink: he was waiting to hear their fate.

"Please . . . eat, drink," Sister Mary Agnus said.

"Children," the priest began, "I am so very sorry that we have
been forced to keep you down here in the darkness and in the cold
without food or water. It's my fault. I should have had better plans
in place before this all happened. I should have had food, blankets,
and water down here . . ." The old priest's voice cracked. Solomon
could not see his face, but from the sound of the father's voice,
Solomon was sure the priest was crying.

"What the good father is trying to say is that he was arrested and
detained. He was just released a few hours ago. The Nazis were
here in the church all night. They went through everything. But they

found nothing. They do not know of your existence. The other children have been told not to ever mention having known you. I have put my trust in God that this will not be too great a task for the young ones," Sister Mary Agnus said.

Father Dupaul cleared his throat. "I am afraid that you will have to stay down here for a while. At least until the suspicion clears."

A little boy named Michael let out a scream. "No, I can't stay down here. I hate it here. I have always been terrified of the dark. And it's so dark down here."

"I am so sorry, Michael," Father Dupaul said, "but you must stay down here for now. Talk to God when you are afraid. He is always with you."

Michael whimpered.

"Now, this is also important that you are very quiet at all times. Just in case anyone is upstairs, you must not scream, shout, or fight. You can speak to each other, but you must keep your voices down."

"I've brought another chamber pot," Sister Mary Agnus said, "I'll bring a fresh one each morning, and I'll take the other one away."

"How long do you think we'll be here?" Solomon asked.

"I don't know, Solomon. I wish I had an answer," the priest said. "If I leave you in charge of a couple of candles I know I can trust you to use them sparingly."

"Yes, Father, you can," Solomon said. "I will only light them when it's necessary."

"I will bring you a Bible and some Bible story books tomorrow when we come back," Sister Mary Agnus said. "Will you read to the others, Solomon?"

"Yes, I will light the candles so I can read," he said even though he hated to read.

CHAPTER 64

THE DARKNESS LOOMED OVER THE CHILDREN, AND EVEN THOUGH their eyes adjusted they became depressed. Every day either Father Dupaul or Sister Mary Agnus brought them as much food as they could scrounge up. Everyone, including Solomon, was always hungry. Each night Solomon lit one of the candles and read a single Bible story aloud. He read the story of Joseph and his wicked brothers. In the middle of the story he stopped and told the children to close their eyes and imagine what Joseph's coat looked like.

"What do you see? What does Joseph's coat look like?" he asked them.

For several minutes the children came alive. They offered their own versions of the coat.

"You see, when you closed your eyes, your imagination took over. So don't be afraid of the dark because you can still see colors in the darkness," Solomon said.

That night after the candle was extinguished, the children all discussed things they'd once seen: a black-and-white puppy, a completely lit menorah on the eighth day of Hanukkah, the performance of a dance troupe with colorful costumes. Each child offered vivid descriptions of them while the others used their imaginations to see everything come alive within their minds.

Then on another night Solomon read the story of Jonah and the whale.

"I'll bet it was as dark inside the whale's belly as it is down here," one of the boys said.

"Yes, I think it probably was. And God was watching over Jonah, wasn't he? When Jonah prayed to God for help, God made the big whale vomit so that Jonah would come back out of its mouth," Solomon offered, sounding far older than his ten years.

"Yes, and he is watching over us, isn't he, Solomon?" Sarah asked.

"Yes, I believe that he is," Solomon said.

"But Jonah went against God's wishes, and that was why he ended up in that whale's belly," one of the older girls said. "What did we do? How did we anger God so much that he let the Nazis do this to us? Why did God let the Nazis kill our families and trap us in this dark basement?"

Solomon shrugged his shoulders. "I don't know. I wish I had answers for you, but I don't."

Another boy who was almost fourteen said, " All I can tell you is that we have to pray. We have to pray together that God destroys the Nazis and we are set free."

"God did send us Father Dupaul and all of the sisters to help us. So he is doing what he can," another child offered.

"God is all powerful. He could stop this anytime he wants to, but he doesn't. He let my parents die. I saw them die. A Nazi beat my mother up with a big stick. He hit her in the head until her face disappeared, and then all this terrible stuff came out and her head was all crushed," another little girl said.

"All right, all right. Now let's not go on about this. Everyone is getting upset, and there are no answers to these questions. These are terrible things that have been done to us, but it doesn't help us to waste our candlelight time talking about them. It only hurts. So why don't we talk about whales. Has anyone here ever seen a picture of a whale?" Solomon asked.

The children began to talk about whales, and then they talked about sharks. They were so animated and enjoying the discussion so much that Solomon allowed the candle to burn for what he figured to be at least another full half hour. Then he said, "All right, everyone, let's get some sleep. Tomorrow we'll read the story of Job, and perhaps that will help us to keep our faith." He blew out the candle and lay down with Sarah at his side. *I never had much faith in God before. I heard all these stories as a child, but they had no meaning for me then. I don't even understand how I found faith. Maybe it's because it's all I have left. But in my heart, for some reason, I am certain that God will not abandon us.*

CHAPTER 65

POLAND, APRIL 1945

Once the cold weather broke and spring was on her way, Tytus was busy planting. But at night after dinner he and Dyta had begun to take long walks alone together. And by the middle of April, Dyta was no longer sharing a room with Ewa. Dyta and Tytus had become lovers and she slept in his bed. He had given her complete access to all of his wife's things, which she generously shared with Ewa.

It was not that Ewa was ungrateful for the clean undergarments and the dresses; she was very grateful, but she couldn't help but wonder how this man was able to give these things to Dyta and not be worried about what his wife would do when she returned. Ewa tried to put these thoughts out of her mind, telling herself that it was none of her business. But she was haunted by questions, and finally one day when Tytus was out working on the land and Ewa and Dyta were busy chopping vegetables for the noonday meal, Ewa asked Dyta, "Have you ever wondered what is going to happen when Tytus's wife returns?"

Dyta looked up at Ewa. She laid the knife down on the cutting board next to the small squares of potatoes she'd been chopping.

Then she said in a slow, deliberate voice, "I doubt she will ever be back."

"What do you mean?"

"If I tell you something, a secret, you can't tell Tytus that I told you."

"Tell me what?" Ewa said.

"Do you like Tytus?" Dyta asked.

"Of course I do. He is a good person. He has been very kind to us, and generous too," Ewa said.

"What I am about to tell you might color your opinion of him for many reasons."

"Go on, tell me."

Dyta looked into her friend's eyes, then she began, "As you know, Tytus was married."

"Yes, I thought he was still married."

"From what he tells me his wife was considered quite the town beauty. She was blonde, and sweet, and he adored her. But she thought she was too good for him. And"—she hesitated for a moment—"she did something that shamed him. She had an affair with a Jewish accountant. He hated her for it, but he didn't throw her out. He tried to break up the affair, that was until she got pregnant. Once she did, he'd had enough. He told her she had to leave. He said he wanted a divorce. But he was hurt, and then to make matters even worse, she moved in with the Jew. The neighbors were talking. Tytus's family was embarrassed. He hated her, but there was nothing he could do. He tried to come up with money for a lawyer for the divorce, but he was afraid that the Jew would take his farm. You know how they are. They steal everything. He was afraid.

But then when the Nazis came into Poland and the Jews were being rounded up, his wife had the audacity to come to Tytus and ask him for help. By that time she had given birth to a little boy who was half Jewish. Tytus still loved her, and because he hoped he could win her back, he took them all in. He hid them in the cellar, and he watched as the Nazis and the rest of the world turned its back on the Jews. Of course, and for good reason, he hated the man who had stolen his wife, and now that the Jew was in trouble, he thought his wife would come back to him. He begged her, even promised her that he would adopt her half-Jewish child and tell the world that it was his, but she refused him. So he went to the Nazis and turned them all in. A few months later, he learned that they'd all been killed."

Ewa could not speak; it felt like a stone was lodged in her throat. *I am a Jew and Dyta doesn't know it. She thinks I am Sylwia, not Ewa. If she knew I was a Jew would she feel differently about me? It hurts to think that she might*, she thought. *Dyta loves Tytus and he hates Jews. I know he has been kind to me. I can't trust him or Dyta. If they ever learned the truth about me . . .*

"You look like you have seen a ghost," Dyta said. "If you're worried about him ever turning us in, don't worry. He won't. After all, the man was a Jew and the child a half Jew. His wife was a cheating good-for-nothing sow who was soiled from laying with a Jew. She brought shame upon his good name. We are not filth like that. We are not vermin. He would never turn on us."

Ewa nodded and mustered a quick smile. Dyta patted her on the back. Ewa tried to pretend that she was all right, but her hand was unsteady as she chopped the carrots. Now she knew why Tytus was so generous with his wife's belongings. Now she had the answers to all of her questions. Everything made sense, but the answers had unnerved her.

CHAPTER 66

Every other week, Tytus made a trip into town for supplies. He was getting ready to leave for his weekly trip when Ewa overheard Tytus and Dyta talking in the bedroom while she was preparing breakfast.

"I wish I could take you with me," he said. "I know how much you would enjoy it."

"I am afraid. It's safe here on the farm, and I've been through so much," Dyta answered. "I don't want to risk anyone asking questions."

"I know, but wouldn't it be nice if we could go into town and have a quick meal or a cup of coffee at a restaurant? I would so love to show you off."

"I would love to go. But it's unsafe. I am happy to be here where I can breathe."

"I agree. But some day . . ."

"Yes, we can only hope."

When Tytus returned from his trip to town that night he was exuberant. He came into the house and called out, "Dyta, Sylwia, come in here." Once they were both in the living room he said, "I have good news. It looks like the end of the war is very close, and soon the Nazis will be nothing but an ugly memory."

Ewa watched him as he walked over to Dyta and kissed her. He was a strange man. In some ways a good man and in many, a bad one.

"I don't know if Dyta told you, but my wife recently passed away. She caught her sister's illness. So as soon as the war is over, Dyta and I plan to marry."

"No, she never mentioned your wife to me," Ewa lied.

"Yes, it happened a few months ago."

"I'm sorry."

Tytus nodded. "Thank you. But my wife and I had our differences. Anyway, you will attend our wedding?"

"Of c-course," Ewa said.

CHAPTER 67

Adolf Hitler found that he'd backed himself into a corner. His lust for power had cost him dearly, and now he knew for certain that Germany would lose the war. Distraught and addicted to narcotics, he decided to go down into his underground bunker and contemplate his options. He took his sweetheart, Eva Braun; Joseph Goebbels, his minister of propaganda; Joseph's wife, Magda, and their six young children along with him.

Then on April 30, 1945, just ten days after his fifty-sixth birthday, Adolf Hitler and Eva Braun Hitler, his newly married wife of one day, committed suicide.

First the Goebbels murdered their six children, and then Magda and Joseph killed themselves.

After Adolf and Eva Hitler were dead, Feldwebel Fritz Tornow who was Hitler's dog handler, gathered all the dogs that had belonged to Hitler into the yard. Then he systematically shot them.

On the seventh day of May 1945, Germany officially surrendered.

CHAPTER 68

When the news that Germany was losing the war reached Hedy and Ludwig, they left Poland and returned home to Berlin. Even though it seemed inevitable that Hitler's reign was coming to a close, Hedy and Ludwig still held out hope that somehow Hitler would turn things around. However, after the führer's suicide became public knowledge they knew that the Third Reich would never see the thousand-year-reign that Hitler had promised. They were lost, frightened. Although neither of them voiced their concerns, they were both quite certain that the Allies would not treat the Germans kindly. Especially the Russians. They found themselves arguing more often but at the same time clinging to each other, terrified as the Russian army marched into Berlin.

It was not long before the streets were filled with Russian uniforms. Hedy and Ludwig tried to pretend they were just regular German citizens who had not been involved with the Nazi Party. However, the Russian army was cruel. They did not take kindly to any Germans, Nazis or not. Russia had just been through a long, hard battle against Germany, and many of the Russian soldiers who were now stationed in Berlin had lost family and friends in the war.

So they hated the Germans, and they took their anger out on the German people every chance they got.

When Hedy first returned to Berlin she went to see her mother who told her that her beloved father had been killed in a bombing. Without him she was lost. All of her confidence was gone. She and Ludwig moved into the apartment with her mother, and she hung on to Ludwig tightly. He and her mother were all she had left of her life before Germany lost the war. The apartment where they lived was missing walls leaving the front of the building open and exposed to the outside. There was no privacy at all.

Hedy and Ludwig, along with the rest of the Germans in Berlin, found themselves at the mercy of the Russian soldiers who had control of all the food and housing. Not only that, but the bombings had left Berlin in shambles with rubble and broken buildings as far as the eye could see. The Germans were responsible for cleaning up the city. If they wanted to eat, Hedy, Ludwig, and Hedy's mother, even though she was old and sick, were expected to get out and work.

Hedy went into town one afternoon in order to get her hands on any extra food that was available and to offer her help in the cleanup efforts.

It was painful for Hedy to see what had become of the places she'd known as a child. Most of them lay in ruins. She felt overcome with sadness. *Everything has gone wrong. Hitler failed us. How could this have happened? He'd offered Germany such promise. We were respected and feared instead of treated like the losers of the First World War. We had pride in our country and in ourselves. And now . . .*

Her stomach rumbled. She put her hand on her belly to quiet it. *We are given so little to eat,* she thought as she looked around shaking her head. The streets of her beloved city were filled not only with soldiers but with ragged refugees of all kinds, German soldiers returning in defeat, orphaned children who had lost their families in the bombings. There were women in tight dresses willing to trade their self-respect for a piece of bread. And she was appalled to see that some of the refugees wandering the streets were displaced Jews who wore Stars of David on their filthy uniforms. Their bones jutted out of their faces sharp as razor blades. Their eyes were deep, dark canyons that she dared not stare into, lest she fall in headfirst and never find her way back to sanity.

Walking a little farther, she noticed the body of a Jew with a bald head, wearing a gray-striped uniform with a Star of David, laying dead on the side of the street. The eyes were wide open, and the mouth of the corpse formed a silent scream as if it had died crying out in horror. *I can't tell if that is a man or a woman, but whatever it was, I am fairly certain that it's dead. It looks so frightening. The Jews are such terrifying people; they look like monsters: demons, walking corpses. And I can just imagine the disease these filthy vermin are spreading throughout the city.*

That afternoon, Hedy worked for over six hours cleaning rubble to receive half a loaf of bread.

One afternoon, Mrs. Klingerman and Hedy's mother were sitting at the kitchen table in Hedy's mother's apartment. Hedy came into the kitchen to pour herself a cup of tea. "Hello, Mrs. Klingerman," she said.

"Hello, Hedy. Have you found work yet?"

"No, but I am still looking. If you hear of anything, please let me know."

"Of course I will," Mrs. Klingerman said as she sipped her tea. Then she added, "Listen to me, Hedy; this is important. I don't know how to say this gently, so I will just tell you what I have to say. My niece Ingrid was raped by the Russians. She is so distraught that she tried to kill herself. Her mother says she sits in a chair all day now and doesn't talk. She hardly eats. It's a dangerous world out there. I know it's none of my business, but you'd better be careful, Hedy. You wander the streets too much. Instead of going out there, you should send Ludwig out to look for food."

A week later, when they had gone through all of their weekly rations, Hedy decided to take her neighbor's advice, so she sent Ludwig out to see if he could find a way to get his hands on some extra food. He was gone for over an hour, but Ludwig returned empty handed. He always seemed to return empty handed. Now whenever she looked at him, she was disgusted. Her father had been right about him. Ludwig was a failure. He'd failed her in so many ways. She had lost all faith in him. But even though she had begun to hate him, she could not let him go. He was all she had left. She looked at him with revulsion in her eyes because it was clear to her she that she could not depend on him. If they were to survive, she must depend on herself. So even though she had been hearing more and more rumors about how unsafe it was becoming for a woman to go out on the streets alone, she went anyway.

It was late spring but still chilly. Hedy pulled her scarf tighter around her neck. Women gathered together in groups cleaning up the rubble. Her heart sank as she watched them. The glory of the Reich was over. She was hungry, so hungry. And her hunger made her bold. When she saw two Russian soldiers standing in front of a tavern, she approached them. She'd heard of German women taking Russian soldiers as lovers in exchange for the comforts that they might provide. The idea was appalling to her, but . . . she was so hungry.

"Hello," Hedy said, smiling at one of the Russians, but her lip was quivering with fear.

"What have we here? It looks like a little German Fräulein to me," the other soldier said, licking his lips.

"How are you today, Nazi girl?"

She felt a lightning bolt of fear shoot through her. Every instinct in her body told her that this was not going to end well. The skin on her neck tingled and the hair stood on end. Her legs trembled. She felt her stomach turn.

"I'm not a Nazi. I was just a secretary, not political at all during the war," Hedy said, but her voice was shaking, and every instinct told her that she should run. She must get away as fast as she could. A tremor of terror rushed through her, and then without another word Hedy began to run. She ran as fast as she could, but she was not fast enough. The soldiers were upon her within minutes. She screamed, but no one came to her rescue. One of them held her while the other one ripped her dress off and then her undergarments. The two of them took turns with her. When it was over, she lay strangled to death on the street in a pool of her own blood.

Several hours passed, and it began to grow dark outside before

Ludwig began to wonder what had happened to Hedy. He hated leaving the apartment. Not that it was a nice place, but the world outside was much more frightening. He considered waiting a little longer, but in a few hours, it would be night. Forcing himself to get up from the sofa, he stuffed his gun into his back pocket and put on his coat. Then he went outside.

It didn't take long before Ludwig was approached by an old woman. It was Mrs. Klingerman. He'd met her before. He knew she lived in the apartment directly upstairs from them. She ran up and grabbed his sleeve. Her body was shaking as she held on to his coat. Then she told him what had happened to Hedy.

"Are you sure? Did you see it happen?" Ludwig asked. He didn't want to believe it.

"I did. I saw it all. But I couldn't do anything. I was afraid. I am an old woman. What can an old woman do?"

"W-where is she?" Ludwig stuttered.

"She's still in the street. Right down there." Mrs. Klingerman pointed. "And she's naked. It's shameful, Ludwig," she said.

Ludwig didn't stop to answer the old woman. Instead, he ran toward the scene. There she was, just as Mrs. Klingerman had described. Her lifeless body lay shameful and naked. He suddenly felt overcome by fear. Would he be punished for all the terrible things he'd done and witnessed during the war? He bent down to touch her face. *Hedy wasn't the best girlfriend. I can't say we had a wonderful relationship or even that I truly loved her. But she was a good German girl, and she did deserve better than to be lying naked in a pool of blood like a filthy Jew.* With trembling hands, he took off his coat and lay it over her to cover her nakedness. He felt like he might vomit. So he got up and looked away. There was nothing more he could do. *Was there?* Ludwig began to walk back toward his apartment with his head bowed, just as a group of Russian soldiers approached him.

"What is that bulge in your pocket?" one of them asked.

Ludwig shook his head.

"It looks like the Kraut has a gun. Do you have a gun, Nazi?"

Ludwig tried to back away, but two of the Russians caught him by the arms. One of them took the gun out of his back pocket and hit Ludwig on the head with it. He fell to the ground. The others kicked him in the belly and chest until blood ran from his lips. *How did things ever get this bad for Germans? All we were trying to do was make this world a better place* . . . Ludwig thought right before he took his last breath.

CHAPTER 69

POLAND, SUMMER 1947

It took two years for Tytus and Dyta to say their marriage vows in a small civil ceremony in town. Lack of funds to get to France, coupled with the chaos in the cities, kept Ewa from leaving the farm. Since she'd learned the truth about Tytus hating Jews, she was cautious of him. Yet she had to admit he had always treated her with kindness and generosity. A kindness she knew he would have forsaken had he learned she was a Jew.

She yearned to go to France and collect the children, but It was easy to stay on the farm. She had a roof over her head and did not suffer the bitter cold of being outside during the winter. There was plenty to eat, so she no longer knew the misery of hunger. And Tytus made it clear that she was welcome to stay as long as she liked. However, Sarah and Solomon haunted her dreams. And Ewa knew she needed to find work in order to save enough money to find a place and bring them back from France to live with her.

But there was another reason she hadn't gone back to the orphanage yet. A secret reason that she hid even from herself. Ewa was afraid of what she might find in France. After all, anything could have happened to the children. They might be there waiting, and then again . . . they might not. She couldn't bear to think of the possibilities.

But the children were always on her mind. And she knew she must face the inevitable whatever it might be. So she told Tytus and Dyta that she needed to go to France and see if she could find the children.

"You can bring them back here with you and stay here if you'd like. I know you and Dyta are best friends, and she would love to have you stay, wouldn't you, Dyta?" Tytus offered.

"Of course I would."

"I might have to do that. I am not sure what I am going to do once I find the children, but it is a very kind offer."

"Well, like I said, you are welcome here. Didn't you say you had a boy? How old is he now?"

"I think he should be about fifteen, and the girl would be around ten."

"A fifteen-year-old boy would be a big help to me on the farm."

"Yes, and he is good boy. A smart boy. I am not sure what I am going find when I get to France. And we just might come back here. I can't say for certain. The truth is, I am hoping I find them alive. The war did a lot of things to a lot of people. Anything could have happened to them."

"Would you like me to go with you, Sylwia? I will. I want to be there in case you need me. You know what I mean . . ." Dyta said.

"Don't even say it, dear." Tytus took Dyta's hand. "Of course, Sylwia's children are fine. But if you want us to go with you, I will put my work aside and go with you too," Tytus said.

"No, no need. You are both so wonderful, so kind, such good friends. I will never forget you, no matter what happens. But I must go alone."

"Do you have any money or valuables to sell?" Tytus asked.

"Nothing," Ewa said. "I'm thinking about going into the city and trying to get work so I can afford train fare to France."

Tytus looked at his wife. "Dyta, may I speak to you for a few minutes?"

She nodded, and the two of them left the room. They went into their bedroom leaving Ewa at the kitchen table with a cup of weak tea. When they returned Dyta was smiling. "It's not much," she said, handing Ewa a small pile of bills, "but it's all we can spare. Tytus and I decided to give you this to help you get to France to find your children."

Tears burned the backs of Ewa's eyes. She was so touched by this kind gesture that she could not speak. And besides that, she felt guilty for having lied to her friends. *How can I love them and hate what they stand for at the same time?* she thought. *They are such good people, yet they hate the Jewish people. I know it's only because they were raised that way, and they don't know any Jews. They grew up to believe that Jews were evil. Yet not knowing I was Jewish, they became like family to me. What do I say? What do I do? Do I continue this lie, or tell them the truth?*

"Slywia, are you all right?" Dyta asked.

"I'm just so touched by this," Ewa said as tears ran down her cheeks. She felt her mouth open to tell them the truth. She felt the words form in the back of her throat, words with the power to change everything. Words that might cause the love her friends felt for her to disintegrate: *I am a Jew.* But she did not utter a sound. She swallowed her secret. Instead, she took Dyta in her arms and held her tightly. Then she looked into Tytus's eyes and then back at Dyta and whispered, "Thank you, my dear friends. Thank you."

The following day, Ewa packed her bags and got ready to set out for France. Dyta and Ewa said a tearful goodbye at the farmhouse. They hugged tightly. "Go and get your children, then come back, and live here forever," Dyta said. "Tytus and I are hoping for the best."

"I know. I can't tell you how much you have meant to me over these years, Dyta. You've been a good friend. And I am so happy you and Tytus found each other. If I don't return, please know I love you both."

They hugged again, and Dyta's tears wet the collar of Ewa's blouse. Then Tytus came from the barn. He was sitting on top of the wagon, which he'd hitched up to his old horse.

Again, the two women hugged. Harder this time. Stronger this time. "If we don't see each other again, I love you, Slywia."

"I love you too."

Ewa climbed up into the wagon. Tytus cracked the whip in the air above the horse once, and they began their journey into town.

CHAPTER 70

EWA TOOK THE NEXT TRAIN INTO FRANCE. SHE ARRIVED AT THE church at dusk the following day. Memories of the last time she'd seen Gunther alive flooded her senses. She remembered the café, the bitter taste of the ersatz coffee, the softness of his lips the last time she'd kissed him. When she closed her eyes she could hear his voice, and her heart ached. Opening the large wooden door to the church, she recalled the day she'd left the children in this quiet house of God with the beautiful stained-glass windows and polished wooden floors. It had been five years. Who were Sarah and Solomon today? More importantly, were they still here? Where they still alive?

The old priest came out of a confessional with his head bowed. He walked slightly bent over and with a limp, but when he looked up and his eyes met Ewa's, a glow of light came over his face and he smiled.

"Father Dupaul," she said. Her eyes burned with tears. Ewa looked at the priest. He was not as she remembered him. He had been a full-bodied man, heavyset, and jovial. But the man who stood here before her was painfully thin. His face was wrinkled with deep lines of worry, but the light that she remembered shining from his eyes remained unchanged.

"Yes, Mother, it's me. The children and I have been waiting for you." He nodded.

"Sarah and Solomon are still here!" Ewa breathed a sigh of relief.

"They are, and they are doing quite well. However, they have missed you."

"I am not their mother. I lied to you. I am sorry. I am not their real mother, but I was their guardian. Can you forgive me?"

"Of course I forgive you. And you were not only their guardian, but you have been a guardian angel." He smiled. "By the way, child, what is your name?"

"Ewa."

He nodded and smiled. "Follow me; you can wait in my office. Meanwhile, I'll send Sister Mary Francis to fetch the children for you," he said. "And by the way, do you and the children have a place to go?"

"I'm not sure, Father. I do have a place. I just don't know if it is the best place to take the children."

"I see. Well, you could stay here if you would like. Or . . . I have a friend in the Jewish Joint Committee who might be able to help you find a place to stay at one of the DP camps where you could register to see if you can find any of your friends or relatives."

"You know we are Jewish? Did the children tell you?"

He let out a soft laugh and his blue eyes sparkled. "I always knew," he said.

"And you helped us anyway? I didn't think priests cared about Jews."

"Every man, priest or otherwise, must decide what he believes. I knew that I could not be a man of God and stand by and watch any of God's children be treated the way the Nazis were treating the Jews."

"What about the old myth that the Jews killed Jesus?"

"Sarah and Solomon were just two young souls lost and alone. They weren't responsible for killing Jesus . . ."

Ewa heard footsteps coming down the corridor and her heart raced. *Will they be happy to see me? Will they be angry at me for leaving them? Can they forgive me?*

"Ewa?" Sarah said as she ran into Ewa's arms. Solomon stood back watching.

"Look at you! You've grown up," Ewa said as she looked at the pretty dark-haired girl with her shy smile.

"I'm ten," Sarah said. She hesitated then she added, "I missed you so much."

"Oh, I missed you both more than I can ever say."

"What took you so long to come back?" Solomon asked, a note of sarcasm in his voice. He'd grown into a tall, big boned, and muscular boy who had just turned fifteen, with dark, wavy hair and deep-set dark eyes.

"I came as soon as I could." Ewa felt a pang of guilt run through her. *I could have come earlier. I should have found a way after the war. But it took me some time to find the courage.*

"Five years? That was as soon as you could?"

"Solomon, please know that I have been through a lot too. I know this must have been hard on you . . ."

"No, not at all. Father Dupaul was wonderful. He took care of us. He even hid us when the Nazis came searching the church for little Jewish orphans. They almost killed him. But he stood up to them. He's a wonderful man. No, it wasn't bad staying here at the orphanage. But we didn't know what happened to you. We thought you died."

"I know. I'm sorry. I was in a work camp, a prisoner of the Nazis. I was raising rabbits."

"Rabbits?" Sarah asked, her face lighting up.

"Yes," Ewa nodded. "Strange, I know, but yes. I was actually very fortunate to have that job. It's a long, drawn-out story. Someday I'll tell you all about it."

"Where's Gunther? Is he outside?" Solomon asked, not looking into her eyes. He wrapped his arms around his chest, refusing to give in to his need to hug her and weep in her arms.

"He's dead," she said somberly. "I'm sorry."

"Are you sure?" Solomon asked.

She nodded.

Solomon swallowed hard. His Adam's apple bobbed. But he didn't speak.

"Oh, Ewa . . ." Sarah said, "that's horrible."

Ewa looked at the children. After a few awkward moments of silence, she turned to Father Dupaul and said, "I would like to meet with your friend from the Jewish Joint Committee." She'd decided it was best not to take the children back to the farm.

"Very well. But it's late. You can spend the night here at the church, and in the morning I'll contact him. His name is Abel Fine."

CHAPTER 71

It took Abel Fine three days to return Father Dupaul's call. But when he did, he agreed to help Ewa and the children in any way he could.

"You are welcome to stay here at the church as long as you like, but Mr. Fine suggested that the three of you go to a DP camp that has been established in the American Zone in Germany. Abel is there. He is helping people restart their lives, and he says he will help you search for friends and family who might have survived," the old priest said.

"What is a DP camp?" Ewa asked.

"Displaced Persons. The Nazis left many, many people without anywhere to go: homeless, orphaned, and alone. These camps have been set up to help those in need find a way back to living as normal a life as possible."

"Oh, Father Dupaul." Ewa sighed. "This is so kind of you . . . but how will we get there?"

"I can help you. You see, my child, it's not kindness. It is my responsibility as a human being."

CHAPTER 72

ABEL FINE WAS AN OLDER MAN. HE WAS SHORT WITH DARK, COARSE hair, a muddy complexion, a large brown wart on his chin, and a warm smile. His eyes were filled with compassion as he helped Ewa search the Red Cross registers for familiar names. They found none. After they finished, Abel added Ewa, Solomon, and Sarah to the unorganized lists of survivors. Then he helped the three of them find a room in the DP camp. They were escorted to a small hut which had been divided into ten small rooms each housing at least two people. There were very few complete families at the camp. Most people were strangers who had come together after the war and after the loss of all of their loved ones.

Ewa heard that there were former Nazis and Jew haters hiding among the survivors in the DP camp, but she didn't meet any of them. Food was still scarce, but it far more plentiful than it had been in the Nazi camps. And although the displaced persons had suffered greatly, there was the air of promise in the camp. Troops of actors offered performances. Musicians gave concerts. Comedians and mimes showcased their talents. Ewa and the children attended most of these events with excited anticipation. And as Ewa watched the

Jewish performers, she couldn't help but wonder why Germany would want to deny the world such wonderful talent.

There were political parties in the DP camp too, mostly socialist and Zionist. Then one day Ewa was on her way back from dropping the children off at school when she passed the center of town. There on a makeshift stage with a crowd gathered around him, stood a young handsome man with curly, black hair. His passion was contagious as he spoke to the group about the formation of a Jewish state called Eretz Israel. Ewa was swept away.

"A Jewish state," he said. "A land where our children will no longer have to live in fear because they are Jews." Ewa listened. She was late getting home, but she couldn't move. She had to hear more.

"Come train with us; prepare yourselves to live on a kibbutz," the handsome man said. Then he continued, "You have no money? I know. You have no home? I know. Your family is gone? Come with us. Come to Eretz Israel. You will not need money. In a kibbutz, everyone works together. Everyone lives together; everyone eats together. And you are a part of a family . . . a family of your own people. A family of people whose ancestors suffered as yours did. A people whose blood runs through your veins. Your people . . . the Jews."

"But there is no Eretz Israel. The land you are speaking of is Palestine. A boat was already sent there. It was filled with Jews. They sent it back," some man called out from the crowd. "How do you know there will ever be an Eretz Israel, a homeland for the Jewish people?"

"Mark my words; there will be! Join us and be ready."

Ewa's heart swelled. And at that moment she became a Zionist. And from then on she began to prepare herself and the children to live on a kibbutz in Eretz Israel.

CHAPTER 73

1948

On the sun-filled afternoon of May 14 in the year 1948, Israel was proclaimed the first Jewish state in two thousand years with David Ben-Gurion as her first prime minister.

And so . . . they came! These were the survivors. They were alive in spite of the Nazis' relentless attempts to annihilate them. God had been with them as they sprung from the jaws of death. They were left penniless; their homes had been stolen. Their families had been murdered. By all rights they should have been paralyzed by depression. But instead they turned their faces to God, to the sun, and they came! Limping bags of bones they were, their bodies broken by starvation, some altered forever by sadistic experiments, and many crippled by disease. Most came alone. Some came with their new spouses who they'd met and married in the DP camps. Some carried newborn infants in their arms. Many were lost and bewildered, unsure of what they would find at the end of their voyage into the desert so far away from everything they knew. Still, regardless of their age, regardless of their condition, they boarded boats and sailed to the land of their forefathers: Israel! The homeland of the Jews!

They came . . .

Tzena, Tzena, Tzena, Tzena come into the fields and we'll begin to
work the land
   Tzena, Tzena join the celebration
   There'll be people there from every nation
   Dawn will find us laughing in the sunlight
   Dancing in the city square
   Tzena, Tzena building a new nation . . .
   By Issachar Miron and Yechiel Chagiz

CHAPTER 74

New York City, Manhattan, The Diamond District 1956

Benjamin Rabinowitz turned the key in his mailbox. He'd just returned from work, tired. It had been a long day. Cutting diamonds and precious stones was tedious work. His eyes burned; he rubbed them hard and then pulled a stack of envelopes out of the mailbox which had been built into the wall in the front hallway of the building where he lived. He put the letters into his back pants pocket and began walking up the three flights of stairs to his apartment. He hated this job. But his Hasidic bosses and their friends from the Hasidic temple had been so kind to him when he needed legal help that he felt that he could not easily quit this job. It was hard on his body. But he owed them all so much. When he was arrested for killing a woman who had been a guard at the concentration camp where his wife died, the entire Hasidic community had come together and gathered enough money to get him a good lawyer.

The lawyer showed the jury that the woman was a monster. She had pretended to be a Jewish concentration camp survivor when she came into the jewelry shop where Ben worked, to sell some diamonds. The woman claimed that the stones had been her mother's. At the time, Ben who was a concentration camp survivor, had been so lonely that he'd taken her out for dinner. They dated for a while, and Ben found himself falling for her. However, when he learned that she was a guard at a concentration camp, and she was responsible for his wife's murder, he lost his mind. This woman, who he had taken into his heart and into his bed, was nothing but a Nazi. The lawyer explained to the jury that Ben had become blinded by insanity, by hate and anger, and because of the madness that had possessed him, he had killed her with his own two hands. During those moments, the lawyer said Ben was unrecognizable even to himself. And to make matters worse, his son, Moishe, who he had only recently reconnected with, had witnessed the entire horrible scene.

The trial was intense, but because the lawyer was excellent, the jury saw his position, and Ben was released by reason of temporary insanity.

As soon as Ben was set free, he contacted the woman who had been raising his son since the end of the war. Her name was Gretchen Schmidt, and she and her husband, Eli, lived in Berlin. He offered to help them all come to live in America. It had taken two weeks to receive their response, and during that time he'd been anxious and worried that they would not bring Moishe back to America after Moishe had witnessed Ben killing that woman. But finally a letter arrived from Gretchen saying that she and her husband, Eli, would love to come to America. They felt it would be good for Moishe to have contact with his birth father. And so they'd come. When they first arrived, they moved in with Ben, but then Eli found a job as a rabbi in a nearby synagogue, and the three of them moved into an apartment that was within walking distance from Ben's.

Ben lay the envelopes on the kitchen counter and then poured himself a shot of bourbon. Looking up, he caught a glimpse of his reflection in the window. As a young man, he had been devastatingly handsome with hair the color of night and eyes as black and sparkling as onyx. He'd had his share of women, that was for certain. And although he and his beautiful blonde wife had never had a good marriage, together they created Moishe, a stunning boy with hair like golden silk. Now, glancing at his reflection, Ben could see how his time as a prisoner in Auschwitz had taken a toll on him. Although his hair was still thick, it was now white, and his eyes no longer sparkled. And all of the years he'd suffered from malnutrition had caused his bones to weaken and a slight hump to form in his back.

Ben took a sip of the bourbon. *I probably drink too much,* he thought. *But sometimes I can't bear the loneliness. I come home to his empty apartment every day. Once or twice a week I have dinner with Moishe and his family. They are kind to me, and I am glad that Moishe has Gretchen and Eli, but sometimes I feel jealous. I see the way Moishe is with Eli, and I know that he thinks of Eli as his father, not me. And why would he think of me as a father? I have not been with him throughout his life. It may not have been of my own choosing, but the fact of the matter is, I was not there when he needed me. And now after what he saw me do, our relationship is clumsy and strained. I don't believe it is salvageable, although I will never stop trying.* Ben pulled out a chair and sat down at the kitchen table to sort through his bills. He began by making two piles, those requiring immediate payment and those that could wait for a week or two. As his fingers skimmed the pile of envelopes, his eyes fell upon a letter that had been addressed to him in a handwriting he did not recognize. He put the other letters aside and tore it open. Inside the envelope, written in careful script in Polish, he read:

Dear Benjamin Rabinowitz,

I don't know if you will ever receive this letter. But I have been searching for you for many years. You see, I have never forgotten you. So when I received word from the Red Cross last month that this was your last known address I decided to write to you immediately.

I truly hope you are well. And I also hope that you will remember me and my sister. I am Solomon Lipman, and my sister is Sarah Lipman. In case you forgot, we are Zelda and Asher's children. I remember you from the Lodz ghetto. You were very kind to my sister, my mother, and to me. I am so very sorry that I must be the bearer of bad news. It is with great sadness that I report that both of our parents are dead. I have received confirmation of this, but I know it to be a fact. I remember how you cared for my mother, and I know this news will be painful for you. Once again, I am sorry. It was also very hard on Sarah and me when we found out.

However, I still smile when I remember how kind you were to me when I was just a child. I often recall an afternoon in the kitchen in the apartment you shared with my family and me in the ghetto. On that particular day, my father was beating me. I felt so helpless because I was young and small and terrified of my father. But you came into the kitchen, and you distracted him and saved me from a terrible whipping. Do you remember this? So, because of your kindness, I have never forgotten you, Ben Rabinowitz. You helped mold me into the man I am today. And I want to thank you.

There is also another reason I am writing. I am getting married in July, and I would be so honored if you would think of attending. You are the closest thing to a father that I have, and I would love for you to stand up at my wedding. Besides that, my sister and I would love to see you again, more than we could ever express.

We live in Israel on a kibbutz in the Jordon Valley, and this is where my wedding will take place. You are probably wondering what a kibbutz is. It is a place where many people live together as a family. We all work together, eat together, and help to build up this wonderful country together. I realize that it is a far distance for you to travel because you would be coming all the way from America. However, I believe that you will love this blessed country and that every Jew should see our homeland at least once. Israel is so magnificent it will bring tears to your eyes, and I promise you if you come you will not be sorry. Please, if you receive this, write to me even if you cannot attend the wedding. A letter from you would mean the world to Sarah and also to me.

Most respectfully yours,
Solomon Lipman

"Zelda," Ben said, his voice barely a whisper. Then he took a long swig from the glass of bourbon. It had been years since he'd said her name aloud, and the sound of it made his heart ache with longing, even now, so many years later. Of all the women he'd known in his life, including his wife, Lila, Zelda had been his one true love. His hands trembled as he held the letter close to his heart. Zelda was dead. He knew it already, but hearing it again ripped the scab off a deep wound that had still not healed. How he'd loved her. He met Zelda after his wife, Lila, escaped the ghetto with his son, Moishe, leaving him behind. They met when Zelda and her husband had moved into the apartment where he lived. He would never have gotten involved with a married woman, and she probably would never have cheated on her husband, except for the fact that her husband, Asher, was a terribly abusive and cruel man. He beat Zelda and Solomon relentlessly. Life in the ghetto was brutal, and any tiny bit of joy was to be grabbed with both hands and held on to very tightly.

Neither Ben nor Zelda had planned it, but somehow they'd fallen in love. It was such a beautiful, fulfilling love. Even though they were faced with starvation, disease, terrible living conditions, and death, the love they shared made the horrors of the ghetto bearable. Ben closed his eyes, and he was transported back to the Lodz ghetto. In his mind's eye, he saw himself as a young man once again, holding Zelda's face tenderly in his hands. A smile came to his face as he heard her laughter, and his heart sang with delight. It had been years since he'd allowed himself to remember this vividly, and as he held Solomon's letter to his chest, he could almost feel her hand caress his cheek. He reached out to hold her in his arms. "Zelda," he whispered, but no one was there. His arms were empty, and when he opened his eyes, his face was covered in tears. *I am alone,* Ben thought. *Zelda is gone. I am alone. I am destined to die alone.* Ben lifted the glass of bourbon to his lips and swallowed the rest of the contents. It burned his throat, but it was warm, and sometimes he felt the only real warmth available to him came from a bottle. *My bubbe used to have an old saying. She used to say, "Only a stone should be alone." Well, Bubbe, maybe I am nothing more than a stone*, he thought, wiping the tears from his face with a kitchen towel. Then he tucked the letter into his jacket pocket, picked up his keys from the table, and left the apartment.

As Ben walked to Gretchen and Eli Kaetzel's apartment, which was less than five minutes away, he thought about Sarah and Solomon. *Solomon must be in his early twenties now and Sarah not far behind. I can't believe it. When I think of him, I think of a young, scrappy boy. Now, he is a man and he is getting married. More importantly, he wants me to attend his wedding.* It was a lovely spring day, and it should have been a pleasant walk. But Ben had too much on his mind to enjoy the weather. He had a request for the Kaetzels, and he wasn't sure how they were going to respond.

When he arrived at his destination, he stood outside for a moment. He could hear Eli and Gretchen and bits of a lighthearted conversation followed by lots of laughter. For a moment, Ben thought about turning around and going back home. He reached into his pocket and felt the letter. Then he knocked.

"Ben!" Gretchen said, opening the door. She always looked genuinely glad to see him. "Come in."

Ben walked in to find Eli sitting at the kitchen table with a large book open in front of him. "Hello, Ben. Welcome. You'll eat by us tonight? Of course you will," Eli said, smiling. Then he turned to Gretchen. "Set another place. Ben is going to eat by us."

"Thank you, I would love to have dinner with you."

"Moishe, your papa is here. Come out and say hello," Eli said in a voice that was filled with welcoming and joy. "All day Moishe practices the violin. I think maybe we have a musician in the family."

"Hello, Papa," Moishe said. Moishe was a quiet boy, not outgoing at all. He had problems; anyone could see that, but he was much more well adjusted than Ben thought he would be considering all he'd been through in his young life. Ben knew that it was the love between Eli and Gretchen and the way they'd raised Moishe with so much love that had saved his son. Ben liked Eli. After all, Eli was always a mensch. He had never tried to take Ben's place in Moishe's life, but he'd been a great friend to the boy. And it was clear to see that Moishe loved him and Gretchen.

"So to what do we owe this honor?" Gretchen said, taking another plate off the shelf and setting it on the table.

"I got a letter today from someone who means a lot to me. It's from someone I knew in the Lodz ghetto."

"Oh?" Eli said, closing his book and looking at Ben, his expression suddenly serious.

Ben cleared his throat. "I want to talk to all of you about the possibility of Moishe accompanying me to a wedding in Israel."

Gretchen looked at him, lines of worry deepening around her eyes. "I don't know, Ben. Israel is far away . . ."

"I know you would be nervous about sending Moishe so far away. I don't blame you. But it would be good for him to see Israel. After all, Moishe is eighteen. He is a man, and perhaps it would be good for him to visit the home of the Jewish people. And I also want him to meet these two young people who were the children of a dear friend of mine who I knew in the Lodz ghetto. Their names are Sarah and Solomon, and they should be about Moishe's age."

Gretchen turned to Eli who sat back in his chair running his hand over his beard as he contemplated the situation. Over the years Eli had grown more handsome. Perhaps it was the wisdom that shined like a beacon of light from his eyes. "I think maybe it's not such a bad idea," Eli said. "Ben will take care of Moishe, and I think it will be good for the two of them to spend some time together without us. Just the two of them."

Gretchen bit her lower lip. "I don't know; it's such a long way away."

"It will be all right," Eli assured her.

She tried to smile.

He smiled at her and nodded his head.

"All right. If you think so," she said, still unsure.

"Gretchen, it's not only what I think we should do. Your opinion is important here as well," Eli said. "What do you think?"

"I think you're right. I am afraid for Moishe to go so far away from us. But I trust Ben. And it is probably good for him to spend time with Moishe."

"And you, Moishe? Do you want to go?" Eli asked.

"I don't know. I am a little afraid."

"What are you afraid of?" Eli asked gently.

"New things. Going so far away from you and Gretchen."

"You know how much Gretchen and I love you. But like a mother bird, we have to throw you out of the nest so you can learn to fly. Do you understand me?" Eli said.

"Yes, I think so."

"And sometimes it's good to do things that scare you. It will give you confidence in yourself and make you strong," Eli said.

"If you think it's best, I'll go," Moishe said.

CHAPTER 75

NEITHER BEN NOR HIS SON, MOISHE, HAD EVER BEEN ON A PLANE before. As they sat together looking out the window, Ben glanced over at his son. Moishe resembled his mother with her golden hair and blue-gray eyes. He was slight of build with long legs and slender fingers, but his personality was not at all like his mother's who was a strong-willed woman. Moishe had his father's kind, gentle nature, but he was clearly damaged by the horrors of his early life. He'd seen his mother murdered in a concentration camp. He'd been raised by Nazis. How much of this did he remember? Ben didn't know. Moishe never said a word. But it was clear that he was an overly sensitive boy who was plagued by constant fears and long bouts of depression.

Eli's influence on the boy was apparent in everything that Moishe did. Even now, on the plane, Moishe wore a kippah, a small skull cap made of black velvet and embroidered with red and white threads. Ben's head was uncovered. He grew up a nonreligious Jew who had never taken the religion seriously. Even now he only celebrated Shabbat or Jewish holidays when he was invited to Eli and Gretchen's home. He enjoyed those visits. There was a warm glow in the Kaetzel's home that made him smile. Eli was kind and wise, and Gretchen was a good soul, a convert who was more of a Jew than Lila, Moishe's mother, had ever been.

"So are you excited?" Ben asked Moishe.

"I'm nervous. I don't do well in crowds."

"You'll be fine. You'll see," Ben said, not knowing how to answer. Then he continued, "From what I hear, Israel is a wonderful place."

CHAPTER 76

ISRAEL, JULY 1956

The first thing Ben noticed when he walked outside the airport was how the dry desert heat slapped him in the face. Sweat formed on his forehead and under his arms within minutes.

"Nu? So have you ever felt such heat?" he asked Moishe, who had already begun to look anxious.

"It's very hot," Moishe answered in a monotone, but his eyes were darting around taking in the unfamiliar sights. His hands were trembling, and his face was pale and covered in sweat.

"Come, let's get our luggage." Ben tried to sound cheerful, but he was beginning to wonder if it had been a mistake to bring Moishe here. After all, Moishe was unstable. He knew this. Eli and Gretchen knew it too. Now, Moishe was in very unfamiliar surroundings with a man who was his blood, but who had yet to win his complete trust. *What was Eli thinking when he said he thought it would be a good idea for Moishe to go with me? Moishe doesn't feel close to me at all. He acts as if I am a stranger. I wonder what Eli was thinking? If he would have said not to take him, I wouldn't have. Well, it's too late for that now.*

Ben handed Moishe his suitcase and then got his own.

"Solomon wrote to me and said he would send a car for us. He told me to look for a man with a sign that said my name. He said the man would be right outside baggage claim. So come, Moishe. Let's find this man."

Moishe followed behind his father, struggling to carry the suitcase. Ben glanced back at Moishe and his heart sank. *He's so weak; his bones never developed right, from malnutrition.*

A tanned-skinned young man with curly hair held up a sign that said Ben Rabinowitz.

Ben walked over to him. He extended his hand to shake. "I'm Ben; this is my son, Moishe."

"I'm Uri, Solomon's friend. I live on the kibbutz too. Anyway . . . welcome to Israel!" Uri said with a wide white-toothed smile. "Follow me."

Uri glanced at Moishe and noticed he was struggling to carry his suitcase. "Let me," Uri said and lifted the case with ease. Then he gave Moishe an open and friendly smile which Moishe struggled to return.

As they approached an open-air truck that was parked on the side of the road, Uri said, "Solomon and Sarah are so excited that you are coming. They can't wait."

"I'll sit in the back, Father," Moishe said.

"I'll sit back there with you."

"No need. You go ahead and sit with Uri in the front." Moishe gave Ben a quick smile. Moishe's lip quivered, and Ben knew that his son was nervous about meeting all these new people. It hurt Ben to see how insecure Moishe was.

"Are you sure? I certainly don't mind sitting in back with you."

"No, please sit in the front. I promise you, I'll be fine."

Moishe climbed up, and Uri put the suitcases in the back. Then Ben and Uri got into the front. The truck was old and covered with a layer of dust. The seats were torn, but when Uri turned the key it sprung to life.

"You know Sol from the war, yes?" Uri asked as they drove out of the airport, and the countryside opened up to them like a mother holding out her arms to embrace her children who had returned home after a long journey.

"Yes, I knew Solomon and Sarah from the Lodz ghetto. Their mother was my one true love," Ben said wistfully.

"She died?" Uri said.

"Yes. She was sent away on a transport. And . . ."

"I know. I know," Uri said. "I've heard these stories many times."

"You were not in the war?"

"Me? No, I am a Sabra. I was born here in Israel."

After spending so many years in the concrete metropolitan city of New York, the open land that was sometimes desolate, struck Ben as both beautiful and frightening.

"There are more cities here than just the small one outside the airport?" Ben asked.

"Of course. Not big cities like New York where you are living. But cities."

"You like it here?"

"Me? Yes, I love it. If someone were to say to me: Uri, here is a ticket to go to America or any other place in the world. I would not go. I would never leave this country. I know living in Israel can be a dangerous place and wars erupt often, but I would give my life for this land. And I think you are going to find that many people living on the kibbutz feel the same."

"Before I got this letter from Solomon, I'd never even heard of such a thing as a kibbutz."

"It's a wonderful way of life. The kibbutz where I am taking you is the oldest kibbutz in Israel. It's called Kibbutz Degania Alef."

"How do you survive? I don't really understand. If no one goes out and works, then where does the money come from?" Ben blurted. Then realizing that he might have been rude, he added "I'm sorry, I hope you don't mind my asking."

"Not at all. We have chickens and livestock. So sometimes, not often, we have meat. But we always have eggs and milk. We press olives to make olive oil. And we also have a garden where we grow delicious vegetables. You'll see how good the food is here. Everything is fresh. What we don't make, we trade for with other kibbutzim."

"And everyone works together?"

"Everyone has a job. If we all do our jobs, the kibbutz runs like a well-oiled clock. You understand?"

"I think so." Ben nodded.

"You'll see. I think you're going to love it. And you will find that your son might just come out of his shell here in Israel. He is a Jew, and this land is his homeland. He doesn't have to prove himself here. He is accepted here just for being Jewish. And besides, Israel is a land of miracles. So keep your eyes open for great things!" Uri let out a laugh.

Ben felt his face redden. This man was very bold and outspoken. He couldn't believe that Uri would have the audacity to mention that he could see how troubled Moishe was. But Uri had addressed Moishe's problems casually as if they were common knowledge, and he'd even offered a possible solution. Ben didn't know what to say so he said nothing.

CHAPTER 77

SARAH AND SOLOMON WERE WAITING WHEN THE TRUCK ARRIVED.
Ben's breath caught in his throat when he saw them. Sarah looked
so much like her mother that Ben felt the tears swell in his eyes. And
Solomon? He was tall and big boned, with large muscles, like his
father had been. But his eyes were kind and warm like his mother's.
*Zelda. You should be here at my side. You should see your babies. They are all
grown up now. And they are beautiful, Keinehora (may the evil eye look away
from them). You would be so proud.*

Ben jumped down from the truck, and Sarah ran to embrace
him. She'd given him a hard time when she was a child because she
felt that her mother had betrayed her father by falling in love with
Ben. But now she realized that her father was gone, and her mother
turned to Ben for comfort. And as a young woman she was glad that
her mother had found someone who made her happy during her
short life.

"Welcome, Ben. Do you forgive me for being a horrible child? I
was so mean to you then."

"You were five years old. A little girl who lost her father. Of
course, I forgive you. And look at you now. How old are you?"

"Nineteen."

"A woman. And so beautiful. You look just like your mother."

"Do I? I don't remember what she looked like, Ben. I wish I had a picture."

"I wish I had one to give you. The only picture I have is in my mind and in my heart. But . . . look in the mirror and you will see Zelda."

Both Sarah and Ben's cheeks were wet with tears.

Solomon came forward. Ben extended his hand to shake Solomon's hand, but Solomon pulled him into a bear hug.

"I've searched and searched for you. Praise God, you are alive."

Suddenly Ben felt guilty. He'd given up searching a few months after he arrived in New York. It was less painful to believe that everyone had perished than to keep waiting for information that never came.

"When we were in that ghetto you were like a father to me," Solomon said. "I am so glad you could be here at my wedding."

"As am I," Ben said.

"Come, I want you to meet my wife-to-be." Solomon put his arm around Ben and began to lead him forward.

Moishe followed, struggling with his suitcase. Sarah caught up with Moishe and smiled at him. "I'm Sarah Lipman," she said, the sunlight sparkling in her dark eyes.

"M-Moishe R-Rabinowitz," Moishe said.

"Let me show you to the room we've prepared for you and your papa."

Moishe followed Sarah quietly. "You are religious?" she asked.

"I suppose you could say that," Moishe said. "How did you know?"

"You wear a kippah."

"Oh," Moishe said, reaching up and touching his yarmulke.

"Yes, I am religious. It's a long story, but the man who raised me is very religious. And I admire him a great deal."

"Your parents are divorced?"

"No, my mother is dead. She was killed in a concentration camp. Ben is my birth father. But I was raised by a woman who converted to Judaism and her husband who was raised Hasidic."

"My goodness, that's quite a story."

"Yes, I suppose it is," he said, but he was thinking *It's even more complicated than that.*

"I'd love to hear the whole story sometime if you ever want to tell me."

He glanced sideways at her. *How could I ever tell her my story? It's so horrible. Would a girl like her ever understand? Besides, she is so pretty. What does she want with me? Don't delude yourself, Moishe. She is just talking to you to be nice because of Ben and his relationship to Solomon.*

He nodded but didn't say anything.

"Oh my, I hope I didn't offend you. I didn't mean to ask too many questions. I'm sorry if I pried too much into your personal business."

He looked over at her again. This time his eyes caught hers. *She is sincere*, he thought. *She wants to know more about me.* "I don't mind you asking. And I'd be happy to try to tell you anything you want to know. At least, I will tell you what I remember. You see, I was very young . . ."

"Tell me about what you did during the war, and then I'll tell you what happened to me. I was very young too. And I am sure that there is a lot I don't remember. But there is plenty that I can't forget."

The kitchen was alive with women cutting fresh vegetables, braiding challahs, and talking all at once.

"Tamar, come here. Ben has arrived," Solomon called out over the voices of the women.

A pretty girl with long, dark, curly hair and skin the same dark tan color as Uri's wiped her hands on the apron she wore. There was a thin veil of sweat on her brow, but her smile was sweet. She walked over and put her arms around Ben. "Welcome to Israel! I've heard so much about you."

"Come on, Tamar. There is no time for you to stand around talking. There is work to be done. It's almost lunchtime, and we aren't nearly ready," an older woman with her hair in a bun on top of her head said.

"I have to finish my work. Go and show Ben to his room. Let him put his suitcase away and freshen up, then I'll see you both in the dining room."

"She's bossy but beautiful." Solomon laughed. "So . . . I overlook her bossiness."

Tamar laughed, shook her head, and then turned and went back to work.

"Sarah and I did not work this morning because we took the time to prepare for your arrival," Solomon said as he and Ben headed to the rooms that had been prepared for Ben and Moishe. "After lunch I have to go into the fields to pick olives. I know you are probably very tired from the flight today. But perhaps you would like to join me tomorrow? It's hard work, but in many ways it's very rewarding to be out in the sunshine. Sometimes I feel that the sun is the face of God smiling down on me," Solomon said.

"I would like that."

"Good, I'll come to your room right before dawn. Have you ever seen an olive tree?"

"I don't think so."

"You're in for a treat. Just wait until you see these trees."

CHAPTER 78

Ewa was already sitting at the table when Solomon and Ben arrived. "So this is Ben?" she said to Solomon. The years she'd spent working out in the sun had highlighted her brown hair with gold.

"Yes," Solomon said, smiling proudly. "This is Ben."

"I'm Ewa." Ewa hugged Ben. And once again he was taken aback by how friendly and open the people here in Israel seemed to be.

"I'm Ben Rabinowitz."

"I know the infamous Ben Rabinowitz. Sol and Sarah have been talking about you since they were little children."

"You raised them?" Ben asked.

"Sort of. When they ran away from the ghetto, they ended up with a group of partisans. I was one the partisans. It's a long story. But for right now, let's enjoy this good food and this wonderful company, yes?"

"Yes," Ben said as Ewa passed him a large platter filled with cheese slices and green-pepper strips. Then he was handed a bowl of chopped cucumbers, parsley, onions, and tomatoes drizzled with dark-green olive oil. It smelled so fresh that his mouth watered.

Next, came a bowl filled with hard-boiled eggs, followed by a platter of hummus and another platter of soft, flat bread.

"You're late," Ewa said as Sarah and Moishe sat down.

"I know. I'm sorry. Moishe and I were talking," Sarah said.

"Nu? So what did you talk about with this handsome young man?" Ewa kidded her.

"Ewa!" Sarah said with mock indignation.

"I'm joking, of course. You don't have to tell me. By the way, the children missed you today in the kindergarten."

"You work in the kindergarten?" Moishe asked Sarah.

"Yes. I want to be a teacher like Ewa."

Ben watched his son. He'd never seen Moishe speak so calmly and openly to someone he'd just met. A smile slipped over Ben's face. *Maybe Uri is right. Maybe Israel is a land of miracles.*

After lunch, Moishe and Ben went back to their room to unpack, and the others went off to their respective jobs.

Ben watched Moishe clean up before dinner. He'd never seen the boy so meticulous about combing his hair. *Life is so strange and wonderful. I'm not much for religion, but I do believe in God. And I have found that sometimes God blesses us in the most unusual ways,* Ben thought as he watched Moishe get dressed. *This boy is my son, and he is clearly attracted to Sarah who looks just like her mother. The look on Moishe's face when he looks at Sarah reminds me so much of myself when I was a young man in love with Zelda.*

After dinner, the group made a campfire and everyone, young and old, including the children, gathered around it. One of the young men who lived on the kibbutz brought out a guitar and he began to play. Another man took out a harmonica and joined in. Then everyone sang along. Even though Ben didn't know the words of the song, which was in Hebrew, he found he was clapping his hands and humming the tune. Sarah and Moishe sat close together. Ben had been worried that Moishe might never have a normal life, but as he watched Sarah and Moishe together he felt encouraged. *Moishe is doing so well here. I really wish that Gretchen and Eli could see this.*

Ewa disappeared into the kitchen for a few minutes. When she returned, she brought Ben a piece of chocolate. "This is the best chocolate I've ever had," she said.

He took it and popped it into his mouth. He closed his eyes and savored the rich flavor. "It's delicious."

"Isn't it?"

"You know what's kind of strange? Every time I taste chocolate, it is a reminder to me of how lucky I am to be alive," Ben said.

"Hmmm," she said.

"That sounds strange, right?"

"A little, I suppose. But I am sure there is a reason."

"There is a reason. You see, when I was in the concentration camp, I used to have dreams of chocolate. Every day, I thought about it at least a dozen times. I would remember how it tasted. And sometimes, if I tried hard enough, I could feel it melting on my tongue and the sweetness trickling down my throat. I was close to death at that time. But somehow, chocolate represented life to me. Does that make any sense? I felt like the taste of chocolate was the taste of life, and I craved it so much that now when I taste it I feel such gratitude to be alive."

They sat outside and listened to the music until it grew dark. Then everyone began to retire for the night. "Time to get some rest," Ewa said as she stood up to leave and go to her room. "It is a full life we live here, Ben. We work hard; we play hard. We eat good, and we sleep well," Ewa said. "Would you like me to walk you back to your room?"

"I would like that very much," Ben said.

They began to walk together.

"You're a teacher?" Ben asked.

"Yes, I was a teacher before the war, and I am blessed to be able to enjoy the work I have always wanted to do right here on the kibbutz."

Ben smiled.

"What do you do for a living back in America?"

"I cut diamonds and precious stones. I work in the diamond district."

"Do you enjoy it?"

"I like the men I work for. They've been good to me. But I don't love the work itself. Some people are mesmerized by the beauty of the stones. Not me. I am more attracted to living things than to stones."

"So am I. I don't care much about inanimate objects. I find my joy in the smile of a child or the beauty of a sunrise. I understand that you like the men you work for. But you should do something you love. You should enjoy every day you are alive. That's what the horror of the Nazis taught me," Ewa said.

"You're right." He smiled.

She tapped him on the shoulder. "Well, we're here. This is your room. And I'm off to bed. I'll see you tomorrow."

"I'm going olive picking with Solomon in the morning."

"Oh yes? Well, good. Enjoy it." She smiled, then she turned and walked away. He stood outside the door of his room just watching her until the darkness covered her silhouette and he could no longer see her.

The following morning just before sunrise, Solomon knocked on the door to Ben's room. Ben let him inside.

"You two are still sleeping?" Solomon asked.

"I guess I didn't realize what time it was."

"Well, it's all right. But hurry and get dressed. Would you like to join us?" Solomon asked Moishe.

"No thank you," Moishe said shyly. Ben thought Moishe seemed to be intimidated by Solomon.

"All right, tomorrow maybe."

"Yes, perhaps.

As the sun rose in the east, the leaves of the olive trees sparkled in the sunlight. They looked as if they were made of pure sterling silver. Ben was awestruck. "You're right. This is magnificent."

"I told you," Solomon said, smiling.

CHAPTER 79

THAT AFTERNOON, BEN AND SOLOMON CAME IN FROM THE FIELDS
for lunch. They smelled of fresh air and hard work. Ben smiled at
Ewa and she returned the smile. Tamar came out of the kitchen
carrying a heavy platter of boiled fish. She sat down beside
Solomon. Ben glanced around the table, but he didn't see Sarah or
Moishe.

"I'd better go and check on my son. He knows that lunch is
served at noon," Ben said, concerned.

"He's all right," Ewa assured Ben. "He and Sarah decided to
take a hike. There's a beautiful waterfall not far from here, and she
wants to show it to him."

"She told you this?" Ben asked.

"Yes, of course. She didn't want me to worry."

"I see," Ben said, but he was quiet for the rest of the meal.
While everyone was clearing the tables, Ewa walked over to Ben.

"Are you upset?"

"Worried, I suppose."

"Why?" Ewa asked with genuine concern.

"Moishe isn't a stable boy. He has a lot of problems. He went through a lot during the war and after the war. He lost his mother. And . . . then . . . well . . . he has problems because of me too."

"What do you mean?"

"I can't tell you here. It's a long story. An ugly story."

"If you want to get it off your chest, we could take a walk after dinner tonight. I'll show you that waterfall I was talking about if you'd like. But we have to before it gets dark."

"All right," Ben said, wondering if he should tell her.

CHAPTER 80

Sᴀʀᴀʜ ᴀɴᴅ Mᴏɪsʜᴇ ᴡᴀʟᴋᴇᴅ sɪᴅᴇ ʙʏ sɪᴅᴇ.

"The terrain is uneven and rocky, so be careful," Sarah said.

Moishe followed her quietly. They walked up steep hills and down into valleys. As they continued on their journey, Moishe heard the rush of water. Then the land opened up, and there stood a magnificent waterfall. Moishe sighed. "It takes my breath away."

"You like it? I knew you would." Sarah smiled.

"Of course I do. I never saw anything like it in either New York or in Germany."

"Come sit beside me," Sarah said, sitting down on a smooth rock.

Moishe did as she asked.

They were quiet for several minutes watching the water. Then Sarah took Moishe's hand. "Are you glad you came to Israel?"

"I am. If I hadn't come here, I would never have met you."

"You are such a shy and quiet fellow."

"I know. I hate myself for it sometimes."

"But why? I find you fascinating. You're sensitive and mysterious."

"Me?" Moishe laughed a short laugh. "Not at all. Just shy and afraid of my own shadow. I'm uncomfortable in crowds. And until I met you, I had never even talked to a girl."

"Well, I'm glad you chose me to be the one to talk to."

"So am I," he said.

They sat quietly again, and Moishe felt his heart flutter. He had never felt this way about anyone before. *Is this love? Is this what love feels like?*

CHAPTER 81

LATER THAT EVENING JUST BEFORE SUNSET, EWA AND BEN TOOK THE same walk that Sarah and Moishe had taken earlier that day. They stopped to sit down and rest. They were only a few feet from the spot where Moishe had Sarah had been earlier that day.

"I see why Sarah wanted Moishe to see this. It's quite the landmark."

"Israel is full of wonderful things. It's too bad you're leaving after the wedding, or I would love to take you to the old city in Jerusalem. It's really something to see."

"The airport was in Tel Aviv. Is it like that?"

"Not at all. Tel Aviv is a big city. Not as big as New York, but big for us here in Israel. But the old city, now that is holy ground."

"You love living here, don't you?"

"It saved me. Israel shot life back into me when I wanted to give up. I was lucky to be able to come here after the war with Sarah and Solomon. The war broke me in some ways. You see, while I was struggling to stay alive I didn't realize how depressed I was, but when the war ended I realized that my heart was broken. I had been so busy just trying to live another day that I didn't realize the impact it all had on me. After the war I had no choice; I had to come to terms with all of it. I had lost my entire family; they died in Poland. My fiancé, who was a German, was dead, and everyone I knew was gone or scattered. All I had left were two little children that were not even my biological children, Solomon and Sarah. But they needed me. They were alone in the world too, and I loved them. So I couldn't just give up. I had to find a way to live again. Israel did that for me."

"You were engaged to a German Jew?"

"No, he was a German. He was a deserter from the German army. He was a good person. You see, not all the Germans agreed with Hitler."

"You're Polish?"

"Yes, a Polish Jew, you can tell?"

"Of course. I hear it in your accent. How did you learn English?"

"I learned it at the university."

"You speak well."

"Thank you." She smiled. "Do you still speak Polish?"

"Of course," he said.

"Me too. And Yiddish."

"Me too."

"They say Yiddish is the language of God," she said seriously.

"It might be."

"Say something to me in Yiddish," she said.

"I really like you," he said in Yiddish.

"I like you too, Ben Rabinowitz."

"By the way . . . remember I mentioned that I have been a big part of Moishe's problems? There is something I must tell you."

"It's all right. Go on. Please, tell me."

"Not yet," he said.

CHAPTER 82

OVER THE REST OF THE WEEK, BEN'S DAYS AND NIGHTS FELL INTO AN easy pattern. He worked with Solomon during the day picking olives. While they worked, they each shared the stories of what had happened to them during the time they were separated. They laughed at sweet memories of Solomon's mother. They talked about her cooking, how she baked bread, and made her own matzo. Then Solomon mentioned the way she always sang him and Sarah to sleep in Yiddish.

"She always sang slightly off-key," Ben said.

"Was she off-key?" Solomon said. "I don't remember that."

"A little. But it was endearing," Ben said.

They both laughed.

"They are good memories. Even if they hurt," Solomon said. "I wish she had lived."

"So do I, but my friend Eli says that no one dies as long as we don't forget them. We must go on with our lives, but as long as we keep their memories safe in our hearts they are still with us."

Ben decided not to tell Solomon about the role he'd played in the murder of Rumkowski. It was a harsh and violent story, and Ben didn't want to spoil the beauty of the day. Even though he knew that

Rumkowski had gotten what he deserved, for some reason Ben felt ashamed of the entire incident.

They had come out to the fields just before dawn.

"So tell me how you met Tamar?" Ben asked as the sun began to rise in a scarlet sky.

"She was here at the kibbutz when I got here. She lived on the kibbutz with her parents. At first we fought all the time. She was such a stubborn little thing. She wouldn't back down. And then one day she and I were having an argument; I can't even remember what it was about, but all of a sudden I looked at her. I mean, I really looked at her, and I was stunned by how beautiful she was. And then it was as if she felt the shift in me, in us, because she looked into my eyes. And, well, something happened. I kissed her. And then, I guess, maybe I grew up? Before I knew it, we were talking about marriage."

The sky was turning from crimson to a deep orange as the sun climbed in the east.

"Tamar's a nice girl. I'm glad you found each other."

"She's a wonderful girl. Don't get me wrong; she's still as stubborn as a goat. But so am I."

Ben laughed. "Yesterday Ewa showed me how you press the olives to make olive oil. Fascinating. That olive oil you put on the vegetables sure is delicious. It's much different than the stuff we buy in the stores in New York."

"You like Ewa, don't you?" Solomon said. His voice was serious.

"I do. She's a good and kind soul."

"If it weren't for her, I don't know if Sarah and I would have made it through."

"And the priest you told me about too?" Ben said. The previous day Solomon had told him a little about Father Dupaul.

"Oh yes, Father Dupaul. God rest his blessed soul. He was a godsend to Sarah and I. He passed away last year. This may sound strange, but Sarah and I sat Shiva for him."

"After what we all went through with those damn Nazis, nothing sounds strange."

Ben felt the sun on his back. It was hot, and he was sweating, but he felt productive. He took a long drink of water, then he and Solomon continued working. As he put the ripe olives into a bucket, he thought about Moishe. His son was a different person here in Israel. He was helping Sarah with the children in the kindergarten during the day. The two of them seemed to have a connection that he had never seen Moishe have with anyone else. Not even Eli.

"Israel is paradise," Ben blurted out.

"Paradise? I don't know about that. It's beautiful, and we Jews are blessed to have this land. But it's not without fault. There are years when our crops don't grow as well and we go hungry. And this country is always on the brink of war."

"If there is a war in your lifetime, would you be required to go?"

"I would go not because I am required but because I love Israel, and I know what it would mean to our people if we lost our homeland. So I would put my life on the line to ensure the safety of this land."

CHAPTER 83

THAT NIGHT AFTER DINNER, BEN AND EWA WENT OFF ON THEIR OWN
again as they had been doing each night since the first time Ewa
took Ben to the waterfall. They walked until the sun set, then they
sat down beside the waterfall and gazed out at the shadows of the
hills as the moon began to rise.

"Remember I told you I had something I had to tell you?"

"Yes."

"I have come to like you very much, Ewa, and so I must tell you
the truth about me. I am not a perfect man."

She let out a small sharp laugh. "Who is perfect?"

"No, I am worse than most."

"Go on, tell me what you have to say," she said, taking his hand
in hers.

And he told her everything. He told her about Rumkowski's
murder and how he and a group of his friends from the sonderkom-
mando had lured the man into the crematorium and then beaten
him to death. He explained why he killed Rumkowski.

"He was a Jew, just like the rest of us. But when we were in the
Lodz ghetto, he tore ten thousand Jewish children away from their
mothers and sent them to their deaths."

Ewa gasped, but she did not say a word.

Then Ben took a deep breath and continued. His body shook as he told Ewa what happed with Ilsa. How she'd posed as a Jewish survivor. How he'd started dating her. And then how he'd found out that not only had she been a Nazi guard at Ravensbrück, but it was she who killed his wife in front of their son.

"I was like a crazy man. Moishe was visiting me; he had been living in Germany at the time. Gretchen had brought him to meet me. This was our first meeting. I should have tried to control myself. But I couldn't. I lost my mind. I killed that woman, that dirty Nazi, with my bare hands. I don't regret killing her. I only wish Moishe had not seen it happen."

"Oh, Ben," Ewa said.

"They say only a certain type of person can kill like that with their hands. I never thought I was that kind of a man. But the Nazis proved me wrong. They taught me that if a man is driven hard enough he can kill. And he can do it with his own hands. I'm sorry I had to tell you this story. I don't know how this makes you feel about me. Can you forgive me?"

"Forgive you? It's not for me to forgive you. Forgiveness comes from God. And I have a feeling God will understand why you did what you did."

"Does this change what you think of me?"

"Not at all."

"Ewa, it's been a very long time since I held a woman in my arms. And . . ."

She looked up into his eyes. "It's been a long time for me too. I haven't kissed a man since Gunther died."

"May I kiss you?" he asked shyly.

She nodded.

The kiss was soft and warm. A breeze blew a spray of water from the waterfall toward them. Ben took Ewa's face in his hands and kissed her again.

"Let's go for a swim," he said.

She was trembling as she stood up. "All right."

They took their clothes off, everything except their undergarments and went into the cool water. They swam under the waterfall.

"You're a good swimmer," she said.

"Yes, I used to go swimming when I was a boy."

"I can't tell you how many times I have walked by this beautiful waterfall in the years I have been here. But this is the first time I've been in the water," Ewa said.

"It's so clean, not like New York. Even the air here is clean," Ben said, smiling.

She nodded and smiled, and he kissed her again. This time he held her close to him. She closed her eyes. Her body trembled in his arms. He lifted her up and carried her to the shore where he lay her gently upon his clothes. Then he made soft, sweet love to her. Slowly, carefully, tenderly, taking his time and savoring every second and every inch of her body.

Once it was over they lay in each other's arms.

"Thank you for making me feel alive again, Ewa."

"Thank you, Ben."

"I want to say so many things, but tomorrow night is the wedding, and then Moishe and I will be on our way back to New York."

She shrugged and turned away from him. Ben had enough experience with women to know she was crying.

He gently turned her back to face him. Ewa's tearstained face touched his heart. "You are so beautiful," he said.

"Will you ever come back to Israel? Will we ever see each other again? I've said so many goodbyes in my life . . ."

"I will return to Israel. Now that I have been here, I know Israel will call to me."

"You'll come only for Israel?" she asked.

"Not only for Israel. Mostly for you."

CHAPTER 84

SOLOMON MOANED IN FRUSTRATION. HE HAD NEVER WORN A TIE before, and now as he was getting ready for his wedding he couldn't seem to tie it properly. Ben had shown him how to do it several times, but now that he was trying to tie it alone the darn thing looked lopsided. He was almost ready to abandon the tie altogether when there was a knock on his door.

"Who is it?" he asked, glad for the distraction.

"It's me, Sarah."

Solomon opened the door.

"Ben sent me." She smiled. "He said you'd be having trouble tying your tie. I think I can help."

"You know how to do it?"

"Yep, I do."

"How do you know how, and I don't?"

"Ben showed me."

"He showed me too," Solomon said. "I still can't get it right. Will you just look at it?" He threw his hands up in the air.

"Come here. Let me do it for you," Sarah said. She took the two ends and wrapped them until the tie was perfect.

"What would I ever do without you?" he said.

She shrugged. "I'm glad we never had to find out. God protected us and kept us together."

"Which reminds me"—he cleared his throat—"I have something for you. I was going to give it to you at the wedding, but I think I'd rather give it to you privately."

She looked at him puzzled. "This is your wedding day, not mine. I should be giving you and Tamar gifts."

He opened the drawer to his desk and pulled out a doll. "I think I owe you this."

"Solomon!" Her face turned pale as the memories of their past flooded back to her. She gasped as the breath caught in her throat.

"Do you remember when we escaped from the farm, and you lost your doll for the second time? I promised you I would get you another one."

She nodded, holding the doll to her chest remembering how she felt as a five-year-old frightened little girl. Tears ran down her face.

"And by the way, you were a real pain in the neck at five years old, but you know me." He tried to sound casual, but his voice trembled with emotion. "I like to make good on my promises."

She nodded.

He continued, "Now, I know that I am kind of late with this because you're too old for dolls. But in a few years, God willing, everyone here on the kibbutz will be making a wedding for you. And then, with God's blessing, there will be children. A little girl, perhaps. You can give this doll to her. And when you do, you can tell her the story of our escape, of how we survived, and at the same time you can tell her the story of our people."

"Oh, Sol, I'll always treasure this doll because of what it means to me . . . to us." She was weeping. "I love you. I am so glad that you are my brother."

"I love you too, Sarah. But I can't get all weepy now because I have to get ready for my wedding. So, go on, get out of here and get dressed." He winked, but she could see how much he cared in his shining eyes.

She was at a loss for words, so she just nodded and hugged him.

"And . . . by the way, thanks for showing up at just the right time and for tying this damn tie."

She giggled. "You can thank Ben for that," she said as she walked out the door carrying the doll in her arms. For a single moment as Solomon watched her walk away, he saw the little girl she had once been when she stood outside the ghetto wall, and he couldn't hold back the tears.

CHAPTER 85

FOUR MEN HELD POSTS COVERED BY A SHEET OF FABRIC TO CREATE A chuppah, a canopy under which the chatan, the bridegroom, and the kallah, the bride, would speak the vows that had been spoken for centuries. The vows of holy matrimony.

Solomon looked handsome as he waited in front of the canopy for his bride to walk down the aisle. He'd borrowed his suit from one of his friends on the kibbutz. How blessed he felt as he let his gaze scan the entire room. All the friends he'd made in Israel were here to wish him and his bride a happy and healthy life together. They might not all be blood, but they were all his family. Then his eyes fell upon Sarah who was sitting beside Ben and Ewa. On her lap, she held the doll.

The young man who played the guitar at the campfires each night was standing on the sidelines playing softly. He was accompanied by an older woman on the violin. Ben couldn't believe his eyes when he saw that Moishe was also standing with the other two musicians, and he was playing a violin as well. Moishe, who had always been so withdrawn, so painfully shy, was making that violin sing with such a sweet and haunting melody that it touched Ben's soul.

Over the week that Moishe had been in Israel, he seemed to change. His skin was now tanned slightly, and he looked healthier than Ben had ever seen him look. Ben, who was sitting beside Ewa and holding her hand, watched as Moishe and Sarah exchanged glances and smiles across the room.

Then the music stopped, and Tamar appeared at the end of the aisle holding tightly to her father's arm. She wore a dress that she'd made with the help of all the women who lived on the kibbutz who had once been seamstresses. *This is life on a kibbutz,* Ben thought as Tamar left her father and walked up to where Solomon waited. Together the two of them walked under the canopy, then Solomon remained still as Tamar walked around him seven times.

The vows were said; the rings were exchanged. The rabbi placed a glass that was wrapped in a towel beneath Solomon's feet. The room grew quiet as Solomon lifted his foot to stomp on the glass. Once he did, everyone yelled "mazel tov," and Solomon kissed Tamar.

As the couple walked away from the ceremony toward the main room where the reception was set up, an old man missing one eye, who had spent the war as a prisoner in Treblinka, raised a bottle of wine high in the air. "L'chaim," he cried out. "To life. We Jews have survived in spite of Hitler. In spite of every pogrom that has tried to annihilate our people . . . we prevail. And this"—he pointed to the newlyweds—"this . . . marriage, family, children, this is what life is all about. L'chaim!"

"L'chaim!" the rest of group called out. "L'chaim!"

Tears were running down Ben's cheeks. *L'chaim,* he thought. *L'chaim.*

Milk and meat were never served at the same meal on the kibbutz. Most of the meals were nonmeat meals which could include fish, cheeses, and milk. But tonight was a special night. Tonight was a wedding dinner, so chicken, vegetables, hummus, and pita were served.

Before they began to eat, Solomon stood up. He clanged his spoon against his wineglass to get everyone's attention. Once the crowd was silent, he spoke: "Tamar and I want to thank every one of you for all of your help in making our wedding possible. We couldn't have done it without you. You! Our dear friends, our family!"

Everyone clapped.

CHAPTER 86

After dinner, Ben was surprised to find that Moishe got up and played the music for the hora dance. Ewa took Ben's hand, and they danced in a line with all the others. They danced until they couldn't dance anymore, and then they sat down, breathless, together. Sarah was sitting across the room beside Moishe who was still playing music.

Tamar and Solomon were dancing.

"You know, I was thinking," Ben said. "I am a lonely man. I have only my son in New York. Yes, I have a job, and it's a good job. But I go home at night to an empty, dark apartment. I was thinking perhaps . . . I might move to Israel. Moishe could come and visit me every summer when school lets out. What do you think?" he asked, looking into Ewa's eyes.

She hesitated for a moment, then she touched his cheek. "I think, like my bubbe used to say, 'Only a stone should be alone.' Come, Ben. Come and move here to Israel. Live on the kibbutz and be with me."

"That's funny, my bubbe used to say that exact same thing about the stone. I was beginning to believe that my heart had turned to stone. That was until I met you," he said, then he kissed her.

"Maybe our wedding will be next? That is if you will have me," he said.

"Yes, if you are proposing, my answer is yes." She swallowed hard. "Oh, Ben, you've made me so happy," she said, and a tear slipped down her cheek. He gently kissed it away.

A NOTE TO THE READER

Thank you so much for reading my book *Sarah and Solomon*!

I always enjoy hearing from my readers, and your thoughts about my work are very important to me. If you enjoyed my novel, please consider telling your friends and posting a short review on Amazon. Word of mouth is an author's best friend.

Please Click Here to Leave a Review

Also, it would be my honor to have you join my mailing list. As my gift to you for joining, you will receive 3 **free** short stories and my USA Today award-winning novella complimentary in your email!!!!! To sign up, just go to my website at... www. RobertaKagan.com

I send blessings to each and every one of you,

Roberta

Email: roberta@robertakagan.com

ACKNOWLEDGMENTS

I would also like to thank my editor, proofreader, and developmental editor for all their help with this project. I couldn't have done it without them.

Paula Grundy of Paula Proofreader
Terrance Grundy of Editerry
Carli Kagan, Developmental Editor

Printed in Great Britain
by Amazon

81792113R00181